THE BACHELOR

THE BACHELOR

CARLY PHILLIPS

WARNER BOOKS

An AOL Time Warner Company

WARNER BOOKS EDITION

ISBN: 0-7394-2787-3

Book design by Giorgetta McRee
Jacket design by Diane Luger
Jacket art by Shasti O'Leary

Warner Books, Inc.
1271 Avenue of the Americas
New York, NY 10020

 An AOL Time Warner Company

Printed in the United States of America

To Mom and Dad for making me believe
I could do anything.

To Phil, who loves and supports me
through everything.

And to Jackie and Jen, who make it
all worthwhile.

Acknowledgments

To the people who made this book possible:
Maureen Walters, agent extraordinaire, who believed in me from day one.
Beth De Guzman, for welcoming me with open arms; and Karen Kosztolnyik, for making the experience the best I could hope for!

Special Thanks

Thanks to the people who contributed their knowledge and answered endless questions: Lynda Sue Cooper, the cop expert, and Terri Hall, journalism expert. Any errors or fabrications are mine alone.

And last but by no means least, to the best critique partners a girl could have. To Kathy Attalla for your plotting brilliance and Janelle Denison for your panty thief expertise—without your endless patience and willingness to reread, I'd have lost it a long time ago!

THE BACHELOR

PROLOGUE

"You're fit, Mrs. Chandler. The cardiogram is normal and so is your blood pressure. Nothing more than a bad case of indigestion. An antacid, some rest, and you should be fine." The doctor slipped her stethoscope around her neck and made another notation in the chart.

Relief flowed through Raina Chandler as strong as the pain had ripped through her earlier. The fiery sensation in her chest and arm had caught her off guard. Ever since losing her husband to a heart attack at age thirty-seven, Raina had never taken unexpected pain lightly. She'd become health-conscious, watched her weight, and started an exercise routine of brisk walking she'd kept up through this very day.

At the first twinge of pain, she'd picked up the phone and called her oldest son. Not even the bad memories of sterile, antiseptic hospital smells or the depressing graying walls could deter her from taking care of her health. She had a mission to accomplish before she left this earth.

She glanced at the attractive young doctor who had met her at the Emergency Room. Any woman who looked good in drab hospital green had potential. "You're new to this town, aren't you?" But Raina already knew the answer before the other woman nodded.

She knew everyone in Yorkshire Falls, population 1,723, soon to be 1,724, when the editor of the local section of the *Yorkshire Falls Gazette* and his wife had their baby. Her general practitioner had been Dr. Eric Fallon, a close friend for years. Widowed like herself, Eric only recently had succumbed to the desire to enjoy life more and work less. As Eric's new partner, Dr. Leslie Gaines was his answer to less stress.

She was new to town, and from Raina's perspective that made her not just interesting, but fresh, potential wife material for her jaded sons. "Are you married?" Raina asked. "I hope you don't mind my prying, but I've got three single sons, and—"

The doctor chuckled. "I've only been here a few weeks and already your sons' reputations precede them, Mrs. Chandler."

Raina's chest swelled with pride. They were good men, her boys. They were her greatest joy and recently the source of continued frustration. Chase, her oldest, Rick, the town's favorite cop, and Roman, her foreign correspondent and the baby brother, who was currently in London covering an economic summit.

"Now, Mrs. Chandler—"

"Raina," she corrected and studied the good doctor. Nice laugh, sense of humor, and a protective nature. Raina immediately discounted the woman physician as a mate for Roman or Rick.

Her no-nonsense demeanor would bore Roman and a doctor's hours would clash with Officer Rick's. But she could be just the right woman for her oldest son, Chase.

Since taking over as publisher of the *Yorkshire Falls Gazette* for his father almost twenty years earlier, he'd become much too serious, bossy, and overprotective. Thank God he had his father's handsome, chiseled face to make a decent first impression before he opened his mouth and started taking control. Good thing women loved a protective man and most single women in this town would marry Chase in a heartbeat. He was handsome, as were Rick and Roman.

Her goal was to marry off all three of her boys, and she would. But first they had to desire more from a woman than sex. Not that there was anything wrong with sex; in fact, it could be more than pleasant, she thought, remembering. But it was her sons' mind-set that presented her with a problem. They were *men*.

And having raised them, Raina knew exactly how they thought. They rarely wanted any female for more than one night. The lucky women lasted a month, no longer. Finding willing women wasn't the issue. With the Chandler good looks and appeal, women fell at their feet. But men, her sons included, wanted what they couldn't have, and her boys had too much, too easily.

The lure of the forbidden and the fun of the chase was gone. Why should a man consider *until death do us part* when he had women willing to give it up without commitment? It wasn't that Raina didn't understand today's generation. She did. But she'd also loved the trappings of a family life—and was smart enough to hold out for the whole package.

But in today's world, a woman had to offer a man a challenge. Excitement. And even then, Raina sensed her boys would balk. Chandler men needed a special woman to pique their interest and keep it. Raina sighed. How ironic that she, a woman who held marriage and children as her ideal, raised three sons who thought the word *bachelor* was sacred. With their attitudes she'd never have the grandchildren she desired. They'd never have the happiness they deserved.

"Some instructions, Raina." The doctor snapped her chart closed and glanced up. "I'd suggest keeping a bottle of antacid in the house, in case of emergencies. Often a cup of tea is the best remedy."

"No more late-night pizza deliveries, then?" She met the younger woman's amused gaze.

"I'm afraid not. You'll have to find another way of entertaining yourself."

Raina pursed her lips. The things she endured for her future. For her boys. Speaking of whom, Chase and Rick would be back any second and the doctor hadn't answered the most pressing question. Raina let her gaze slide up the doctor's slender physique. "I don't mean to push, but . . ."

Dr. Gaines grinned, obviously still amused. "I'm married. And even if I weren't, I'm sure your sons would appreciate finding their own women."

Raina tamped down her disappointment, then waved her hand in the air in response. "As if my boys would ever find their own women. Or should I say *wives.* Nothing short of a life-or-death emergency would force them to pick one woman and settle down. . . ." Raina's voice trailed off as the import of her own words sank in.

Life-or-death emergency. The only thing that would convince her sons of the necessity to get married. *Her* life-or-death emergency.

As the plan began to form, Raina's conscience begged her to dismiss the idea. It was cruel to lead her sons to believe she was ill. On the other hand, it was for their own good. They couldn't deny her anything, not when she truly needed them, and by playing on their good natures, she'd ultimately be leading them to happily ever after. Not that they'd know or appreciate it at first.

She gnawed on her lip. It was a risk. But without grandchildren, loneliness loomed large in her future, just as, without a wife or family, it loomed large for her sons. She wanted more for them than empty homes and emptier lives—the kind of life she'd had since her husband died.

"Doctor, my diagnosis here . . . it's confidential?"

The younger woman shot her a slanted glance. No doubt she was used to that question with only the most dire of cases. Raina checked her watch. She was running out of time before the boys returned. Her newly formulated plan as well as her family's future depended upon the woman's answer, and Raina waited, tapping her foot impatiently.

"Yes, it's confidential," Dr. Gaines said with a good-natured laugh.

Raina relaxed a bit more. She hugged her cotton hospital gown closer. "Good. I'm sure you don't want to have to evade my sons' questions, so, thank you for everything." She extended her hand for a polite shake, when she really wanted to shove the other woman through the curtain before the cavalry arrived with pointed questions.

"It was a pleasure and an experience meeting you. Dr. Fallon will be back in the office tomorrow. If you have any problems before then, don't hesitate to call."

"Oh, I won't," Raina said.

"So what's the story?" Rick, the middle child no one had ever been able to ignore, barreled through the drawn curtain with Chase on his heels. Rick's brash nature echoed his mother's personality. His dark brown hair and hazel eyes resembled Raina's before her hairdresser had gotten hold and changed her to a honey-blond to obliterate the gray.

In contrast, Roman and Chase were the bookends with jet-black hair and blazing blue eyes. Both her oldest and youngest were the spitting image of their father. Their imposing builds and dark hair never failed to remind her of John. Only their personalities were uniquely their own.

Chase stood in front of his agitated sibling and faced the doctor head-on. "What's going on?"

"I think your mother's condition is something she'd like to explain herself," the doctor said, then slipped beyond the awful multicolored curtain.

Ignoring the tug of guilt in favor of the greater good, and assuring herself they'd thank her in the end, Raina blinked back tears and placed a shaky hand over her heart. Then she explained her frail health and long-standing desire to her sons.

Chapter One

Roman Chandler glared at his oldest brother, or more accurately he glared at the quarter in Chase's right hand. After getting the phone call about his mother's heart problem, Roman had grabbed the first flight out of London. He'd flown into JFK Airport, taken a connecting flight to Albany, and then rented a car so he could drive an hour to his hometown of Yorkshire Falls, just outside of Saratoga Springs, New York. He was so tired even his bones ached from sheer exhaustion.

And now he could add stress to his problems. Thanks to his mother's heart condition, one of the Chandler brothers would have to sacrifice his freedom in order to provide Raina with a grandchild. A coin toss would decide which brother would shoulder the burden, but only Rick and Roman would be involved. Having already done his family duty by giving up college to run the paper and help his mother raise his younger brothers, Chase wouldn't take part in the toss—despite his argument to the contrary. He'd wanted things equal. Rick and Roman had insisted he opt out.

He'd play executioner instead.

"Call it. Heads or tails," Chase said.

Roman glanced at the unpainted ceiling, toward the upstairs of his childhood home where his mother was resting, as per doctor's orders. Meanwhile, he and his brothers stood waiting on the dusty, dirt-smeared floor of the garage that was attached to the family house. The same garage where they'd stored their bikes and balls as kids, and where Roman had snuck beers when he thought his older brothers weren't around. And the same house they'd been raised in and their mother still held on to, thanks to Chase's hard work and his success with the newspaper.

"Come on, guys, someone call it," Chase said in the wake of the surrounding silence.

"You don't have to sound like you're enjoying this," Rick muttered.

"You think I'm enjoying this?" Chase twisted the coin between his fingers, frustration tugging at his lips. "That's bullshit. I sure as hell don't want to see either of you lose the life you chose just because of some whim."

Roman was certain his oldest brother felt so strongly because Chase hadn't chosen his own life path. Instead he'd been thrust into the dual roles of publisher and parent overnight. At seventeen and the oldest sibling when their father died, Chase had felt a duty to take his father's place as head of the family. And that was the motivating factor for Roman's participation in the coin toss now. Roman had been the one to leave Yorkshire Falls and follow his dreams, while Chase had stayed behind and given up his.

Both Roman and Rick looked to Chase as their role model. If Chase thought their mother's dire health and her deep desire for a grandchild warranted a sacrifice, then

Roman had to agree. Not only did he owe his brother, he shared the same sense of devotion to family.

"It's no whim Mom suffered," Roman said to his siblings. "She said it's a weak heart that can't handle stress."

"Or disappointment," Rick said. "Mom didn't use that word, but you know damn well she meant it. We've disappointed her."

Roman nodded in agreement. "So if grandchildren will make her happy, then it's up to one of us to give her one to coddle while she's still around to enjoy being a grandmother."

"Knowing one of us is happily married will take the edge off that stress she's supposed to avoid," Chase said. "And a grandchild will give her life direction."

"Can't we just get her a puppy?" Rick asked.

Roman understood the sentiment. At thirty-one, his lifestyle precluded settling down. Marriage and family hadn't been in the future. Until now. It wasn't that Roman didn't like women. He did. Hell, he loved women, how they smelled and how their soft skin felt gliding against his aroused body. But he couldn't imagine giving up his career in favor of looking at the same female face across the breakfast table every day for the rest of his life. He shuddered, amazed that his life choices had come down to this one moment.

He turned to his middle brother. "Rick, you've tied the knot once. No need to do it again." Though Roman had no desire to announce himself the man for the job, he couldn't let his sibling repeat his past—marrying to help someone else while sacrificing himself in the process.

Rick shook his head. "Wrong, baby brother. I'll take part in the coin toss. Last time has nothing to do with this. *This* is about family."

Roman understood. The Chandlers were all about family. So he was back to where they left off. Would he return to his job as foreign correspondent for the Associated Press, continue to land in political hot spots and get the untold stories out to the rest of the world, or would he settle down in Yorkshire Falls the way he'd never planned? Though sometimes Roman wasn't sure whose dream he was actually pursuing—his, Chase's, or a combination of both—Roman lived in fear of replicating his brother's life, of being closed in with no options.

But despite his churning stomach, he was ready and nodded in Chase's direction. "Get it over with."

"Whatever you say." Chase flipped the coin high into the air.

Roman inclined his head toward Rick, giving him the choice, and Rick called out, "Heads."

As if in slow motion, the quarter circled and flew in the air. Roman's carefree life passed before his eyes the same way: the women he'd met and flirted with, the special ones who'd lasted long enough to constitute a relationship but not a life mate, the occasional hot, steamy encounter, less often now that he was older and more discriminating.

The sound of Chase's palm slapping against his hand stunned Roman back into reality. He met his oldest brother's solemn gaze.

A life change.

The death of a dream.

The severity of the situation hit Roman in the gut. He squared his shoulders and waited, while Rick sucked in an exaggerated breath.

Chase lifted his hand and glanced down, before meeting first Rick's, then Roman's gaze. Then he did the job the way he always did, without backing down. "Looks like you'll be needing a drink about now, baby brother. You're the sacrificial lamb in Mom's quest for grandchildren."

Rick heaved a heavy sigh that was nothing compared to the ball of lead sitting in Roman's stomach. Chase walked up beside Roman. "If you want out, now's the time. No one's going to hold it against you if you don't want to do this."

Roman forced a grin, emulating Chase at eighteen. "You think scoping out women and making babies is a tough assignment? By the time I'm through, you're going to wish you were me."

"Make sure she's a babe," Rick said helpfully, but no real humor tinged his words or tone. He obviously felt Roman's pain, though his own relief at not being the chosen one was tangible.

Roman appreciated the attempt to lighten his mood, even if it didn't work. "More important that she doesn't expect too much," he shot back. Any woman he married had to know up front who he was and accept what he wasn't.

Chase slapped him on the back. "I'm proud of you, kid. This is a once-in-a-lifetime decision. Be certain you can live with her, okay?"

"I don't plan to live with anyone," Roman muttered.

"Then what do you plan?" Rick asked.

"A nice long-distance marriage that doesn't change my life much at all. I want to find someone who's willing to stay at home and raise the kid, who'll be happy seeing me whenever I can make it back."

"You've got enough baggage as it is, is that it?" Rick asked.

Roman scowled at him. His attempt at mood-lightening had gone too far. "Actually, we had a damn good life while growing up and I want to make sure anyone I marry can provide the same thing for my kid."

"So you go on the road, the wife stays home." Chase shook his head. "You'd better watch your attitude. You don't want to scare potential candidates off too early in the search."

"There's no chance of that happening." Rick chuckled. "There wasn't a girl in high school who didn't lust after the kid, before he left for a life of adventure."

Despite the situation, Roman laughed. "Only after you graduated. Yours were big shoes to fill."

"That goes without saying." Rick folded his arms over his chest and grinned. "But fair's fair. I had to walk in Chase's footsteps, and they were huge. Girls loved his strong, silent bit. But once he graduated, they turned their sights on me." He tapped his chest. "And once I was gone, the field was open for you. And they were *all* interested."

Not all. Without warning, the memory of his high school infatuation resurfaced, as it often did. A beautiful girl with jet-black hair and green eyes, Charlotte Bronson had made his teenage hormones run wild. Her stinging rejection lived within him, as sharp now as it had been back then. He considered her the one who'd gotten away, and he'd never forgotten her. Though Roman would like to label it a teenage crush and leave it there, truth dictated he admit his feelings had run deep.

Not that he'd admitted it aloud to his brothers then, nor would he now. A man had to keep some things private.

Last Roman had heard, Charlotte had moved to New York City, the fashion capital of the world. Though he shared a rent-controlled apartment in the same city, he'd never run into her, nor had he looked her up. Roman was rarely in town long enough to do more than sleep one night, change clothes, and head out again to his next destination.

He hadn't heard any gossip from his mother lately, and curiosity won out now. "Charlotte Bronson back in town?" he asked.

Rick and Chase exchanged surprised glances. "She sure is," Rick said. "Owns a little business on First."

"And she's single," Chase added with a smile at last.

Roman's adrenaline kicked in hard and fast. "What kind of business?"

"Why don't you stop by and see for yourself?" Rick asked.

The notion tempted him. Roman wondered what Charlotte was like now. If she was still as quiet and sincere as she'd been way back when. If her jet-black hair still hung down her back, tempting a man to touch. He was curious to know if her green eyes were still expressive and open, providing a window to her soul for anyone who cared enough to look.

He'd cared and had been shot down for his effort. "Has she changed much?"

"Go have a look." Chase added his prompting to Rick's. "You can call it your first chance at scoping out potential candidates."

As if Charlotte would be interested. She'd walked away with ease after their one date and let him move on, apparently without an ounce of remorse. Roman had never believed her proclamation of disinterest, and he didn't think it was his ego talking. The sparks had been strong enough to light the entire town, the chemistry so hot an explosion had threatened. But sexual attraction wasn't the only thing they'd shared.

They'd connected on a deeper level, connected enough

for him to share his dreams and hopes for the future, something he'd never done before. Revealing such an intimate part of his soul had left him open for hurt and made her rejection that much more painful, he realized now, thanks to the adult wisdom he'd lacked in his youth.

"Maybe I will look her up." Roman remained deliberately vague. He didn't want to give his brothers any more indication of his renewed curiosity in Charlotte Bronson. Especially when he needed a different kind of woman, one who'd agree to his plan.

He let out a groan, recalling why this conversation had begun in the first place. His mother wanted grandchildren. And Roman would do his best to give them to her. But that didn't mean he could provide a spouse with all the strangling emotions and expectations a typical marriage entailed. He was a man who needed his freedom. He wasn't a husband for all seasons. His potential wife would have to want kids more than a husband and enjoy being on her own. An independent woman who adored children would do just fine.

Because Roman intended to get married, get his wife pregnant, and get the hell out, while doing his damnedest not to look back.

Sunshine shone through the plate-glass storefront window, bathing Charlotte in incredible warmth and heat. A perfect setting for the tropical display she was setting up. She tied the back of a string bikini around the mannequin that would be featured prominently in the window, and turned it toward her assistant. "So what do you think?"

Beth Hansen, also Charlotte's best friend since childhood, chuckled. "I wish I were built so fine."

"You are now." Charlotte glanced at Beth's petite figure and enhanced breasts.

Yorkshire Falls was a small town, four hours from New York City—far enough to remain a small town, but close enough to make travel to the big city worthwhile if the reason was good enough. Apparently bust alteration was good enough reason for Beth.

"And you could be. You don't even need to use too much imagination." Beth pointed to the mannequin. "Take a look at her and imagine yourself like this." She outlined the curvaceous shape with her hands. "An uplift would be a start, but an extra cup size would do even more to attract male attention."

Charlotte exhaled an exaggerated sigh. "Considering the interest this store's been getting, I don't need help attracting more attention of any kind."

As for men, she hadn't had a date since her New York City days six months before, and though she was sometimes lonely, she wasn't ready to begin the dating routine again—the long meals with drawn-out silences or the obligatory good-night kiss in which she inevitably had to grab her date's wandering hand before any real groping could begin. Although, if she were ever to complete her life with a husband and kids added to her career, she'd have to get back into the dating game one day soon.

"Every woman needs more male attention. It's an ego boost and who can argue with that?"

Charlotte frowned. "I'd rather a man be—"

"Interested in your mind instead of your face or body," Beth parroted, hands on her hips.

Charlotte nodded. "That's right. And I'd give any man the same respect in return." She grinned. "Am I beginning to sound like a broken record?"

"Maybe a little."

"Tell me something. Why is it the men who attract me are only interested in the packaging and don't stick around for the long haul?" Charlotte asked.

"Because you've dated the wrong men? Or maybe it's because you don't give them a chance. Besides, it's a proven fact that the packaging attracts a man first. A smart guy, the right guy, will get to know you and then you can blow him away with your brilliant brainpower."

"Men who go for looks first are too shallow."

"There you go again. Jumping to generalized conclusions. And I beg to differ." Beth placed her hands on her hips and scowled Charlotte's way. "It's the packaging that makes the first impression," she insisted.

Charlotte wondered why Beth could assert one thing when she was living proof of another. If Beth believed in a man being attracted to packaging first and then getting to know and appreciating a woman for who and what she was, why had she undergone plastic surgery *after* meeting her fiancé? Charlotte cared too much for her friend to hurt her by asking.

"Look at this store, for example." Beth waved a hand through the air. "You sell the packaging, and hence you're responsible for the rejuvenation of many relationships and marriages that have gotten stale."

"I can't argue with you there." Charlotte had been told the same thing by many of her customers.

Beth grinned. "Half the women in this town are getting lucky, thanks to you."

"I wouldn't go that far."

Her friend shrugged. "Whatever. The point is, aren't you sending the message that packaging is important?"

"I'd rather think I'm sending the message that it's okay to be yourself."

"I think we're saying the same thing, but I'll drop it for now. Did I tell you David offers packages? Eyes and chin, uplifts and implants."

Charlotte rolled her eyes. As far as she was concerned, Beth had been perfect before going under the knife, and Charlotte still didn't understand what had compelled her to think she needed to change. And Beth obviously wasn't talking. Just advertising her soon-to-be husband's services.

"Has anyone mentioned you're beginning to sound like an advertisement for your plastic surgeon?"

Beth smiled. "But of course. I plan to marry the man. Why not boost his business and our joint bank account at the same time?"

Beth's mercenary words were at odds with the sweet, down-to-earth woman Charlotte knew her to be. Another subtle change in Beth that Charlotte had noticed since her return. Like Charlotte, Beth had been born and raised in Yorkshire Falls. And like Charlotte had once done, Beth would move to New York City soon. Charlotte hoped her friend enjoyed the bright lights and big city. She remembered her own experience there with mixed feelings. At first, she'd loved the busy streets, the frantic pace, the glow of light and life even late at night. But once the newness faded, an emptiness grew. After living in a close-knit community like Yorkshire Falls, the loneliness had been overwhelming. Something Beth wouldn't have to deal with, since she was moving to New York to be with her husband.

"You know I'm never going to be able to replace you," Charlotte said wistfully. "You're the perfect assistant." When Charlotte had decided to leave her sales manager job at a posh New York City boutique and open Charlotte's

Attic back home, it hadn't taken more than one phone call to convince Beth to leave her job as a receptionist at a real estate office to come work with Charlotte.

"I'm going to miss you too. This job has been more rewarding than anything else I've done."

"That's because you're finally putting your talent to use."

"Thanks to your vision. This place is incredible."

Charlotte merely blushed. She'd been worried about a chic boutique succeeding in her small, upstate hometown. It was Beth who'd pushed and supported her emotionally during the preopening stages. Charlotte's concern had been unwarranted. Thanks to television, the Internet, and magazines, Yorkshire Falls' women were ready for fashion. Her store was a hit—if somewhat of an oddity among the old-time shops that still remained.

"Speaking of talent, I'm so glad we chose this aqua color instead of black." Beth fingered the strings tied tightly around the back of the mannequin.

"It's the exact color of the water off the Fiji Islands. The Koro Sea, and the South Pacific Ocean." Charlotte closed her eyes and envisioned the setting depicted in the brochures she had in her backroom office.

Not that she planned to travel, but the dream of faraway places had beckoned to her for as long as she could remember. As a young girl, pictures of idyllic resorts nurtured her hope that her errant father would return and share what she'd perceived as his glamorous life. Today she couldn't squelch the occasional urge to see exotic places, but she feared that desire made her too much like her father—selfish, shallow, and ungiving—so she settled for photos instead. Like the ones in her office portraying glistening water, white frothing waves, and hot sun heating bare skin.

"Not to mention the aqua color will complement the rest of the summer window display?"

Beth's voice intruded on Charlotte's thoughts and she opened one eye. "That too. Now be quiet and let me return to my daydream." But the spell had been broken.

"It's hard to get used to looking at bathing suits when we're just coming off winter."

"I know." Besides luxurious and basic undergarments, Charlotte also sold some fashionable eclectic pieces—sweaters in the winter, bathing suits and matching cover-ups in the summer. "But the fashion world works on its own schedule."

And so did Charlotte. The cold air had barely begun to give way to a slight March warming trend, but Charlotte dressed for the summer season anyway, in shockingly bright colors and light fabrics. What had started as a bid to lure people into her store had worked. Now word of mouth brought people to her store, and she'd grown to love the clothes she wore.

"I was thinking we could put the bathing suits in the right-hand corner of the display," Charlotte told Beth.

"Sounds like a good plan."

Charlotte dragged the mannequin toward the window overlooking First Avenue, Yorkshire Falls' main strip. She'd been fortunate in nabbing the perfect location, formerly Guy's Clothing Store. Charlotte wasn't worried about putting another retail store in the space because her merchandise kept up with the times. She'd had six months at the old rental before a rent increase kicked in, time enough to get her business off the ground, and her success told her she was on the right track.

"Listen, I'm starving. I'm going to grab some dinner

next door. Want to join me?" Beth grabbed her jacket off the rack in the back and slipped it on.

"No, thanks. I think I'll stick around and put some finishing touches on the window display." Charlotte and Beth had accomplished an almost complete overhaul of inventory today. It was easier to get things done when the store was closed than during business hours. The customers didn't just enjoy shopping, they enjoyed chitchat as well.

Beth sighed. "Suit yourself. But your social life is pathetic. Even I'm better company than those mannequins."

Charlotte started to laugh, then glanced at Beth and saw something more in her friend's eyes than a good joke. "You miss him, don't you?"

Beth nodded. Her fiancé had come up almost every weekend, staying Friday through Sunday night before returning to the city for the work week. Since he'd missed this weekend, Charlotte figured Beth probably wasn't looking forward to another lonely meal.

Neither was Charlotte. "You know what? Go get a table and I'll meet you there in five . . ." Her voice trailed off as she caught sight of a man outside the window.

Jet-black hair gleamed in the sunlight and a pair of sexy sunglasses were perched on the bridge of his nose, obscuring his face from view. A worn denim jacket covered his broad shoulders, and jeans hugged his long legs. Charlotte's stomach did a flip, bringing a warm sensation to her belly as recognition flickered with possibility.

She blinked, certain she'd been mistaken, but he'd backed far enough away that he was gone from view. She shook her head. Impossible, she thought. Everyone in town knew Roman Chandler was off traveling and reporting the news. Charlotte had always respected his ideals, the burning desire to expose unreported injustices, even if she didn't understand the needs that kept him far from home.

His aspirations had always reminded her of her actor father's. So had his good looks and charm. A wink, a smile, and women swooned at his feet. Heck, *she'd* swooned, and after a lot of flirting and lingering looks, they'd gone on their first date. One night—a night in which she'd connected with Roman on a meaningful level. She'd fallen hard and fast, as only a teenage girl could. And a night during which she'd discovered Roman's intention to leave Yorkshire Falls as soon as the opportunity arose.

Charlotte's father had abandoned his wife and child for Hollywood years before. With Roman's declaration, she'd immediately recognized the devastation he could leave in his wake.

She had only to look to her mother's lonely life to find the nerve to act on her conviction. She'd walked away from Roman that same night, lying that he didn't "do it" for her. And she hadn't let herself look back, no matter how badly she hurt—and she had hurt.

Look, don't touch. Smart rules for a girl who wanted her heart and soul intact. She might not feel like dating now, but when the right man showed himself, she would. Until then, she'd abide by her rules. She had no intention of following the same path her mother had taken, waiting for the wanderer to sporadically return, so she wouldn't involve herself with a restless soul like Roman Chandler. Not that she had to worry about such a thing. No way was he in town, and if he were, he'd steer clear of her.

Beth's hand on her shoulder caught her by surprise and she jumped.

"Hey, you okay?"

"Fine. I just got distracted."

Beth flicked her blond hair out from beneath her collar, then opened the door to the street. "Okay, then. I'll grab a table and see you in a few minutes." She let the door close behind her and Charlotte turned back to the mannequin, determined to finish the job—and calm down—before heading out to dinner.

There was no way Roman was back in town, she told herself. No way at all.

CHAPTER TWO

Dusk was setting on the horizon when Roman entered Norman's Garden Restaurant, named in part for Norman Hanover senior, who'd first opened the place, and in part for the gardens across the street. Norman's was now run by Norman, junior, owner and chef. The morning after the coin toss and his first full day back in Yorkshire Falls, Roman slept in, then kept himself busy playing cards with his mother and making sure she stayed off her feet. He'd also spent the time pondering an offer that had been relayed to him that morning from the *Washington Post* to take over an editorial job in D.C.

Any journalist would kill for the position, Roman knew. Though he had to admit he might enjoy the political intrigue and change of pace, settling in one place had never been on his agenda. He'd done his share of traveling, but there was more to see, more news to report, and injustices to expose—though with the corruption in Washington, D.C., Roman figured he wouldn't be bored there.

He doubted he'd feel as confined living in the nation's capital as he had in his small hometown, and might even have taken the offer more seriously had he not lost the coin toss. Now that he had a potential wife to contend with, one who'd undoubtedly want to live with a husband who made his home within the United States, he had good reason not to take the job. At this point a return abroad sounded even more appealing.

By early evening, his mother had dozed in front of the television and Roman had finally been able to leave the house knowing she was resting and he didn't have to worry about her trying to overdo.

Because it was late, he walked quickly through town until color in a storefront window—lots of vibrant color—caught his eye, causing him to stop and check out the change. He squinted for a better look, bringing him nose to glass with women's lingerie.

Frilly, sexy nighties, garters, and whatever else the opposite sex wore to attract a man—and he'd seen plenty of those getups in his time—decorated the display. The items in the window were sensual and decadent, including enticing animal prints.

Apparently some things in his small hometown *had* changed. As he wondered who was responsible for knocking conservatism to its knees, last night's conversation with his brothers came back to him. *Is Charlotte Bronson back in town?* he'd asked them.

Owns a little business on First. . . . Stop by and see for yourself. His brothers' replies had been deliberately vague, definitely amused, Roman thought now.

He allowed himself another glance at the provocative panties in the window and shook his head hard. No way Charlotte Bronson owned this shop. The Charlotte he remembered had been more quiet than outgoing, more innately sensual than overtly sexy. The combination had always intrigued him, but regardless, her personality type didn't strike him as one who'd open such an enticing and erotic shop. *Or would she?*

A horn honked, jerking Roman back into reality, and he turned to see Chase's truck pull into an empty spot down the street. He glanced at his watch. Rick would already be inside. Plenty of time to check out the shop after he met up with his brothers. He headed into the restaurant and strode to the back, bypassing the tables by the windows up front.

Roman met Rick by the old jukebox machine, which featured the jazzy reggae beat of the newest hit on the charts. He glanced around, taking in the familiar atmosphere. "Except for the music, nightlife in Yorkshire Falls is as exciting as ever."

Rick shrugged. "Did you really expect things to change?"

"I guess not." Even the decor was the same, he noted. Thanks to Norman senior's obsession with bird-watching, the restaurant's motif was comprised of wooden hand-painted birdhouses lining the walls, while pictures of varying species in their natural habitat hung in between.

The place had been and still was home to the older teens seeking independence from their parents, the singles in town, and the families needing a bite after Little League practice. Tonight, the patrons included the Chandler brothers. After living out of hotels for weeks on end and rarely seeing his New York apartment, let alone his family, Roman had to admit coming home felt good.

"Just tell me the burgers are as good as I remember and I'll be a happy man."

Rick laughed. "Takes so little to make you happy."

"What would it take to make you happy, Rick?" Years had passed since Rick's marriage ended in a devastating divorce, his wife leaving him for another man. To his credit, Rick had remained the happy-go-lucky brother, but Roman often wondered what pain he hid inside.

Rick folded his arms across his chest. "I'm already a satisfied man."

After all Rick had been through, Roman hoped his brother meant what he said.

"Hi, handsome. What can I get for you?" a high-pitched female voice asked.

Roman rose to give Isabelle, Norman's sixty-year-old wife and everyone's favorite waitress, a swift hug. She smelled like a unique mixture of home cooking and the good old-fashioned grease Norman used in the kitchen when she wasn't looking.

He stepped back. "Good to see you, Izzy."

She smiled. "Your mother's over the moon that you're home."

He settled himself back into the chair. "Yeah, just wish the reason were different."

"Your mom's a tough one. She'll be fine. Norman and I sent over enough prepacked meals to get her through the week."

"You're the best."

She grinned. "Don't I know it. So what can I get you? Cheeseburger deluxe?"

Roman laughed. "You've got a memory like an elephant."

"Only when it comes to my favorite customers." She shot Roman a wink, then turned to Rick. "Steak and mashed potatoes, that I know. Soda tonight, Officer?"

Rick nodded. "I'm on duty."

"I'll have the same."

"So what are you up to while you're home?" Izzy asked.

"One day at a time. Tonight I'll see if Chase needs any help while I'm around."

She stuck her pen behind her ear. "You Chandler boys work too hard."

Rick shrugged. "It's the way we were raised, Izzy."

"That reminds me. Put a burger up for Chase. He'll be here any minute," Roman said.

"I'm here now." His older brother came up behind Izzy.

"Perfect timing. One cheese, one burger, and a steak. You have a seat and I'll bring your drinks." Isabelle started to leave.

"Coke for me, Izzy." Chase shrugged off his jacket and hung it over the back of the chair, then settled into his seat. "So what'd I miss?"

"Rick was telling me how happy he was with his life," Roman said wryly.

"He ought to be. You'd be amazed, the predicaments the women in this town find themselves in just so they have an excuse to call and have the cop come to their rescue," Chase said. "We could donate a full page of the paper to Officer Rick's exploits."

Roman smirked. "I'm sure he doesn't find it a hardship, do you?"

"No more than Chase finds it tough fending off the women with picnic baskets who try to coax him out of the office and onto his back. I mean onto the picnic blanket." Rick laughed and eased back in the vinyl-covered chair, satisfaction etched on his face. "So many women, so little time."

Roman laughed. "But there's a bigger choice outside of Yorkshire Falls. How come you never made the move?" He always wondered why his middle brother was content policing the small town when he could make better, more varied use of his talents in a big city.

Lord knew, during the summers Roman had spent reporting for Chase, he'd felt confined by the small and often trivial stories he'd been assigned, while the outside world pulled at him, beckoning him toward bigger and better . . . what, exactly, he hadn't known at the time. He still wasn't sure what the draw was, but he wondered if his brother ever felt similar dissatisfaction, or the pull to move on.

"Roman? Roman Chandler? Is that you?"

Apparently he wouldn't be getting his answers anytime soon. He pushed his chair back, glanced up, and found himself face-to-face with one of his old high school girlfriends.

"Beth Hansen?" He rose from his seat.

She squealed with excitement and wrapped her arms around his neck. "It *is* you. How are you? And how'd I miss the fact that you were home?"

"With my mom out of commission, things are a little slow on the gossip mill." He returned the friendly hug and stepped back to look her over.

Professionally touched-up blond hair fell to her shoulders, well styled and making her look more chic and less like the relaxed, California-type girl he remembered. And was it his imagination, or had her breasts grown tremendously since he'd been gone?

"I heard about Raina. Is she okay?" Beth asked.

He nodded. "She will be, if she takes it easy and listens to the doctor." And she'd be even better if Roman married and impregnated a woman as soon as possible. No way could Roman think of his mission in terms less than clinical, not when love and desire had nothing to do with it.

He appraised Beth once more, this time as a potential candidate. He'd always liked her, which would help in accomplishing his goal. They'd been good friends, nothing more, but back in high school, he'd asked her out anyway. They'd gone out a few times and had had sex in the back-seat of Chase's car—because she was willing and he'd been horny. But mostly because he'd been in desperate need of ego-soothing after Charlotte Bronson's rejection. If he didn't "do it" for Charlotte, he'd decided he was damn well going to "do it" for Beth.

And that had been all male ego, he admitted now. But he and Beth had stayed together till graduation because it was fun and easy, going their separate ways after. Neither had been hurt and their camaraderie obviously remained.

"Give Raina my love, okay?" Beth asked.

"Will do."

"So how long are you here for this time?" Her bright eyes sparkled with curiosity.

Beth didn't attract him like Charlotte had, but she had a good heart. Was she still interested? Roman wondered. And if so, would she settle for a friendly but loveless marriage? He leaned closer. "How long do you want me here?"

She laughed and punched him in the shoulder. "You're still such a tease. Everyone knows you don't stick around any longer than you have to."

From behind him, Chase cleared his throat, a noise that sounded more like a warning. "Give Beth congratulations, Roman. She's gotten herself engaged to a big-city doctor. A plastic surgeon."

Roman gave his brother a grateful smile for the heads-up before he made a bigger ass of himself by actually making a move on Beth.

"I hope he knows what a lucky guy he is." Roman grasped her hands, noticing for the first time the huge rock on her finger. "Wow. I hope his heart is as big as this ring. You deserve it."

She looked at him through honest eyes. "That's the sweetest thing anyone's ever said to me."

If that was the sweetest, her fiancé had to work on his delivery, Roman thought.

"Listen, I've got to go take my seat. Don't want to lose our table." She gave him a friendly kiss on the cheek. "Don't be a stranger while you're in town, okay?"

"Okay."

He slipped back into his seat, hoping his brothers would forget that he'd obviously been scoping out Beth as a potential candidate. He watched as she walked away and settled into a table out of earshot before glancing back at Rick and Chase.

The brothers looked at each other, neither breaking the silence until Rick let out a smothered laugh. "You hope his heart is as big as that ring?"

Roman grinned. "What other comparison was there?" Without stating the obvious, he thought.

"For a minute there I thought you were going to mention the size of her . . . Never mind." Rick shook his head, an amused grin still on his face.

"You know I have more class than that."

"Think they were worth ten grand?" Chase asked. "Not that her fiancé charged her or anything."

"They were . . . impressive," Roman said.

"Obviously impressive enough to make you consider taking the plunge." One side of Chase's mouth lifted in a smirk.

So much for hoping they'd back off. They'd always been good-natured jokers, that much hadn't changed. "So I considered her for a minute. I was falling back on the good times we had, not the size of her . . . You get the picture."

The brothers all nodded in agreement.

Izzy stopped by with their drinks, ending that conversation.

"How 'bout Alice Magregor?" Chase asked as soon as Izzy was out of earshot. "She came by the paper the other day with a home-cooked meal in a picnic basket and a bottle of Merlot. When I wasn't interested, she asked about Rick. There's an obvious sign she's looking to settle down."

"With you two," Roman muttered. There wasn't a single available woman in Yorkshire Falls who hadn't attempted to bait and entice both Chase and Rick with her wares—baked and otherwise. "Wasn't Alice the one with the big hair?"

"That was her," Rick said.

"I don't remember her being interested in more than hairstyles and makeup," he recalled. And even if her hair had calmed down, he didn't remember anything they had in common. "I need intelligent conversation," Roman said. "Can she hold up her end, or is she still into the superficial?"

Chase groaned. "Roman's right. There is a reason she's still single in a town that pairs up right after graduation."

Roman grabbed the cold, damp glass. "I've got to get this right the first time." He leaned his head backward, feeling the blood rush to his temples, before he lifted his head and met his brother's gaze. "I need to pick someone Mom will like too. She wants a grandchild for emotional reasons, but she also wants to feel a part of things again. I mean, the people in this town were good to her after Dad died, but let's face it, she became the widow no one knew what to do with."

"She epitomized every wife's greatest fear," Chase added.

"Speaking of Mom . . . I just want to make sure you two remember the deal. Either of you blow the whistle on this plan and snitch to Mom, and I'm on the first plane out of here, leaving you two to hold the bag. You got it?"

Rick let out a low growl. "You sure know how to take all the fun out of winning the coin toss."

Roman never let his glare waver until Rick finally conceded. "Yeah, yeah. My lips are sealed."

Chase shrugged. "Mine too, but you do realize she's going to be forcing women down all three of our throats until Roman unveils the bride."

"That's the price you pay for being single," Roman reminded them.

"Then we'd better get serious before Mom's up and around town again. Marianne Diamond?" Chase asked.

"Engaged to Fred Aames," Rick said.

"The fat kid everyone made fun of." Fat Freddy, Roman remembered now.

"Except you. You beat up Luther Hampton for stealing his lunch. I was too proud of you to give a shit that you'd gotten suspended," Chase recalled.

"So what's Fred up to now?" Roman asked.

"Well, he's not Fat Freddy anymore, that's for sure," Chase said.

"Well, good for him. Overweight's unhealthy."

"He followed in his old man's footsteps. He's got his own plumbing business. Everyone in town likes him and you started the trend." Rick sucked down the last of his soda with a loud slurp.

Roman shrugged. "I can't believe you two remembered that."

"There's other things I remember too," Chase said, a combination of humor and seriousness in his big-brotherly gaze.

"Dinner, boys." Izzy had arrived with their meals. The mouthwatering aromas of Norman's burger and fries reminded Roman his stomach was empty. He snagged a fry before she'd had a chance to put the plate in front of him and popped it into his mouth. "My compliments to the chef. His staple items are the best."

"Enough with the fancy words. Just make sure you finish what's on your plate. That's the only compliment Norman needs." She said she'd be back with refills on the drinks, and disappeared once more.

"Now, where were we?" Chase asked.

Roman took a bite of his burger without waiting for Chase to finish with the ketchup. He chewed and swallowed.

"Discussing women." Rick dove right in to the topic at hand.

"But looks like you're in for another reunion first," Chase said before any of them could offer another candidate.

Roman turned in his seat and saw a woman walking down the aisle of the restaurant, a vision in a tangerine-colored skirt and low-necked tank, with lustrous black hair falling past her shoulders.

A rush of familiarity hit him in the gut at the same time Rick leaned close and whispered in his ear.

"Charlotte Bronson."

The moment Roman focused on her face, he knew Rick was right. The warmth spreading through him made sense now, he thought, studying her. Her body was no longer a girl's but that of a woman—lush, full, and oh-so-tempting.

Her porcelain skin was still as radiant, her smile as vibrant, as he remembered, and the tug of a full-fledged grin pulled at his mouth. She'd always made him smile just by being in a room, and that hadn't changed. But she had. More cosmopolitan clothes and a more confident stride, she'd obviously grown into herself.

His high school crush had become one hell of a beautiful woman. His mouth grew dry and beneath the table, he had one hell of an erection he'd never be able to hide. This woman always had the damnedest effect on him, Roman thought, and his pulse kicked into high gear as he waited for her to stop at his table.

All the while, Rick muttered in his ear, reminding Roman of why he'd hated having big brothers. "Five, four, three, two . . ."

And just when she'd have to stop and acknowledge him, she cut a sharp right turn and headed for the table where Beth had settled in to wait.

He groaned and turned back to face the firing squad he called his siblings.

"Looks like she's going to make you work for it, little brother."

Hadn't she always?

Chase laughed. "Bet you're not used to being ignored. It's got to be hell on the ego."

"Shut the hell up," Roman muttered. He hadn't forgotten that one night in high school. Though he'd always considered Charlotte the one that got away, he'd never forced the issue between them. It wasn't that he was afraid of hard work or even another rejection. He'd always had the inclination to pursue her; he'd just never had the time.

Things had changed. Back for a prolonged stay, Roman

was no longer content to let her deliberately ignore him. It was time to push the issue.

Roman *had* returned. Charlotte's stomach churned; disbelief and shock rippled through her. Her initial glimpse through the store window and the hunch she'd tried to ignore hadn't prepared her for the impact of seeing him again.

Drat the man anyway. No one on God's green earth had the ability to affect her the way he had. One look, and she felt like a hormonal teenager all over again.

The passage of time had affected his good looks—for the better. Age had defined him in incredible ways. His face was leaner, more chiseled, and, if possible, his eyes were a more striking shade of blue. She shook her head. She'd been too far away to know for sure—at first because she'd been in front of the restaurant, giving him time alone with Beth, and afterward because her palms were sweating and she was mortified she couldn't regain her composure.

But Charlotte was certain one thing about Roman hadn't changed—his reporter's instincts. With one glance, he not only saw, he dissected. And she didn't want him dissecting her.

"Your hands are shaking," Beth said.

Charlotte took another hefty sip of the soda her friend had ordered for her. "It's the caffeine."

"I think it's testosterone overload."

Somehow Charlotte managed to keep from spitting her cola at a grinning Beth. "You mean hormone overload?"

"Whichever. That table of hunky male flesh has you hot and bothered." She gestured with a flip of her hand toward the corner occupied by the Chandler brothers.

"Don't point, " Charlotte said.

"Why not? Everyone else in Norman's is staring at them."

"That's true," she said, then realized she'd missed her opportunity to deny having seen them. Ignoring the brothers had been her plan. At least until she'd eaten something and steeled her defenses against Roman's unsettling impact.

She folded her damp palms, one on top of the other. "But not me. I'm immune."

"You always were. Or you pretended to be," Beth said with the wisdom she'd lacked in her youth. "*Not* that I understand in the least." She shook her head. "Never had, never will."

Charlotte hadn't ever told her best friend the truth about why she'd rejected Roman. In high school, she'd had her defenses a mile high, and next thing she knew, Roman had turned from Charlotte's rejection to Beth's willing arms. Despite the pain and the jealousy, Charlotte had encouraged her friend's interest, pretending to be immune, as Beth had just said. Then they'd graduated and Roman had taken off for parts unknown.

Charlotte hadn't asked how serious their relationship had been. She often told herself it was out of respect for Beth's privacy, but the truth was more selfish than that. Charlotte hadn't wanted to know. And unlike the news of her plastic surgery, Beth had been discreet on the topic of Roman.

But times had changed and Beth was engaged to another man now. Roman was so far in her past, Charlotte contemplated tackling the topic tonight.

"He's still really good looking," Beth said.

Charlotte changed her mind about a heart-to-heart talk.

"Hey. If you're still interested in Roman, have at him. If Dr. Implant doesn't mind, then I don't."

"Liar." Beth tossed her napkin on the table and folded her arms across her chest, a smile pulling at her lips. "I saw the way you looked him over before he turned and noticed you. And I saw how you shifted your gaze and walked right by, like you didn't even see him there."

Charlotte twisted uncomfortably in her seat. "Is it too late to ask, see who where?"

"Chicken."

"We all have our weakness, so quit ruffling my feathers. Now, if you'll excuse me, I have to go to the ladies' room." Charlotte made a quick escape without a glance in Roman Chandler's direction. But as soon as she hit the narrow hallway that led to the restrooms, she wiped her damp palms against her gauzy skirt.

Five minutes later she'd touched up her lipstick and reminded herself of all her achievements, so if she absolutely had to make polite conversation with Roman, she'd be able to do so with poise and ease.

With a new attitude, she pushed open the door and walked smack into Roman's broad chest. The incredible scent of musky aftershave and potent male surrounded her. Aroused her. She sucked in a surprised breath.

As she stepped back on unsteady feet, he grabbed her forearms with both hands. "Easy."

Easy? Was he kidding? His palms felt warm, solid, and too good on her bare skin. She looked up into his blue eyes. "This is the ladies' room," she said inanely. She sighed. So much for poise, sparkling conversation, and wit.

"No, this is the hallway. The ladies' room is behind you and the men's room is down the hall." He grinned. "I should know. I practically grew up here."

"I need to get back to my table. Beth's waiting. Beth Hansen, you remember her, right?" Charlotte rolled her eyes This was getting worse and worse.

To her chagrin, he laughed. "Well, at least now I know you remember me."

She didn't pretend to misunderstand him and couldn't bring herself to lie. "I was late, in a rush, Beth was waiting." She lifted her hands, then let them fall to her sides.

"So you didn't mean to ignore me."

A burning flush rose to her face. "No. I . . . I have to go. Beth's waiting for me. Again."

His rough hand brushed her cheek and a tremor of awareness shot through her body, a quiver he couldn't possibly miss. "I'll let you get back to your table as soon as I ask you a question. It's been ten years and the attraction between us is still going strong. When are you going to give in?"

When hell freezes over came to mind, but she clamped her mouth shut. Because she didn't really mean it, for one thing, and because he didn't deserve such a crushing rejection, for another.

She licked her dry lips. "When are you going to give up trying?"

He grinned. "When hell freezes over."

He *would* have to mimic her thoughts. She leaned back against the wall for support and protection, but it meant little when Roman took another step forward, locking her body between the wall and his lean, hard, masculine frame.

Years melted away as his hands bracketed either side of her head and his lips hovered near her jaw. The warmth of his breath against her cheek and the pressure of his body against hers felt tantalizingly good, making her wonder why she'd resisted him for so long. Her eyelashes fluttered closed and she allowed herself to enjoy the erotic sensations pulsing through her veins. For the moment, she reminded herself. No longer.

He was attractive and out of reach, like the exotic destinations she researched and dreamed about but would never visit. Because she wasn't her father and her life was here. Stability and a solid future were tied to this town, to having roots. But Roman's lips nuzzling at the soft spot between her jaw and her ear made her want to forget safety and routine. Warmth trickled through her veins, moisture dampened her panties, and she wanted so much more than she'd let herself admit before.

"Have dinner with me on Friday." His throaty voice reverberated in her ear.

"I can . . ." His lips settled on her earlobe, his teeth nuzzling exactly the right spot. White hot arrows of desire shot to other, more private, sensitive areas and the wash of sensation made her body come alive. She moaned aloud, ending her sentence and cutting off any negative contraction she'd intended.

His teeth nipped, then alternated with delicious laps of his tongue, at once fierce yet feather-soft and light, and more seductive than the deepest desire she'd ever harbored inside her. If his intent was to sway her, he was doing an amazing job. His lips lingered, damp and warm, undemanding yet so very seductive at the same time. A small voice in her head tried to rebel, reminding her this was Roman and he'd leave as soon as his mother was well, or as soon as he grew bored with this town. With *her.*

She ought to walk away. Then he caressed the shell of her ear with his tongue and blew lightly on her damp skin. Oh, but he tempted her, and a moan escaped her barely parted lips.

"I'll take that as a yes," he whispered.

She forced her eyelids open. Yes to a date with him? "No."

"That's not what your body's telling me."

He didn't step back, which made this rejection harder than any she'd delivered in the past—because he was right. "My body needs a keeper."

A charming grin touched his lips. "Now, that's a job I wouldn't mind taking."

"Only while you're in town, of course." She forced an easy smile.

"Of course." He finally stepped back, giving her much-needed breathing room. "You should know, I'm a man who appreciates a challenge, Charlie."

She stiffened at the use of her father's nickname for her. He'd chosen her name, Charlotte Bronson, in honor of his favorite actor, Charles Bronson. "Charlotte," she corrected Roman.

"Okay, *Charlotte,* you pique my interest. You always have. And if I can admit it, so can you."

"What's the difference what I'm willing to admit? You don't always get what you want in life." Lord knew *she* rarely had.

"But if you try sometime, you just might get what you need." He propped one shoulder against the wall and grinned.

"I'm impressed. You know the Rolling Stones." She applauded for effect.

"Better. I know how to apply their words to life." He pushed himself off the wall and rose to his full height. "Mark my words, Charlotte. We *will* have another date." He started down the long hall, then turned back. "And based on your reaction and mine, we'll probably share a whole lot more." His voice rang with certainty and promise.

"Okay, sure, Roman. We'll have that date, all right."

At her words, his eyes opened wide.

"The day you decide to stay in town." And since *that* would never happen, Charlotte thought, neither would his proposed date. He posed no threat to her at all. *Yeah, right.*

"The more you challenge me, the more determined I get." He laughed, obviously not believing she meant what she had said.

Little did he realize she was deadly serious. Nothing more could happen between Charlotte and the carefree world traveler, unless, of course, she wanted to end up alone and abandoned, like her mother.

But Roman had thrown down the verbal gauntlet. Now all she had to do was remain strong enough to resist.

Chapter Three

By the time Roman walked out of Norman's and into the cooler night air, he had a job to do.

Chase had gotten an emergency call from his editor, Ty Turner, who needed to miss the town meeting in order to accompany his pregnant wife to the hospital. The last thing Roman wanted to do was take over *that* assignment, but he did want to lighten his brother's load. So he volunteered to cover the meeting.

And so, while Rick headed to a pay phone to call and check on Raina before heading back to work, and Chase retired to do some work for next week's edition, Roman was on his way to tonight's bickering session.

He glanced at his watch, noting he had a few minutes to kill. A few minutes to browse the seductive shop next door and figure out who owned it. One look at Charlotte, and he'd nearly forgotten his own name. No way he'd been focused enough to ask her about her new business.

He focused on the window display and his mouth opened wide. Were those crocheted panties on the amazingly lifelike mannequin? In the conservative town of Yorkshire Falls? He couldn't have been more astonished. He felt a distinct rush of arousal when he realized that raven-haired mannequin bore an uncanny resemblance to Charlotte. Suddenly realizing he looked like an old lech leering at women's lingerie, he stepped back. God, he hoped to hell no one was watching, or he'd never live down the embarrassment.

Roman took another step back and bumped against something hard. He turned around to find Rick, arms folded across his chest, grinning at him. "See something you like?"

"You're a laugh riot," Roman muttered.

"I figured you were revisiting your youth."

Roman couldn't mistake Rick's meaning. Leave it to his middle sibling to remember Roman's high school prank, done back when his idea of fun had been a panty raid at a friend's house, where the girls were having a slumber party. Not only had it been his idea, but he'd been so damn proud he'd hung a pair from his rearview mirror for about twenty-four hours. Until his mother had found them and given him a blistering lecture and punishment he'd never forget.

Raina Chandler had a unique way of curing her sons' most incorrigible habits. After a summer of rinsing his boxers and hanging them to dry in *front* of the house, he'd never subject anyone to that same humiliation again.

With any luck, the rest of the town had long forgotten. "I can't believe a shop like this is making it here," he said, changing the subject.

"It is. Young and old, slim and the more . . . robust—they all shop here. The younger ones anyway. Mom's on a crusade to get the older women in here too, and she's one of the most loyal customers."

"Mom *wears* these panties?"

The brothers shook their heads at the same time, neither wanting his imagination to travel down that path. "How *is* Mom?"

"Hard to tell. She sounded winded when I called, like she'd been running, which is impossible. So I'm heading on over to check myself."

Roman exhaled hard. "I've got my cell phone. Call me if you need me."

Rick nodded. "Will do." He then walked along the street by the store, turned right at the corner leading to the apartments above, and returned soon after.

"What's going on?" Roman asked, recognizing a walk-by when he saw one. His brother was patrolling the area and Roman wanted to know why.

Rick shrugged. "Yorkshire Falls had a couple of break-ins over the weekend."

Roman's reporter's instincts kicked in. "What was stolen?"

A smile Roman could only describe as wicked settled on his brother's mouth. "If I weren't with you myself at the time of both break-ins, you'd be my only suspect. But I've got squat."

"*Panties?*" Roman shifted his gaze from his brother to the assortment in the window, then back again. "You're telling me some idiot broke into a house and stole women's underwear?"

Rick nodded. "I'd have filled you and Chase in over dinner but Norman's was too crowded to talk privately. It seems the good people of Yorkshire Falls have an actual crime spree on their hands." Rick filled Roman in on the details of the thefts. It turned out that all of the stolen panties had been purchased at the store they were standing in front of now.

Roman glanced at the window once more. The panties in question were there for the world to see. *Who owned this place?* The Charlotte he'd known might not have been brazen enough to open this shop, but the one he'd seen dressed in bright colors and who'd laid down that challenge, well, she was another woman entirely.

"Are you going to tell me who owns this place?" he asked Rick.

A gleam danced in his brother's eyes and Roman's instincts went on high alert, confirming what he'd already suspected. When Rick remained silent, a knowing look on his face, Roman did the obvious. He took a step back and glanced up at the awning.

A burgundy overhang with hot pink trim and bold calligraphy stared back at him. CHARLOTTE'S ATTIC—HIDDEN TREASURES FOR THE BODY, HEART, AND SOUL.

"Hot damn." Apparently he'd been too quick to discount the possibility. Charlotte, *Roman's* Charlotte, owned this sensual, erotic shop.

Because she was a sensual, erotic woman, as she'd proven to him in Norman's back hall. He'd proven something to himself as well. He was a man with healthy carnal appetites, and it had been too long since he'd indulged those.

"Don't you have someplace to be?" Rick asked.

Roman ignored his brother's laugh, slapped Rick on the back, and headed off to town hall.

Twenty minutes later, Roman was overwhelmed by complete and utter boredom. The things he did for family, he thought and yawned as he waited for the architectural review portion of the evening to end. Though he could barely concentrate, he jotted notes just the same. He waited, pen hovering over his pad.

"Next up. Petition for variance to put dog door in the front entrance of 311 Sullivan Street, in the Sullivan Subdivision. Neighbors complain said door will destroy uniformity and beauty of subdivision—"

"My beagle Mick's entitled to have free access to his home." George Carlton, petitioner, rose to his feet, only to be jerked back down by his wife, Rose.

"Hush up, George. It's not our turn to speak."

"Go on," a man on the board directed.

"We're getting older and so's Mick. Having to get up and down each time he needs to relieve himself is wearing on us." She took her seat and folded her hands into her lap.

People were starving in Ethiopia and being killed in the Middle East, but here in Yorkshire Falls, canine concerns ruled the day. Roman remembered that the itch to leave town had started during his apprenticeship with Chase, and had grown with each meeting he'd attended that had degenerated into petty arguments between neighbors with too much time on their hands.

Back then, Roman's imagination had traveled a dual path in search of excitement, from foreign locales with more intriguing, fast-paced stories, to Charlotte Bronson, his crush. Now that he'd visited most of the places in his dreams, he had but one focus. His mind returned to Charlotte and the attraction he'd proven was mutual.

He'd intended to corner her, to make her admit to avoiding him tonight and find out why she'd ditched him in high school. He had a hunch, but wanted to hear it from Charlotte. He hadn't intended to seduce and arouse them both. Not until he'd looked into those eyes and seen the same emotional connection sizzling in the depths.

Nothing had changed. She was glad to see him, no matter how she fought that truth. Then there was the fresh coat of glossy coral color on her full, pouty lips. No red-blooded man could resist. He'd inhaled her scent and nuzzled her soft, fragrant skin. He'd gotten close enough to tease but not satisfy.

Roman groaned, because though her body screamed, *Take me*—and he'd wanted to—her mind rebelled. And now he knew why. She'd finally given him a reason for rejecting him that he understood. One he'd suspected all along. *We'll have that date, all right. The day you decide to stay in town.*

She wanted a home in Yorkshire Falls. She needed stability and security, to live happily ever after in the way everyone knew her parents never had. He'd been too young and rushed to see the truth before, but he understood it now. And that meant she was the last woman he could turn to with his agenda. He couldn't hurt her, and that meant he needed to take a lesson from Charlotte and steer clear.

"Next." A gavel banged against the wooden platform on the desk up front.

Roman jumped in his seat, startled. "Dammit, I missed the outcome," Roman muttered. Because he was preoccupied with *her.* This time he'd only missed out on the doggy dilemma, but next time he could miss much more. And that was something he couldn't let happen.

"Is that you, Chandler?"

Roman turned at the sound of his name to see a familiar-looking guy slip into the seat behind him.

"Fred Aames, remember me?" He stuck out his hand.

Chase and Rick hadn't been kidding. Fred no longer resembled the fat kid everyone had bullied. "Hey, Fred, how are you?" Roman shook his hand.

"Couldn't be better. How 'bout you? What are you doing back here?"

"I'm back in town for my mom; I'm here now for the *Gazette.*" Roman glanced forward. No one had introduced anything new for discussion yet.

"I heard about Raina's hospital trip." Fred ran a hand through his dark hair. "Man, I'm sorry."

"Me too."

"You covering for Ty?" He leaned forward and placed an arm behind Roman's chair, nearly knocking him forward in the process. Fred had lost weight but not upper body strength. He was still one hell of a big guy.

Roman stifled a cough and nodded. "His wife went into labor and he couldn't be in two places at once."

"That's nice of you. Besides, these meetings are as good a place as any to get caught up on what's going on around here."

"True enough." If he paid attention, Roman thought. But he hadn't a clue if Mick the beagle had been granted his freedom or locked behind closed doors for the duration of his doggy life.

The sound of a gavel hitting the table let them know the meeting had adjourned for a short recess. Roman rose and stretched in an attempt to wake himself up.

Fred stood, joining him. "Hey, you involved with anyone right now?"

Not yet. Roman shook his head, refusing to go that route with anyone but his brothers. "Not at the moment, why?"

Fred stepped closer. "Sally's been eyeing you. I thought she had a thing for Chase, but now she's locked in on you." With a generous wave that made a mockery of his whisper, Fred gestured to where Sally Walker sat in her seat, taking notes for the county record.

Sally half raised her hand in salutation, a blush staining her cheeks.

Roman waved back, then looked away, not wanting to encourage her obvious interest. "She's not my type." Because her name wasn't Charlotte. The thought surfaced unbidden. "Why don't you go after her yourself?" Roman asked.

"Guess you didn't hear I'm engaged," Fred said proudly. "Marianne Diamond's going to be my wife."

One of his brothers had mentioned it earlier, Roman recalled now. He grinned, raised a hand to slap Fred on the back, but refrained. He didn't want the big man to reciprocate the gesture. "Well, good for you. Congratulations."

"Thanks. Listen, I've got to talk to one of the councilmen before things heat up again. I've got a few jobs on hold pending a permit . . . well, you don't need to know details. See you around."

"Sure thing." Roman pinched the back of his neck. Exhaustion threatened to overwhelm him.

"How'd your first day back in the trenches go?"

He turned to see Chase standing beside him. "What's wrong? Is it Mom?" He hadn't expected to see Chase again tonight.

"No." Chase laid a quick, comforting hand on Roman's shoulder, then withdrew it.

"What, then? You don't trust me to do my job?" Which wouldn't be unfair, Roman thought. He still didn't have an answer to the Carltons' beagle's problem.

Chase shook his head. "I just figured you'd be antsy sitting at one of these things and thought I'd relieve you in case it ran long." He pinched the bridge of his nose. "I overheard you and Fred. Looks like you've got yourself a candidate."

"From what Fred said, Sally was interested in you first."

"Trust me, the field is open. I wouldn't hold it against

you for stealing her away from me," Chase said wryly. "Sally's too serious for me to even think about. She's the type to be dreaming about a house and kids after one date." He shuddered.

"If she likes a loner like you, she's not gonna be interested in an outgoing guy like me." Roman grinned, only too happy to rib his brother about his lone wolf qualities. Rick had been right in saying women were drawn to their older brother's brooding silence.

But Chase stared him down, obviously unwilling to buy in to Roman's excuses. "Sally's ready to settle down. Everything she wants right now would make her the perfect candidate for you. So why'd you tell Fred she's not your type?"

"Because she isn't."

"Forgive me for pointing out the obvious, but isn't that what you want? Sally's interested in you and you don't return the sentiment. See if she'll accept your arrangement."

Roman glanced over his shoulder again and took in Sally Walker, an innocent, blushing type of woman. "I can't." He couldn't marry Sally. Sleep with Sally.

"I suggest you be careful, little brother. If you pick out a lady who actually is your type, you might not be in such a rush to get the hell out." Chase shrugged. "Just something to think about."

Leave it to Chase, Roman's father figure, to point out the obvious. Also leave it to Chase to remind Roman of his priorities. His wife hunt. His brother was right. Roman needed a woman he could leave behind, not one he'd be drawn back to over and over again. Yet another reason Charlotte was all wrong for him. He wished like hell he could get her out of his system once and for all. But damned if he knew how. Touching her, tasting her, only made him want her more, not less.

An hour later, Roman headed home, Chase's words in his mind, but Charlotte in his subconscious. In bed later that night, he woke more than once in a heated sweat, Charlotte Bronson the cause.

Ten years, and the flame burned hotter than ever. Which only proved one thing: Temptation or no temptation, Roman couldn't afford to get involved with Charlotte. Not now. Not ever.

The sun woke Roman early the next morning. Despite a splitting headache, he stretched and climbed out of bed with a renewed sense of determination and purpose. After a quick shower, he headed for the kitchen. Food wouldn't kill the pain, but at least something to eat would fill his empty stomach. He reached into his mother's pantry, pulled out a box of Cocoa Puffs, poured a bowl of cereal, added mini-marshmallows, then drowned the mixture with milk.

His stomach growled at the same time he settled in, sitting in the same chair he favored as a kid. Pulling out the latest copy of the *Gazette,* he looked over the new and improved layout, and a tug of pride lodged in Roman's throat.

Chase had managed to grow the paper along with the increased population in town.

The sound of someone running down the stairs startled him and he turned to see his mother come to a quick halt as she entered the kitchen.

"Roman!"

"You were expecting someone else?"

She shook her head. "It's just . . . I thought you'd left the house already."

"And you decided to run a marathon while I was gone?"

"Weren't you supposed to have breakfast with your brothers?"

He narrowed his gaze. "I couldn't get out of bed this morning, and don't change the subject. Was that you running down the stairs? Because you're supposed to be taking it easy, remember?" But hadn't Rick said she'd sounded winded last night too?

"How could I forget something so important?" She placed a shaking hand to her chest, then walked slowly into the room, coming up beside him. "What about you? Are you feeling okay?"

Other than disoriented from this circular conversation, he was fine. "Why wouldn't I be okay?"

"Because your ears are obviously still clogged from the plane ride if you're thinking you heard something as ridiculous as me *running,* of all things. Do you want me to make an appointment with Dr. Fallon for you?" she asked.

He shook his head hard enough to clear his ears had they been blocked and met his mother's gaze. "I'm fine. It's you I'm worried about."

"No need." She slowly lowered herself into the chair beside him, then stared at his cereal bowl, a frown puckering her face. "Well, I see some things haven't changed. I can't believe I actually keep that garbage on hand for you. It's going to—"

"Rot my teeth, I know." She'd told him often enough as a kid. But she loved him enough to indulge him anyway. "You do realize I haven't lost one yet?"

"*Yet* being the operative word. A single man needs all his teeth, Roman. No woman finds it attractive to wake up in the middle of the night and discover you soaking your dentures on the nightstand."

He rolled his eyes. "Good thing I'm a respectful man

and don't let women spend the night." Let his mother chew on that, Roman thought wryly.

"Respect has nothing to do with it," she muttered.

As usual, his mother had a point. Women didn't stay overnight because he wasn't currently involved and hadn't been in a while, and because women who spent the night took it for granted they could spend another one. And another. The next thing a man knew, he was in a relationship—which Roman supposed wouldn't be a bad thing, if he could find a woman who interested him for more than a couple of weeks. Chase and Rick felt the same way. At this point, Roman figured the Chandler brothers' hearts were stamped NO TRESPASSING. Any intelligent woman read the fine print before getting involved in any way.

"You're too smart for your own good, Mom." As he rose from his seat, he realized Raina was completely dressed for the day. She wore navy blue slacks, a white blouse with a tie, and the pin with three baseball bats, a diamond in each, clipped into the center—a gift from his father after Chase's birth, and added to with each son she'd delivered. Other than her slight pallor, she looked great. The way his mother always looked, he thought with pride. "Going somewhere?" he asked.

She nodded. "To the hospital to read to the children."

He opened his mouth to speak, but she cut him off.

"And before you argue with me like Chase and Rick tried to do, let me tell you something. I've been in bed since late Friday when your brothers brought me home. It's a beautiful morning. Even the doctor said fresh air would do me good as long as I take it easy."

"Ma—"

"I'm not finished."

She waved a hand in front of his nose and he lowered

himself back into his chair, knowing better than to attempt to get a word in edgewise.

"I always read to the children on Monday and Friday. Jean Parker has chemotherapy treatments on those days and she looks forward to hearing *Curious George Goes to the Hospital.*"

Bless his mother for caring, he thought. Even ill, she put others first. She'd always had more than enough room in her heart for any kid who'd walked into their home.

As if she'd read his mind, she placed her hand over that heart and rubbed gently. "And besides, there's nothing like *children* to make a heart feel decades younger."

He rolled his eyes. "More rest will do the same thing, so after you read, I expect you home and in bed." No way would he touch the dig regarding kids. Not when he was about to embark upon a hunt to find a mother for his. "Are you finished with the monologue?" he asked politely.

She nodded.

"I wasn't going to argue. I just wanted to know if I could make you breakfast. I wouldn't want you to wear yourself out before you start your volunteer work."

A smile worked its way onto her face. Considering she was over sixty, her skin still held a glow most women would envy and the lines weren't as deep as many others' her age. Fear of losing her suddenly washed over him. He stood again and held out his arms. "I love you, Mom. And don't you *ever* scare me like that again."

She rose and hugged him in return, her arms and her grip strong and sure. This was his mother, the woman who had raised him, and though they touched base only once in a while because of his schedule, he adored her. He couldn't imagine life without her in it. "I want you around for a long, long time."

She sniffed. "Me too."

"Don't wipe your nose on my shirt." Female tears made him uncomfortable and he wanted her perky and strong again. "The doctor said you'll be fine as long as you take care of yourself, right? No stress, no overdoing it?"

She nodded.

"I suppose reading couldn't hurt. Can I drive you into town?"

"Chase is picking me up."

"How are you getting home?"

"Eric is dropping me off after lunch."

"How is Dr. Fallon?" Roman asked.

"Fine. Looking out for me just like you boys." She stepped backward, dabbed her eyes with a napkin she'd swiped off the table, and though she didn't meet his gaze, she was his composed mother again.

"How about a bagel and a cup of decaffeinated tea?" Roman asked.

"Don't spoil me. I'll be lost when you're gone."

He grinned. "Somehow I doubt that. You're the strongest woman I know."

Raina laughed. "And don't you forget it."

An hour later, Roman slipped out of the house for a walk to town, grateful his mother's breakfast discussion had included only town gossip and no more baby talk. He knew what he had to do and neither needed nor wanted a reminder.

The job ahead wouldn't be a simple one. The women of this town were raised to be wives and mothers—working or stay-at-home, it didn't matter. It was the wife part that made Roman nervous, and had him wondering how the hell he'd find someone willing to accept his untraditional needs. He needed an untraditional woman who'd accept his absences and wondered if that person could be found in Yorkshire Falls.

There was always the possibility of choosing a more cosmopolitan woman, one who understood Roman's needs better. He'd have to check his PalmPilot when he got home, but a few women he'd met in his travels and knew more intimately in the past came to mind. There was Cynthia Hartwick, an English heiress, but Roman immediately shook his head. She'd hire nannies to care for her children, and Roman wanted any kid of his to know a loving motherly upbringing.

He'd always liked Yvette Gauthier, a pretty redhead with a bubbly personality and the ability to make a man feel like a god. Then, just as he recalled how that same personality trait had nearly smothered him, he also remembered she'd become a flight attendant, which meant she wouldn't be around if his kid fell and got hurt or needed help with homework. Raina had always been home for her boys. Though Roman didn't mind if his wife worked, a long-distance job for both parents was out of the question.

His mother wouldn't approve of either woman. It made him laugh thinking of Raina's reaction to the cool Englishwoman or the sultry French tigress. His mother was the crux of this situation—*she* wanted grandchildren, so the woman would have to live or be willing to settle in Yorkshire Falls.

So much for the women he'd met along the way, Roman thought wryly. He felt somewhat relieved. He couldn't imagine marrying any of them anyway.

The glare of the sun beat down on his aching head. He definitely wasn't in the mood for people yet. Not until he'd had some caffeine, but as he approached town, his solitude was interrupted. A high-pitched voice called to him and he turned to see Pearl Robinson, an older woman he'd known forever, rushing toward him dressed in her housecoat and her hair in the same gray bun she'd always favored.

"Roman Chandler! Shame on your mother for not telling me you were in town. Then again, she's got more on her mind than gossip. How is she feeling? I baked a tray of brownies to bring over this afternoon. Is she up for company?"

Roman laughed at Pearl's rambling. She was such a sweet woman, harmless if you didn't mind chatter and nosiness, and after being away for so long, Roman was surprised to find he didn't mind either.

"Mom's okay, Pearl, thanks for asking. And I'm sure she'd love to have a visit today." He gave the older woman a quick hug. "How've you been, and how's Eldin? Still painting?"

For an older couple, Pearl Robinson and Eldin Wingate had had an unconventional living arrangement for years. Unmarried, they shared an old house owned by Crystal Sutton, another friend of Raina's, who'd had to move to a nursing home a year or so ago.

"Eldin's still painting, though Picasso he isn't. But he's fine, thanks for asking, and healthy, knock on wood." She banged on her head with her fist. "Though his back still acts up on occasion and he still can't carry me over the threshold. That's why we're still living in sin," she said, citing her favorite description of their relationship.

Pearl loved announcing their status to anyone who'd listen, as many times as they'd allow in the course of one conversation. Obviously that idiosyncrasy hadn't changed. But Roman's reaction to it had. Instead of being annoyed by her single-minded, self-oriented focus, he realized he'd missed his small town and all the different people who occupied it.

Even the peaceful quiet of his morning walk had been a refreshing change from his hectic daily life. How long, though, before the boredom and confinement he'd felt in his youth resurfaced and took over? How long would his enjoyment last once he got hitched? He shuddered to think of his imminent doom.

"Are you sick?" Pearl put a hand to his forehead. "You can't possibly be chilled on such a nice day. Maybe your mother should be taking care of you instead of the other way around?"

He blinked and realized he'd gotten lost in thought. "I'm fine, really."

"Well, I'll let you get going. I'm just going to the bank and then on home. I'll be by to see your mother later."

"Say hi to Eldin for me."

Pearl headed for the bank on First and Roman picked up his pace too. So much in town had stayed the same, but it was the new and different things that interested him now and he headed straight for Charlotte's store. Now, *she* was a woman who always drew him, no matter how many times she fought the idea.

Though they were mismatched opposites, she tempted him. Unfortunately, she didn't meet the one criterion that mattered most, her willingness to accept his travels. His desire to storm the shop and her defenses was strong, but reality asserted itself. Any contact between them could only cause them both pain.

Resigned, he turned to find Rick standing where he'd been last night, watching him with a speculative gleam in his eye. "On patrol again?" Roman asked.

"Just looking out for suspicious characters like yourself." Rick grinned.

Roman let out a groan and rubbed his burning eyes. "Don't start."

Rick eyed him warily. "Someone's testy this morning."

Roman hadn't been until Rick started bugging him. "Later, brother. I need coffee."

"Ah, yes. To help you wake up so the wife hunt can begin."

At Rick's words, Roman's head began to pound harder.

"Good luck." Rick walked past him and started for the panty-filled store.

"What gives?"

Rick turned, not a hint of amusement in his gaze. "Business."

"The panty thief."

He nodded but said nothing more. He didn't have to. He'd already given Roman more information than he should have, all off the record. Someone was breaking into the store customers' homes and stealing one particular brand of panties. Rick figured Charlotte could provide pertinent facts the police needed for their investigation.

"Want to join me?" Rick asked.

Roman looked for signs Rick was having fun at his expense. After all, this was the brother who as a teenager had answered the phone and agreed to blind dates in Roman's place. But Rick stood waiting, not a grin in sight.

Roman assessed his options. He had none. The woman of his dreams was inside. Roman shot his middle sibling a grateful glance. Though gut instinct and self-preservation told Roman to steer clear, curiosity pushed him inside.

So, he admitted, did his desire to see Charlotte once more.

* * *

At the sound of the door chimes, Charlotte stopped in the middle of folding lavender lace underwear. She glanced up to see Officer Rick Chandler saunter inside.

She gave him a friendly wave, but her hand froze in midair as Roman followed him in. She licked her dry lips as she watched them walk through her feminine store.

Side by side, the contrast between the brothers couldn't be more clear. All three Chandler men were beyond breathtaking. But no matter how handsome, Rick didn't have the same devastating impact on Charlotte as Roman did. Ever since her return to town, they'd become good pals, nothing more. Even Chase, who resembled Roman in looks, didn't come close to tipping Charlotte's Richter scale the way Roman did.

Something about the youngest Chandler brother, his jet-black hair, his confident stride, and his compelling blue eyes, captivated her. Made her yearn for things beyond her control or understanding. She shivered, then let reality return. No matter how good-looking the Chandler men were, none of the brothers were interested in settling down. It was part of town lore. Charlotte couldn't let it be her downfall.

She shook her head, and then wiggled her arms, fingers, and toes. "Relax," she muttered aloud. Roman had always been perceptive and she didn't want him to think her nerves had anything to do with him. Last night had proven Roman was too cocky for his own good and he didn't need additional ego stroking.

"Hi ya, Charlotte." Rick strode up to her, ignoring the panties strewn about, and rested an elbow on the counter, as confidently and casually as if he were surrounded by baseballs and mitts in the sporting goods store down the road.

Roman stood beside him, devouring her with a single, sexy look.

"Hi, Officer." She managed a friendly wink meant to encompass both men. "So what can I do for you this morning? Are you here to check out the newest in thong underwear?" She tossed the joke she always used on Rick, attempting normalcy.

Rick grinned. "Not unless you plan on modeling for me."

She laughed. "In your dreams."

Roman cleared his throat, obviously meant to remind them that he was in the room. As if she could forget. "Come on, Roman. You have to know your brother here likes all women. He'd have a harem if it were legal, wouldn't you, Rick?"

Rick merely chuckled.

"Can we get down to business?" Roman asked.

"Police business, unfortunately." Rick's mood suddenly sobered.

Charlotte didn't like the intense sound of his voice. "Why don't we sit?" She led them to the oversized velour Queen Anne–type chairs near the fitting room.

The two men overpowered the frilly, feminine decor. Her gaze settled on Roman. He epitomized the magnetic lure of the Chandler brothers, she thought. Every female felt his presence when he was in a room.

Though Roman remained standing, Rick sat, hands clasped between his legs, looking like a man with a secret.

"What's going on?" she asked.

The brothers exchanged silent glances. Static broke through the quiet, Rick's police radio calling for his attention. He shot Charlotte a regret-filled look. "Excuse me." While he unhooked the two-way radio from his belt and discussed business, Roman's piercing gaze never left hers.

Rick glanced up. "I'm sorry. A disturbance at the general store, and backup's needed."

Charlotte waved him off. "You go." *And take your brother with you,* she silently pleaded.

"Roman, can you fill her in? She needs to be aware of what's going on." Rick shattered her hopes.

Roman nodded. "My pleasure," he said in that sexy voice.

She shivered with awareness. Blast the man for his effect on her, she thought, but by the time Rick took off, leaving Roman and Charlotte alone in the back of her store, she hoped she'd schooled her face into a polite mask of friendliness. With Beth off this morning and the lull in customers, there was no one to interrupt them, so she'd be safer if she pushed the attraction to the back burner. "If such a thing were possible," she muttered.

"Is what possible?" Roman asked.

She shook her head, then swallowed hard. "Not a thing. Is this about the panty thief?"

Roman nodded. "It's about your merchandise." He leaned against the wall beside her.

"Which items?" Rick hadn't given her specifics on his last visit.

Roman coughed once and flushed before answering. "Ladies' panties."

Charlotte grinned. "Well, I'll be darned, there is a subject that can make a Chandler man blush." His embarrassment let her see a more vulnerable side to Roman than his normal, confident demeanor. She was grateful for the privilege, and a traitorous part of her heart opened to him.

"I'm serious," he said, unaware of the effect his embarrassment had on her.

She had to keep it that way.

"This guy's apparently got a fetish of some sort."

A fetish for panties. She shook her head wryly, then Roman's words sank in. "You said this *guy's* got a fetish. Why assume it's a man? Do the police think it's a man?"

"You'll have to talk to Rick about that."

She nodded, giving the matter more thought. "You do realize only a woman could wear the stolen property—without anyone noticing. Unless, of course, he's a poorly endowed man." She met his amused gaze and caught him laughing.

"Behave yourself, Charlotte."

His grin filled her with warmth and curled her toes. Clichéd as the expression was, it was true. "So what brand of panties? I sell dozens."

"Again, Rick's got the details, but he mentioned the crocheted ones in the window. He said they're handmade?"

By her. Her garments were exclusive, fashionable, personal, and not meant to become an object of obsession or ridicule for a perverted man. She had her reasons for pursuing the hobby that had become a staple in her business. But Charlotte couldn't imagine divulging personal secrets with Roman when distance seemed the safest route. Not when the details connected to those garments would lead to an emotional minefield.

Crocheting provided a window to her soul and discussion would reveal her deepest pain and disappointment. Because along with knitting, Charlotte had learned to crochet from her mother. They were skills Annie had developed as a means of escape, after Charlotte's fame-seeking father had abandoned them when Charlotte was nine. Hollywood was waiting, he'd said one morning, and walked out, only to return at disparate intervals. His revolving-door habit had become a pattern in her life. It was a pattern Charlotte had always feared falling into with Roman, so strong was the magnetic pull he exerted over her.

He cleared his throat and Charlotte blinked. "I know the brand," she said at last. "What can I do to help the police?"

"For now Rick just wants you more informed. I'm sure he'll be in touch with what he needs."

She nodded. As silence reigned, she sought a neutral topic. "How's your mother?"

His features softened. "Hanging in. She's allowed one activity outside the house a day, then she comes home to rest and keep off her feet. I feel better having seen her myself. Chase's phone call scared me to death."

Her heart reached out to him, the desire to help him past his fear and pain strong and overwhelming. But she couldn't afford to connect with him any deeper than she already had. "When did you get into town?" she asked.

"Early Saturday morning."

And Raina had been rushed to Emergency late Friday night. Charlotte admired Roman's fierce protective streak, one shared by all the brothers when it came to their beloved mother. Though a part of her longed for him to turn that caring her way, she knew even if he did, it couldn't last.

He exhaled, then strode toward her. Powerful and sure, he came up beside her. Her heart beat more rapidly in her chest, her pulse picking up rhythm. His body heat encompassed her, along with a rush of warmth and emotion that surpassed mere desire. The man had hidden depths and an innate goodness that came with his family name. He could give her everything she desired except forever, she thought sadly.

He reached out and tipped up her chin, forcing her to meet his gaze. "Be careful. Let's face it, Rick can't say for certain whether this is a freak incident or if a fruitcake's at large."

A chill raced through her. "I'll be fine."

"I'll make sure you are." His husky voice was filled with the caring she'd desired and a lump rose to fill her throat.

"One last thing," he said. "Rick wants to keep all this quiet. The cops don't need a panicked town or rumors of a panty thief spreading like wildfire."

"As if you can control gossip around here." She pursed her lips. "But word won't come from me."

She escorted him to the door, torn by the desire to have him stay and the logical need to see him gone. He held her gaze one last time, then let the door shut behind him. Charlotte's palms were damp, her pulse was racing—and the panty thief wasn't the reason.

Heading back to the lavender panties she'd left on the counter, Charlotte recounted reality in her mind. There couldn't be two more different people on the face of the planet than she and Roman. He thrived on transience and challenge, she needed permanence and the comfort of routine. Even her brief stint in New York, as exciting as it had been, had been necessitated by fashion school and apprenticeship. She'd returned to Yorkshire Falls as soon as possible. Roman made it his life's goal to stay away.

She'd broken up with him once because his excitement at leaving Yorkshire Falls behind had convinced her he'd provide her nothing but pain. Nothing he'd done in his life since had convinced her he'd changed. She gripped the panties, wishing with all her heart things between them could be different but accepting reality as only someone who lived it could.

Then and now, her sole consolation lay in the fact that she had no choice. She'd done the right thing. She didn't want to repeat her mother's life, living in limbo until a man returned and deigned to give her attention on his terms, only to disappear again.

She couldn't afford to admit to the sexual feelings Roman inspired inside her or acknowledge the truth hidden deep in her heart—that both his daring persona and impermanent lifestyle enticed her. And so she'd ruthlessly squelched the part of her that desired Roman Chandler, and the seeds of discontent that lurked in her soul.

Even now.

CHAPTER FOUR

A spring breeze floated through the early morning air, bringing unaccustomed warmth to Yorkshire Falls and filling Raina's lungs with incredibly sweet, fresh air. As fresh as her sons in their teenage years, she thought wryly.

She left Norman's, walked across First and onto the grassy mound in the center of town with a gazebo in the corner. She was meeting Eric here during his lunch hour, before he had to return to the office to see his afternoon appointments. Although he'd done the inviting, she'd chosen the place and picked up lunch. Who could resist a picnic in the outdoors? She had the most delicious grilled chicken sandwiches for them.

She paused in the center of the median, surprised to see Charlotte Bronson and Samson Humphrey, the duck man, as the children in town called him, standing together. Samson lived on the outskirts of town, in a run-down house that had been passed down from generation to generation in his family. Raina had no idea how he got by or what he did with his time other than sit in the park and feed the ducks, but he was a staple fixture in town.

She walked up beside them. "Hello, Charlotte. Samson." She smiled at them both.

"Hi, Raina." Charlotte inclined her head. "Nice to see you."

"You too." When Samson remained silent, Raina prodded again. "Nice weather we're having. Perfect for you to feed the ducks."

"Already told you it's Sam," he grumbled, barely loud enough to be heard. "Can't you remember a damn thing?"

"He's grouchy because he hasn't had lunch yet. Isn't that right, Sam?" Charlotte asked.

Raina laughed, knowing full well he was always grouchy. Leave it to Charlotte to try to smooth over even the surliest disposition.

"What would you know about it?" he asked.

Raina knew Charlotte was probably right and she'd packed a separate sandwich for him just in case.

"Well, I know your bark is worse than your bite," Charlotte said. "Now, here. Take this." She held out a brown paper bag, beating Raina to her good deed.

From the time Roman had a crush on Charlotte in high school, Raina had always known the girl had a heart of gold. She remembered the two had shared one date and her son had been a bear the morning after. More existed between Roman and Charlotte than an awful date. Raina had known it then. She knew it now. Just as she also knew Charlotte Bronson and her heart of gold were perfect for her youngest son.

"Go on, Sam, take it," Charlotte said.

He grabbed the bag and muttered a barely audible "Thanks." He dug past the foil wrapping, taking a huge first bite. "Would've preferred mustard."

Both Raina and Charlotte laughed. "Norman refuses to

put mustard on grilled chicken, and you're welcome," Charlotte said.

Obviously the condiment on the sandwich didn't matter, Raina thought, because he'd devoured half of it in two bites.

"I've got to get back to work." Charlotte waved to Raina, then Sam, and headed back toward her store.

"Nice girl," Raina said.

"Ought to have more sense than to bother with me," he muttered.

She shook her head. "That just shows her good taste. Well, enjoy lunch." Raina walked past him, to settle on the far edge of the bench.

She knew better than to join Sam. He'd just walk away, as he'd done in the past. He was an antisocial loner. The younger kids were afraid of him, the older kids made fun of him, and the rest of town generally ignored him. But Raina had always felt sorry for Sam and she liked him despite his gruff outer shell. When she bought herself food at Norman's, she always picked up something for Samson, too. Obviously Charlotte felt the same way. Something else Raina and the younger woman had in common, apart from Roman.

"I should have known you'd beat me here," a familiar male voice said.

"Eric." Raina rose to greet her friend. Dr. Eric Fallon and Raina had grown up together on the same street in Yorkshire Falls. They'd been friends as married couples and remained friends now that their spouses had died, Eric's wife long after Raina had lost John.

"You'd better not have walked all this way or driven into town well past the speed limit. Indigestion or not, you can't be too careful." Wrinkles of concern furrowed his brows.

Raina didn't want him worrying about her, but she had another, more pressing issue to take care of first. She'd have to remind her dear friend of his medical ethics before he accidentally slipped and told one of her sons she'd suffered no more than glorified heartburn. "Chase dropped me off, and I take it you've either been through my file or heard about my hospital trip through the grapevine?"

"You should have told me yourself when I called this morning."

"If every friend bothered you with health crises the minute you got back from vacation, you'd go running back to Mexico."

He sighed, drawing a hand through his salt-and-pepper hair. "You're not just any friend. When are you going to understand that?" His dark eyes bore into hers.

She patted his hand. "You're a good man."

His tanned, weathered hand covered hers, his touch surprisingly warm and tender.

Shaken, she changed the subject. "I suppose you heard Roman's back in town?"

Eric nodded. "Now tell me why I also heard your sons are tiptoeing around you like you might shatter at any moment. Why Roman's taken a leave of absence from his job. And why when you're not out about town, you're home *resting* as per doctor's orders. Because I know darn well Leslie didn't say a thing about added rest. Added Maalox, maybe."

Raina glanced around to see if anyone would save her from a lecture, but no white knight was in sight, not even Samson, who'd moved behind them and was weeding the flower beds. "Eric, how old are the boys? Old enough to be married," she said without waiting for him to answer. "Old enough to have children."

"So that's what's been bothering you. You want grandchildren?"

She nodded, finding it difficult to speak, to acknowledge the truth without giving away the growing emptiness in both her life and her heart.

"The boys will get married when they're good and ready, Raina."

"What's wrong with upping the time frame? Lord knows Rick needs to see that just because one woman hurt him doesn't mean all will. And then there's Roman—"

"Forgive me, but I'm not understanding," Eric interrupted her. "How does pretending to be sick relate to your desire to see the boys settled with families of their own?"

She glanced upward. Heaven help her when dealing with obtuse men—it seemed she was surrounded by them. "My sons would never deny me my fondest wish, one that will complete their lives too. Not if they thought . . ." She wrinkled her nose and cringed, hesitating.

"Your health was at risk?" At her barely perceptible nod, he rose from his seat. "Good God, woman, how could you do that to your children?"

"I did it *for* my children. Sit down, you're making a scene." She jerked on his sleeve and he followed her command.

"It's wrong."

Raina ignored the twinge of guilt. Okay, it was more than a twinge, but if her plan worked, no one would get hurt and everyone would benefit. "You can't tell them."

"Those boys love you. Give me one good reason why I shouldn't."

"Your Hippocratic oath." She folded her arms across her chest. "Do you need me to quote it for you? Because I can, you know. Verse for verse," she added for good measure.

"I don't doubt it," he said through clenched teeth.

"Fifth century B.C. 'I swear by Apollo, the Physician—' "

"You win, Raina, but I don't like it."

"I know you don't." Normally she enjoyed sparring with him, and when she'd committed the passage to memory she'd wanted to impress him with her knowledge, but the victory wasn't at all sweet. "The boys don't know what they're missing in life. What's so wrong with wanting to show them? You have two beautiful granddaughters of your own, both of whom live in Saratoga Springs, not twenty minutes from here. I'll bet you can't imagine life without them. I'm positive you'd be distraught if your daughters weren't settled yet."

"I couldn't tell you, since they're both married, with children. But I doubt I'd be leading them blind. It's your methods I disagree with, not your feelings. And there's something else."

His thumb began a lazy glide over the top of her hand, and for the first time, Raina realized he was still holding on tight. She swallowed hard. "What's that?"

"You've been alone too long. Studies show that widowed women, women with workaholic husbands, and women without interests of their own are more likely to meddle in their children's lives."

There were many things in life Raina hated. Being patronized was one of them. "I have outside interests. I jog every morning outside or on the treadmill in the basement."

He raised an eyebrow. "You're still jogging with a *weak heart?*"

She shrugged. "When I'm sure I won't get caught, and it hasn't been easy, believe me. Those boys have minds like a steel trap, and with three of them, they seem to be everywhere at once. The basement's my only refuge, but that's not the point. I also volunteer at the hospital," she said, seeking to convince him she had outside, healthy interests.

He frowned. "In the *children's* ward. It's a wonderful gift you give those kids, but as far as you're concerned, it's an extension of the same obsession. Meddling in your children's lives isn't healthy."

She squared her shoulders, but her heart beat painfully in her chest and a lump rose to her throat. "I'm not obsessed and I don't meddle. I'm stretching the truth to get my sons to broaden their horizons. That's all."

"Let's say, on that subject, we agree to disagree. But on the subject of *you,* it's time I spoke up, and not just as your doctor."

Raina wasn't sure why, but her adrenaline picked up in a way she hadn't experienced in years. Distinct butterflies took up residence in the pit of her stomach.

"There are other studies I can quote, but did you know that an emotional and physical connection to another human being is an essential part of life?"

"I'm connected," she told him. "To my sons, my friends, to you . . . to everyone in this town."

"I'm not talking about friendships, Raina."

She met his gaze and for the first time found herself looking at him. Really looking at him, not just as her friend, but as a man. An attractive, attentive, eligible man.

He'd aged well, the salt-and-pepper hair making him distinguished-looking, not old. His skin was tanned and weathered, in a rugged, handsome way that defied aging and wrinkles. And his body had maintained, if not the firmness of youth, then at least the outward appearance of a virile man.

She wondered what he saw when he looked at her, and was surprised to discover she cared. This conversation had personal, sensual undertones she'd never heard before from Eric. She wondered if she was mistaken. She was too old to be thinking men looked at her with any kind of real interest. Not anymore. Not since John.

But hadn't she just appraised Eric in—dare she even think it—an intimate way? Flustered, she curled her hands into fists and he released his hold on her at last.

"I have patients at two. I think it's time to eat."

Raina gratefully nodded and dug into the picnic basket she'd picked up at Norman's.

"So tell me what other schemes you've got going on," Eric said as he began to eat.

"You heard about Bridge Night, didn't you?" One night a month, Raina insisted the women shop at Charlotte's Attic instead of playing bridge. Ladies' night out, she called it.

He laughed. "Of course I heard. You've made it your mission to help Charlotte succeed." He gestured over the lawn, to Charlotte's Attic across the street.

Raina shrugged. "Why not? I always liked the girl."

"Mothering again," Eric said between bites. Raina frowned at him and would have said more, but he softened his words with an admiring smile. "Come with me to the St. Patrick's Day dance Friday night."

He'd never asked her out before. Never offered to accompany her anywhere unless they were in a group. Babysitting the widow, she called it, and nobody had ever disagreed. Eric's wife had been gone three years now and he'd thrown himself into his work, so his invitation surprised her.

"I'd like to go, but the boys will be there, and—"

"They might think you're healthy, heaven forbid?"

Heat rose to her cheeks. "Something like that."

"I'll have to prescribe a night out, then."

His eyes twinkled, and she had to admit she was tempted. Not just by his offer, but by him. "Who's doing the babysitting this time?" She needed clarification. Was she going with him as his date, or was he just seeking to get an old friend out of the house?

He met her gaze with a steady, assessing stare. "Nobody's babysitting. We're going on a date."

"I'd be delighted." The butterflies picked up rhythm once more and this time Raina not only recognized the passionate sensation, but she welcomed the feeling with open arms.

Three days after Roman had visited her shop, Charlotte still hadn't been able to shake him from her thoughts. In her dreams, she knew better than to try. But during the day, when the shop bell chimed, her stomach fluttered at the possibility he might walk back in. If the phone rang, her pulse skipped, thinking she'd hear his deep voice on the other end.

"Pathetic," she muttered. She needed to stop thinking about Roman.

She parallel parked at the curb across from her mother's house. Visiting Annie was a weekly ritual. When Charlotte had moved back to town, she'd already been on her own too long to live with her mother, and besides, she hadn't wanted to fall into the depression and frustration caused by living with Annie and her irrational hopes and dreams.

But she refused to let her mother depress her today, for she was determined to keep her mood as bright as the day. The sun shone in the clear blue sky and spring fever had her floating. And she'd keep floating if she didn't think about how tonight she'd be at the town hall dance, inhaling the smell of corned beef hash and listening to town gossip, instead of on a real date with Roman Chandler. A girl had to make smart choices and she'd made hers.

Charlotte pushed the doorbell once more, not wanting to use her key and scare her mother or have her think Russell had returned. Annie had never changed her locks and never would. She lived in an eternal state of limbo.

Finally the door to the old house swung open wide and her mother stood in her housecoat. "Charlotte!"

"Morning, Mom." She drew her mother into a huge hug before entering.

The house smelled stuffy, as if the windows hadn't been cracked open to enjoy the early spring weather, and her mother looked as if she planned to spend her one weekday off work inside. Again.

"Don't you have to be at the store?" Annie asked.

Charlotte glanced at her watch. "I do, but Beth can open for me. As a matter of fact, Beth can handle things until later." An inspired idea struck Charlotte. She'd wanted a day out, and now she had the perfect idea for them both. "Get dressed," she told her mother. "We're going to have a mother-daughter morning." While she spoke, she prodded her mother up the stairs and into her bedroom. "I'll bet Lu Anne can fit us in for hair and nails. We'll buy outfits for tonight's St. Patrick's Day dance, and then we'll go to Norman's for lunch. My treat."

Her mother glanced around the darkened room. "Well, I wasn't planning on going tonight, and as for leaving the house today . . ." She trailed off.

"No excuses." Charlotte snapped up the shades, letting light in. "We're going to have fun and enjoy." She folded her arms across her chest. "And I'm not taking no for an answer, so get dressed."

While Charlotte wondered what she'd have done if

Roman stormed her fortresses this way, to her surprise, her mother blinked and complied, sans argument. Half an hour later, they sat in Lu Anne's Locks, a salon owned by another mother-daughter team. Lu Anne handled the blue-haired ladies' style and sets, while her daughter, Pam, took care of the funky teens and style-conscious younger women.

After Lu Anne's, they ended up in Norman's for lunch, then tackled shopping. Charlotte couldn't recall the last time she'd actually gotten her mother out of the house and was glad she'd made the time.

She picked a few dresses for her mother off the rack and after Annie grudgingly tried them on, they agreed on one. "It looks gorgeous on you. With the new hairstyle and the makeup, this dress brings out the green in your eyes."

"I don't see why tonight's so important to you."

"Other than the fact that it's an annual Little League fund-raiser? Because getting out of the house is important. Hey, you might even run into Dennis Sterling. I know for a fact he's interested, Mom. He hangs around the library much more than even a veterinarian needs to."

Annie shrugged. "I don't go out with other men. I'm married, Charlotte."

Charlotte sucked in a frustrated breath. "Mom, don't you think it's time to move on? Just a little? And even if you don't agree, what would it hurt to test the waters? You might even enjoy it." And when Russell deigned to show up again, which he always did, it would do the man good to see her mother was no longer sitting around waiting for him to make his grand entrance.

"He loves me. He loves you too. If you gave him a chance . . ."

"A chance to do what? Come home, say hello in one breath and good-bye in another?"

Annie held the dresses close to her, as if the layers of material could protect her from Charlotte's words. Charlotte winced. She didn't need to see her mother's retreat to know she'd been too harsh. As soon as the words had left her mouth, she regretted her harsh comment and tone. She placed a soothing hand on her mother's arm, not knowing what else to say.

Annie broke the silence first. "People have different ways of showing love, Charlotte."

And her father showed his lack of the emotion with every departure he made. "Mom, I don't want to hurt you and I don't want to argue." How many times had she had some version of this conversation with her mother? She'd lost count.

But each time she thought she'd gotten close to a breakthrough, her errant father would waltz into town once more. It was like the man had radar, Charlotte thought. He obviously didn't want Annie, but he didn't want her to get over him, either. As a result, her mother lived her life in limbo. By choice, Charlotte reminded herself. Which was why her own decisions had to be the clear-cut opposite of her mother's.

Annie held out the dress, acknowledging everything but her daughter's words, giving Charlotte a chance to appraise her mother anew. The new hairstyle and color covered the gray and the makeover lit her features. She looked as if she'd lost ten years.

"Why are you staring at me like that?"

"You look . . . beautiful." An adjective Charlotte rarely used to describe her mother, if only because Annie so rarely took pains with her appearance.

But looking at her now, Charlotte recalled the wedding photo on her mother's dresser. Russell and Annie hadn't had a lavish wedding, but her mother had still been dressed in a traditional white gown—and with the glow of youth and love, her mother hadn't just been beautiful. She'd been exquisite. And from the glow in her cheeks and light in her eyes, she'd been deliriously happy too. She could be happy again, Charlotte thought. If she chose to, which made the situation that much more frustrating.

Charlotte blamed her mother for her refusal to get help as much as she blamed her father for his disappearing act. But Annie was the more fragile of the two and Charlotte loved her mother. She touched Annie's hair. "You're really beautiful, Mom."

Annie waved away the compliment, but to Charlotte's surprise, her mother reached out and touched her cheek in return. "You're beautiful too, Charlotte. Inside and out."

It was rare for Annie to come out of her fog long enough to see the world around her. The compliment was so unlike her mother, a lump formed in Charlotte's throat and she found herself at a temporary loss for words. "I look like you," she said when she'd recovered.

Annie merely smiled, and fingered the soft ruffles on the dress with obvious longing. Her mother was wavering.

"Come to the dance, Mom."

"Tell you what. I'll go to the dance if you'll drop the discussion about your father."

Charlotte knew when to grab and run. A night out was progress. Who cared what Annie's reasons were? "Okay." She held up her hands in submission. "What do you say we pay for these things and head back to my store? We'll pick out some undergarments, finish our ladies' day out, and then I'll take you home."

At the word *home,* her mother's eyes lit up and Charlotte made a mental note to put a call in to Dr. Fallon. There had to be more driving Annie's need for home, and maybe Dr. Fallon could talk to her mother.

By the time they walked into the Attic, Charlotte was determined to show her mother another half an hour of fun *outside* of the house. And from the expression on Beth's face when Charlotte ordered her to pull out their most skimpy, eclectic undergarments, her assistant was only too happy to oblige.

Charlotte hung a BACK SOON sign on the front door and turned to her mother and friend. "Fashion show, anyone? Come on, Mom. You can pick out anything you want. Release the inner you to go with the new outer you. What do you say?"

"I'm too old to go parading around in my skivvies." Annie laughed, though, and the sound warmed Charlotte's insides. "But I'll watch you two."

"And promise to take home at least one pair?"

Her mother nodded.

The afternoon proceeded like a pajama party, with Charlotte and Beth trying on the most seductive bras and panties. Even Annie seemed to enjoy not just the show, but the idea of treating herself right for once.

Progress came in various forms, but Charlotte believed she'd made some more today. "Last one," she called out to her mother and Beth, who waited in the private showing area right outside the individual dressing rooms.

"Okay. I'm dressed and your Mom's still waiting in the chairs enjoying the show, right, Annie?" Beth asked.

"Right. You girls make me envious for my youth."

Which she'd wasted on a man who didn't deserve it, Charlotte thought, but she knew better than to speak aloud and ruin what had been a perfect day. Instead she slipped on the panty set she'd saved for last, one from her handmade, crocheted line. She'd never told her mother she'd been using her talent for work, never thought Annie would come out of her shell long enough to care. But Annie had today.

A loud knock sounded at the shop door. "I'll get it," Beth called out. "We've been closed long enough to have the townfolk curious."

"Whoever it is, get rid of them for another few minutes, okay?" Charlotte didn't care as much about business as she did about the bonding time she'd shared with her mother. This last part of their day could bring them even closer.

"Will do."

Charlotte heard the two women go up front to see who was knocking. In the meantime, she fastened the matching bra, a new addition to her line. These garments weren't meant for anything other than intimate seduction.

She glanced in the mirror. She hadn't counted on the arousing effect of wearing these garments. Her nipples puckered, peeking through the insubstantial fabric, while an empty, aching feeling settled in the pit of her stomach.

And once aroused, her thoughts drifted to Roman. She smoothed her hands over her hips and turned to the side, taking in her profile, her long legs and flat stomach. She had to admit, she filled out the bra well. If only she possessed the same nerve she tried to impart to clients, she'd . . . what? Charlotte asked herself and forced her mind to play out the answer.

She'd reach out to Roman Chandler. She'd indulge in the feelings she'd possessed since high school. What had started out as a childhood crush had metamorphosed into adult curiosity and longing. What was he like now? What kind of man had he become? She had his devotion to his mother to begin the sketch, but there were many more depths she'd like to plumb.

The only way to indulge that curiosity was to give in to her feelings. Accept whatever he offered, for as long as he offered it—and then have the courage to go on with her life once he was gone. Unlike her mother, who had never taken the steps to move forward, Charlotte would indulge her deepest passion, then walk away.

But while Roman was here, she thought, continuing with the fantasy, while he was hers, she would go for it all. She'd model her handmade creations in front of him and watch as his eyes dilated with longing and need. As if she were enacting reality, her body shook in reaction to her brazen thoughts. Refocusing on the here and now, Charlotte wondered if she had the nerve to act out her fantasies. She could certainly justify the need. After ten years, she obviously wasn't going to get Roman out of her system by pretending he didn't exist or she wasn't attracted to him.

She hadn't gotten over him by ignoring the feelings. Why not try to get over him by acting on those feelings instead? She wasn't doomed to repeat her mother's mistakes if she learned from them.

Her heart picked up rhythm as she contemplated the idea of allowing herself to indulge. In Roman. With Roman.

"Okay, we're set." Beth's voice rang out from the front of the store and the jangling of the store bells jolted Charlotte back into reality. Unfortunately, arousal didn't dissipate as quickly.

Charlotte shook her head. Time to concentrate on her reasons for wearing these undergarments. To show off her crocheting skills to her mother and perhaps get Annie to use these same garments to break out of her own private prison.

Both mother and daughter had huge steps to take in their lives, Charlotte thought.

Footsteps, obviously Beth's, traveled to the back room.

"Ready or not, here I come," Charlotte called and stepped out of the small, enclosed room and into the open area with the Queen Anne chairs. But instead of her mother and Beth, she had an audience of one.

One incredibly sexy, virile male named Roman Chandler.

Roman stared at Charlotte's practically nude body in complete shock. The most erotic bra and panty set he'd ever laid eyes on hugged the supple curves of the most gorgeous woman he'd ever seen. The same one he'd wanted for what felt like forever.

No way in hell was he prepared for this. He'd finally made up his mind to keep his distance, and now this.

"Roman?" Her eyes opened wide, and to his relief, she began a dive for the protection of the swinging café-type doors. Unfortunately, she paused.

Waiting? Debating? He didn't know, but he had a perfect view of her pale, slender back, tapered waist, and enticing hints of skin on her delectable behind.

And then she turned, slowly, placing one hand on top of the slatted door. Her milk-white breasts pushed upward over knitted black material, full and lush, calling to him. Begging him to forget his newly made vow to steer clear.

She faced him without running to get dressed. Roman hadn't known she possessed such courage. Yet another facet of her discovered. But brazenness wasn't all there was to this incredible woman. The trembling and her uneven breaths told him she was far from composed. Definitely not the ultimate seductress, he thought, and thank God. Her softer, innocent side would keep him centered and restrained. Something had to, because his body was fighting him every step of the way.

"Where's my mother and Beth?" she asked.

Those amazing green eyes met his and a fall of tousled black hair hung over one bare shoulder, causing him to wonder what the silk strands would feel like on his bare skin.

"Beth said to tell you she was taking Annie home and she'd be back later. Much later." Obviously the soon-to-be-married Beth had seen an opportunity to play matchmaker and she'd taken it.

"A setup," Charlotte murmured, obviously realizing the same thing Roman had. "And you're here because . . . ?"

"You've got something I need." He cursed silently. He hadn't meant to sound so damn suggestive.

She inhaled deeply. For courage? Roman didn't know, but he needed a dose himself, because she stepped forward, not stopping until she was close. So close he could smell her fresh as spring scent and wanted more.

"So what can I get for you?" she asked.

"Rick said he'd called and asked you to leave a list of customer names in an envelope for him." Something related to the panty thief, though Roman hadn't asked specifically what.

She nodded. But she didn't make a move to get the envelope Rick promised would be waiting for Roman, nor did she make a move to get dressed. He didn't know what had prompted Charlotte's change of heart since the last time he'd seen her, but there was no doubting she'd approached and cornered him now. Apparently she had an agenda of her own, but damned if he knew what it was.

Roman let out a sharp exhale. The tables had turned.

Predator had become prey, and he didn't miss the irony. "Where are your clothes?" he asked.

"Why do you care?"

Desire trod a heavy beat inside him, powerful and consuming. All his concentration went into keeping his eyes trained on her face and not on her luscious body. "What's going on, Charlotte?" Damn. Her name sounded like a caress and a heated warmth rushed through his veins.

She lifted one delicate shoulder. "Why are you suddenly fighting what you said you wanted? What you dared me to give?"

She'd avoided his question, asking one of her own instead, her voice hesitant despite her bold stance. But he couldn't answer her without betraying his brothers, their coin toss or Roman's own plan. He could barely face it himself.

He refused to reveal it to Charlotte. "You turned me down flat. What's with the change of heart?"

She was barely dressed and offering him his heart's desire. But he had to fight it or risk jeopardizing the job he loved and the future he wanted.

"I didn't think you'd care about the hows or the whys." She reached for the collar of his denim shirt and ran a shaking finger down one pointed edge.

He actually broke into a sweat. "I do have morals and standards, you know."

"You're also up front about your intentions. You aren't sticking around. I appreciate your honesty."

"I'll always be honest with you, Charlotte."

"Well, I decided that works fine for me." A hesitant smile tipped her lips. "You want to acknowledge the attraction? So do I." She swallowed hard. "I . . . I want you, Roman."

"Oh, damn," he muttered. What kind of man could resist a declaration like that? His hand came around the back of her neck, his fingers threaded into her hair, and he sealed his mouth tight over hers.

This first kiss began gently, indulging the need to explore, but quickly flared out of control, thanks to the hunger of too many pent-up years. A driving need to make up for lost time consumed him. Hot and ravenous, he ran his tongue over the seam of her lips, demanding entry, and she gave it to him. She was moist and damp inside, sweet and pure, and she tasted too damn right.

A throaty moan escaped her lips. He wasn't sure who moved first, but she backed up and he followed, his mouth never leaving hers. They hit the wall behind them. Once they were in the small, enclosed dressing room, the swinging doors closed shut, sealing them inside. His hands traveled from her neck to grip her waist, pulling them into intimate contact. His groin nestled into the vee of her legs and his erection grew, swelling with need as he found a warm and welcoming home.

Her damp feminine heat cushioned him through the rough denim of his jeans. "Sweet Jesus," he muttered, his body full to bursting. The barrier of clothing was restricting and a sweet yet painful ache begged for fulfillment. He shifted from side to side, seeking deeper access than was possible.

As if she'd read his mind, her legs slipped open wider, and he sucked in a ragged breath. They were cheek to cheek, her hands gripping his shoulders, her fingertips digging into the skin beneath his shirt, and her breath came in shallow, uneven gasps.

She surrounded him. Physically, her body cradled his, and when he inhaled he was enveloped in her essence. Her scent fulfilled him in a way that surpassed mere sexual need, and *that* was the notion that brought reality surging back. "What the hell are we doing?" he managed to ask.

She let out a shaky laugh, her breath hot on his skin. "I don't know what you'd call it, but I'm getting you out of my system."

As if such a thing were possible, he thought. Ten years later, and this was still the only woman who jumbled his emotions along with his hormones. She had the ability to make him throw his resolutions to hell and back.

Her head resting against the wall, she studied him through glazed eyes. "You have to admit, the idea's got merit."

He stepped back and ran an unsteady hand through his hair. The idea had merit—if he had the time to play around until he tired of her. Assuming he ever tired of her. Roman had his doubts.

He also had his plan. A destiny he hadn't intended but had to fulfill, thanks to the flip of a coin and strong family obligation. Right now he hadn't a clue how he was going to accomplish his objective, but this woman was hazardous. She didn't want a long-term commitment with a man who didn't plan to stay in Yorkshire Falls. That alone put her off limits.

But Roman also feared she had the ability to pull him back to her, to this town, and make him forget the dreams and life goals he'd always had.

The more he indulged, the deeper she drew him in. "Getting you out of my system's a damn good idea. I haven't a clue how to go about it, but this . . ." He gestured between her nearly naked body and his thoroughly aroused one. "Isn't the smart way of doing it."

Before he could change his mind, he turned and stormed

through the swinging doors, the hinges creaking in his wake. He didn't let himself look back.

Only after he was safely back on the street did he realize he'd forgotten Rick's list of possible suspects. And no way was he walking back into the fire now.

CHAPTER FIVE

The streets of Yorkshire Falls were empty as most of the town gathered inside town hall. After getting a breath of fresh air, Charlotte walked inside to her volunteer workstation, where she acted as punch bowl lookout. On a typical day, no smart adult would touch the punch bowl filled with green liquid, but at the Annual St. Patrick's Day dance, everyone indulged in the colored Kool-Aid.

She told herself she was better off concentrating on making sure no one spiked the punch bowl than on Roman. Just remembering their sensual run-in earlier that day caused goose bumps to prickle along her skin.

She'd gathered every ounce of courage she possessed to turn back toward him and reenact her fantasy. To reach out for him first. To accept and give in to his kiss despite knowing he could hurt her badly. And he had. The man had given her ego a huge bruising she wouldn't soon forget. Now she knew how he'd felt all those years ago. Payback sucked royally, she thought.

And yet she couldn't deny his lingering appeal. She let her gaze wander across the packed room. He was scrumptiously alluring in black jeans and a white pullover shirt. He stood out from the crowd, and not just by defying convention and not wearing green. Her eyes were drawn back to him again and again. Apparently the problem wasn't mutual, because he hadn't once glanced her way.

Instead he drifted from single female to single female, plying his charm, easy grin, and sex appeal. It galled Charlotte to see that he had an extremely receptive audience. She was merely one of many. And it hurt.

She arrived back at her station to find she had company. Raina Chandler sat behind the long table serving as a makeshift bar. "Hi, Raina."

The older woman graced her with a huge, welcoming smile.

"Let me look at you." Charlotte stepped back and took in the older woman's appearance. She was slender as always and a makeup-induced glow radiated in her cheeks. From looking at Raina, Charlotte couldn't tell she'd been in the hospital. "You look wonderful!"

"Thank you. I'm trying not to let my health get me down." Raina's glance darted sideways, then back again.

"Well, haven't seen you all week. I hope that means you're taking good care of yourself. One hospital trip is one too many."

Raina nodded. "I'm learning to be more cautious," she acknowledged. "Now back to you. I've come to relieve you. Go mingle."

"Oh, no." Charlotte shook her head. "I'm not going to let you stand on your feet and handle punch bowl duty. You need rest."

Raina waved a hand in the air, dismissing the possibility. "I'm not your replacement."

Charlotte glanced around, but she didn't see anyone with her. "Who is? Not my mother, I hope?"

"Last I saw, your mother was doing quite nicely. Socializing, even."

"Dennis Sterling?" Charlotte asked, unable to hide the hope in her voice.

"Unfortunately, Dennis is going to be late."

"Darn." As the town's only veterinarian, any animal emergency fell into Dennis's lap.

Raina patted her hand. "Don't worry. If the man's interested, once he takes a look at your mom tonight, he'll be persistent."

"Isn't she gorgeous? I picked her dress myself."

"Your taste is impeccable, as always. You look beautiful too."

"Thank you." Knowing she'd picked out this outfit with Raina's youngest son in mind, Charlotte felt the heat rise to her cheeks. Especially since she'd decided to go with something daring, an outfit she'd purchased during her New York City days.

Maybe he'd been able to resist her enough to pull away, but not before she'd felt his body's reaction to her. The man wasn't immune. And tonight she needed the ego boost of having his appraising eyes focused on her. Unfortunately, that blue gaze wasn't nearly as interested in her tonight as she'd hoped.

"I understand you and my youngest had a run-in," Raina said, as if she could see into Charlotte's innermost thoughts.

The flush turned into a full-fledged burn in her cheeks. Who could possibly have seen her with Roman? she wondered, this afternoon's events playing out in erotic detail in her mind. "I . . . uh . . . we . . ."

"Met up again in Norman's a few nights ago. Rick told

me." Raina ignored Charlotte's exhale of relief and merely patted her hand once more. "You never know what might develop after years apart. I'm here to give you a chance to put that sexy outfit to good use. Sam's going to watch the punch bowl, aren't you?" Raina reached behind her and pulled the town's ultimate loner into view.

"Hi, Sam." She was surprised he'd ventured into a crowded function, but free food and drink might explain that.

"I wanted to ask you how you two were acquainted," Raina said.

"She's just a sucker for an old man," he muttered. Charlotte nodded. She'd always had a soft spot for the loner.

"And Sam sometimes does errands for me." Mailing letters and such in return for cash that enabled him to buy food, she thought, but she didn't say that out loud.

He was a proud man few in town bothered to know or understand. But even as a little girl, she'd remembered seeing her mother reach out to him. Charlotte was saddened, on her return to Yorkshire Falls, to see Sam's solitary life had stayed the same, and she'd gone out of her way to help him without directly offering charity.

"Well, now he's going to watch the punch bowl," Raina said.

"Freeing you to dance with me." Rick Chandler appeared on the opposite side of the table, cornering her in front of his mother with a wink.

The last thing Charlotte needed was time alone with another Chandler man. "As long as I'm being relieved, I think I need some air."

"You just got some, didn't you?" Raina called her on her bluff.

Rick met her gaze. "I need you to bolster my reputation around here. The women are turning me down left and right." He eyed her pointedly and she understood he wanted to talk without creating a scene or a distraction. Police business, probably. She still owed him the list of customers who'd purchased or ordered the handmade panties from her shop.

Better cooperate with Yorkshire Falls' finest, Charlotte thought. "I think a dance will do me more good than fresh air."

Rick pushed the table back to make room for her to slip through.

"And that means I can get back to my . . ." Raina's voice trailed off and she placed a shaky hand on her heart.

"Mom?" Rick asked.

"I'm okay. It's just that maybe coming out tonight wasn't such a good idea. Palpitations." She glanced away, toward the far wall. "I'll just get Eric to sit with me until he can take me home. He's my . . ."

"Date," Rick offered, guiding his arm around his mother's waist. He shot Charlotte a worried glance, but pasted a smile on his face, obviously playing it light with his mother. "You can say it. You're here with your date."

"I'm here with my doctor."

"Who's suddenly paying exclusive attention to one patient?" Rick smiled knowingly at his mother, then gestured across the room, calling the doctor over.

"It's like you said, I'm his patient."

But Charlotte noticed Raina couldn't meet her son's gaze.

"Who's the lucky woman tonight?" Raina asked in an obvious subject change.

"I told you they won't have anything to do with me." He winked Charlotte's way.

"What happened to Donna Sinclair?" his mother asked.

"She only wanted me for my body."

Raina rolled her eyes and Charlotte couldn't help but laugh at the byplay, though she too was concerned about Raina's health.

"Erin Rollins?"

"Last month's news, Mother."

"Then maybe you could try cheering up Beth Hansen."

At the mention of Beth's name, Charlotte started, then grew concerned. "Why? Isn't she with David?" Charlotte didn't expect Beth and her fiancé here, not when they hadn't seen each other going on two weeks.

"I haven't seen Beth but I hear her fiancé's a no-show and figured she'd need a shoulder," Raina said. "But that could just be hearsay."

Charlotte sighed. "I'll stop by on my way home and talk to her."

Raina nodded. "One of you should. Now, Rick, since Charlotte's taken that job, how about you ask Mary Pinto to dance? She's over there by her mother's wheelchair."

He shook his head.

"Lisa Burton?" She pointed to the conservative schoolteacher standing by the wall.

He sighed. "I can find my own dates, Mom. And I'm here talking with Charlotte now. Are you trying to scare her away?"

"Funny. From what I hear of your brother's behavior when Charlotte's near, I thought Charlotte was his concern, not yours."

Before Charlotte could react, Dr. Fallon came up beside them. He promised Rick he'd sit with Raina until she got her strength back, and then he'd drive her straight home. He steered Raina away with a firm hand at her back.

Rick stared after them, amused by the new couple, but obviously very concerned about his mother's health. "She can't be in better hands," Charlotte said.

"I know."

"Anyone ever tell you you Chandlers are like hurricanes?" she asked, speaking of Raina's references to Roman.

Rick shook his head. "Not lately, but it's as good a description as any."

"I adore your mother, but sometimes she can be . . ."

"Blunt," Rick said.

"An admirable trait when aimed at others," Charlotte said with a laugh. "Twice as admirable when she's accumulating business for me. It's just that . . ."

"She embarrassed you talking about Roman."

Charlotte nodded. "Before we dance, do you want to make sure your mother's okay?"

"No. You said it yourself. She couldn't be in better hands than her doctor's. So may I have this dance?" He held out his hand. "You can whisper customer names in my ear."

She laughed. "Why not?"

He swung her into his arms and onto the dance floor in time for a slow dance. It wasn't the most orthodox place to discuss the panty thief. They bumped into many couples on the crowded floor, Pearl and Eldin included. The living-in-sin duo were slow dancing together, too slow in deference to Eldin's bad back. Watching them, happy at their age, should have given Charlotte hope for her own future, but increased her longing for Roman instead.

"Customers, Charlotte," Rick whispered, bringing them cheek to cheek.

"You're one smart cop." She laughed and whispered the needed information in his ear. He had his list of her customers at last.

But the best part of the dance had to be the fact that dancing with Rick had done what Charlotte and her outfit could not. She finally had Roman's attention. He was looking their way, a scowl on his handsome face.

If Roman strangled his brother, he'd burn in hell, but it might be worth the sacrifice just to get Rick's hands off Charlotte's bare back.

Roman clenched his fists at his sides, taking in her green leather pants and the handkerchief-style top that wrapped around her like a sarong and was tied in one knot in the back. One freaking knot that could open with the slightest breeze—or the nimblest fingers. Damn her for wearing an outfit that chic and suggestive anyway. This was a family event in town hall, not a New York City singles dance, for God's sake.

"Yoo-hoo, Roman." A feminine hand waved in front of his face. Terrie Whitehall. He'd forgotten he was deep in conversation about the rudeness of patrons to bank tellers. "What?" he asked, never taking his gaze from Charlotte and Rick. The traitor.

"I'm still not sure what I think of her," Terrie said.

"What you think of who?" Roman had long ago perfected the art of repetition without truly paying attention.

"Charlotte Bronson. You're staring at her, so who else would I be talking about?"

Caught in the act, Roman forced himself to refocus on the brunette looking at him as if he'd lost his mind. "What about her?"

"She's older than I am, mind you . . ."

"Just a year," he reminded her.

"Well, she's never done anything to me. Still, to come home and open up such a *brazen* shop . . ."

"I was under the impression most of the women, young and old, appreciated the cosmopolitan feel she's brought to the town."

"Some women, yes."

But not the jealous, repressed ones, he thought, taking in Terrie's severely pulled-back hair, spare makeup, and ruffled blouse buttoned up to her neck. What the hell had he been thinking, considering her for the mother of his child?

Roman knew darn well what he'd been thinking—that he'd find a woman the distinct opposite of Charlotte in looks. One who worked nine to five in a respectable job, who could provide him with the intelligent conversation he sought. Okay, so he'd found conversation. Some of it intelligent, most of it gossip, and too little of it savvy enough to hold his interest.

He'd also wanted to prove to himself that looks weren't everything—and they weren't, as long as the woman in question had a healthy respect for others, their occupations, and dress. This woman looked down her nose at Charlotte's choices. Scratch her off his list of wife candidates.

Along with the other half dozen women he'd spoken to or been cornered by tonight. After he'd left Charlotte in her shop, he'd gone home to take a long, cold shower and mentally distance himself from the one woman he wanted, so he could hit on the women he didn't.

Backass logic, but then Roman figured this baby scheme was a backass plan to begin with. He looked across the room and spotted his mother. Raina was resting in a chair, deep in conversation with Eric Fallon, the family doctor. He hoped his mother hadn't exerted herself by coming out to a party so soon after her trip to the hospital.

Someone ought to check on her and have a word with the doctor. He excused himself to Terrie. An idea in mind, Roman walked up to his brother and, without a word to Charlotte, grabbed Rick by the shoulder. "I think you ought to check on Mom. She looks kinda pale and she's been sitting in one place most of the night."

Rick inclined his head toward Roman. "Check her yourself. Can't you see I'm busy?"

"She doesn't listen to me. Because I'm not normally around, she thinks I'm fussing too much." Which was true—as far as it went. Raina didn't listen to anyone, all three of her sons included. But if it got his brother's hands off Charlotte's back and waist, Roman would consider the half-truth worth telling.

"Take a hike," Rick shot back.

"I think Roman's got a point."

Charlotte's soft voice hit Roman in the gut, but he ignored the burning sensation. "If you're the one who Raina will level with, go make sure she's okay," she said to Rick.

"She's sitting with her very own doctor, for Pete's sake."

Point to Rick, Roman thought and met Charlotte's gaze. If she knew he wanted only to relieve her of his brother's company, she wasn't letting on. In fact, when she looked at him, her normally warm eyes were cold as ice.

He'd wanted her anger. On some level, he'd courted it intentionally so that he could more easily put her behind him and go on with his mission. But talking to the women in this town had left him empty inside. And his feelings for Charlotte were as strong as ever.

How the hell could he find another woman to marry—

and sleep with—when the only one he desired drew him back to her over and over again?

"Rick, please? If Roman's worried, he obviously sees something worth checking on."

When Rick didn't move, Charlotte spoke. "Tell you what. You two talk. *I'll* check on Raina."

Before either brother could react, Charlotte disengaged herself from Rick's grasp and sauntered over to the other side of the room, far away from either Chandler brother.

"You're lame, pathetic, and obvious," Rick muttered.

"So are you. And it's not like you're interested in anything more than a good time, so keep your goddamn hands off. She deserves better."

Rick studied his brother. "I like women's company. All women, and there's not one in this town who doesn't know the score. They don't get involved if they're looking for more. I enjoy them, they enjoy me, and no one gets hurt."

"Especially you?"

"Including me." Rick shrugged, but the flicker of hurt flashed in his eyes.

Roman immediately regretted the pointed barb he'd shot his brother's way. No one deserved to be used and hurt the way his middle brother had. Especially since he had everyone's best interests in his heart at the expense of his own.

"Rick . . ."

"Forget it." He brushed away Roman's concern with his easy Chandler grin.

Roman groaned. He knew he'd overreacted. He wasn't worried that Charlotte wanted anything more from Rick than a friendship. But rational knowledge didn't mean Roman wanted to watch Rick's too-friendly touches on Charlotte's skin.

"Any chance you could enjoy someone else's company?" he asked his brother.

"Why? Because she's yours?"

When Roman didn't respond to the bait, Rick stepped back, appraising him with the cop look that said, *I'm figuring things out. "You're* the one in the market for a long-distance wife, little brother. If you're so worried about Charlotte deserving better, seems to me you'd better take your own advice."

"No shit," Roman muttered.

"Back off. You're hurting her with mixed messages."

Roman knew Rick better than anyone, and he recognized that his brother was looking out for Charlotte's best interest, and pushing Roman in the right direction at the same time. Rick didn't care if Charlotte went into Roman's arms or away from them as long as neither Roman nor Charlotte got hurt. It was his brother's protective nature at play. The same protective nature that had gotten him in trouble once before.

But much as Roman hated to admit it, Rick had a good point. Roman *was* sending out mixed messages. Charlotte had spent over ten years avoiding him and then, when she finally took him up on his overt signals, what did he do? He rejected her out of self-preservation—at her expense.

Rick slapped Roman on the back. "Now that we've cleared that up, I think I'll set your mind at ease and check on Mom." He turned and headed for Raina and Charlotte, leaving Roman to choke on his own words, the taste of them sour in his mouth.

After another half an hour of attempting to interest himself in the single women of Yorkshire Falls, Roman knew he was failing miserably. And all because of the green-eyed woman who'd bewitched him from day one. Then there was his middle brother, who was hanging around Charlotte, baiting and aggravating Roman—intentionally, no doubt. If Rick was looking to get a reaction, he was too damn close to succeeding.

Especially when Roman turned toward the door in time to see Charlotte and Rick walk out together, his brother's hand on the small of her *naked* back. He'd worry about self-control tomorrow, while self-preservation, he decided, was way overrated.

He stormed outside and into the dark night without looking back.

Raina watched her middle son leave with Charlotte to check on Beth Hansen while her youngest ran out of town hall, all eyes on his abrupt and angry departure. Her sons knew how to make an entrance, but they had to work on their exits.

Still, she couldn't deny the sweeping sense of relief she felt with their departures. She'd have to sit tight. Though she'd love a dance, she couldn't afford gossip to reach her boys. They were too smart and might just figure out her scam if she wasn't careful. Keeping up the charade of poor health was more difficult than she'd imagined when she'd concocted this idea.

She shook her head, then glanced over at the punch bowl. Samson had long since disappeared to be replaced by Terrie Whitehall, Roman's leftovers. She sighed. Much as she adored her boys, she hated the devastation left in their wake. Raina felt particularly protective toward Charlotte. And the last thing she wanted Charlotte Bronson to be was a Chandler casualty.

A daughter-in-law, now, that was another story. "Looks like there are renewed sparks between Roman and Charlotte," Raina said to Eric, pleased her youngest had shown emotion where Charlotte was concerned.

She didn't put much stock in the way he'd sashayed from female to female tonight, ignoring the one who interested him most. And she knew Rick's interest in Charlotte was purely platonic, meant to rouse his sibling's jealousy and perhaps get him to make a move sooner rather than later.

Raina liked that idea. It just might work—if Roman didn't kill Rick first. "Those boys will be the death of me," she said aloud.

Eric bit into the carrots they'd loaded onto a plastic plate earlier. "You're mothering again."

"Do you think Roman's gone after them?"

"Do you think he wants us speculating?"

Raina shrugged. "I'm sure the rest of the room's doing the same. He wasn't exactly discreet about his departure." She tapped her fingernail against the seat of the metal folding chair. "Come to think of it, neither was Annie. Poor Charlotte. Do you think Annie's depression is curable?"

He sighed. "Do you think I'm going to discuss a patient with you?"

"Potential patient. Charlotte said she wants you to treat her mother—assuming she has any kind of condition other than lovesickness. Charlotte's a sweet, caring woman. She'd make a wonderful wife and mother. Speaking of babies . . ."

"Let's not." Eric picked up another carrot from the plastic plate he held on his lap, dipped it into low-fat salad dressing, and popped it into Raina's mouth.

She would have been offended if his tone weren't so deep and compelling and his touch weren't so warm. A long-forgotten heat rose inside her, starting in the pit of her stomach and spreading wide.

She chewed and swallowed the carrot, giving herself time to accept and adjust. "You're trying to distract me," she said when she'd finished eating.

"Your boys are gone. You don't need to act so frail anymore. How am I doing?" He dipped and held up another carrot. "In the distraction department, I mean."

"Not bad, for an old man." She smiled, unable to believe she was flirting. Raina didn't care if distraction was Eric's intent, she liked the male attention and discovered she'd missed it more than she'd realized.

"Who are you calling old?" He dotted the carrot on the tip of her nose and quickly kissed off the bit of dip he'd left behind.

Desire she couldn't mistake swelled in her chest. "You certainly don't make me feel old," she murmured. She didn't even care that they were in a public place where anyone could see.

"I should hope not." He laughed and leaned closer, so he could whisper in her ear. "And I'm betting in time I can make you feel even younger. So young you'll forget your quest for grandchildren and think about only me."

"I'd like to see you try." And try, and try. As long as he continued to make her feel young, vibrant, and alive, he had her permission to experiment all he wanted. She hoped Roman intended to do the same.

With Charlotte.

Charlotte left town hall with Rick and together they went to check on Beth. She rented a room in an old house on the outskirts of town. With its wraparound porch, trellis, huge front lawn, and the sunlight that shone into the kitchen, the house had the ambience of home. It was the exact type of place Charlotte had always dreamed of living in one day, when she had a family of her own. It was the dream she'd had when she wasn't fantasizing about faraway places with exotic names and incredibly beautiful scenery illuminated by glistening water and the sun's glorious rays.

Sometimes Charlotte thought she had a split personality, two people living inside her craving two different things. Still, both scenarios included sunshine and a happy ending, something she wanted for Beth too.

And there was no hint of either in her friend's expression, which made Charlotte want to strangle Dr. Implant. "Why couldn't he make it this weekend?"

Beth shrugged. "He *said* he had an unexpected speaking engagement."

Beth turned and stared out the window.

"Is that new language for *something suddenly came up?*" Charlotte whispered to Rick.

He shot her a warning look, which she heeded. But she just didn't understand why Beth's fiancé didn't bring her to the city or pay more attention to the woman he claimed to love.

"Maybe something suddenly did come up. Like a speaking opportunity he couldn't turn down." Rick walked up beside Beth and put a friendly arm around her shoulder.

"Then why didn't he ask me to join him in New York?" She turned to look at Charlotte.

Charlotte inclined her head, having no answers. Her friend had a valid point, but she wasn't about to admit it now.

"Maybe he didn't want you to be bored," Rick said. "And maybe—"

"He'll make it up to you," Charlotte added, picking up

on his list of possible explanations. He obviously sought to protect Beth's already bruised feelings, and he was right. There was time enough for Beth to face and accept the truth—whatever that was. Tonight she just needed her friends.

Charlotte glanced over to where Rick was showering Beth with attention in a futile attempt to restore her humor and self-esteem. Beth was even smiling at his bad jokes. At least someone was helping. Charlotte was in too foul a mood to do her friend much good.

First her mother disappeared out a side door just as Dennis Sterling walked in the front entrance, then Beth missed the town's big night because she'd been stood up again. Charlotte didn't know what was worse, a woman relying on a man for happiness or being manless and miserable.

Her stomach cramped and her heart lodged in her throat. Charlotte knew she was comparing herself with both Beth and Annie, fearful of being just like them. Both women were unhappy over a man. Even if *miserable* was too strong a word for how Charlotte was feeling now, she couldn't deny that the emotions Roman evoked within her were strong.

He treated her to sexy come-ons, encouraging and emboldening her to act, then he shut her down without reason, and followed up the insult by first ignoring her and then showering other women with his charms. If only sexual attraction were at work, Charlotte could deal with this better. But her reaction to Roman went beyond the physical. She wanted to know the man inside the gorgeous body, and that frightened her.

Damn the man anyway. She rubbed her bare arms, wanting to go home. Her two friends were engaged in conversation, Rick providing a friendly distraction for Beth.

Charlotte slipped out without being noticed. The full moon in the night sky guided her way, the stars providing a glittering backdrop to the inky background above. The scent of the outdoors—new grass and flowers—accompanied every breath she took. She tried to give the panty thief some thought. Rick said things had been quiet during the week, but he didn't consider the case over or forgotten. Charlotte drew a blank on who could be responsible, so she gave up trying.

Twenty minutes later, she was home and had shed her party clothes and changed into lounging wear—her favorite outfit, a white tank dress that hung to midcalf with a thick lace ruffle around the hem. She'd snagged it out of the box before Beth could hang the garment or sell it to a customer. It was one of the few items Charlotte had taken home instead of selling—because in it she felt feminine yet comfortable, and completely herself.

After mixing a glass of iced tea, she grabbed her favorite book, pushed open the window that led to the fire escape, and climbed out. The cool breeze brushed over her skin, but she didn't mind. From the moment she'd seen this apartment, the hidden escape had been her favorite part of the deal—if she didn't count the ability to roll out of bed and walk downstairs to work.

Anytime Charlotte climbed out here, she found herself alone, and she adored the solitude. She sat down, the oversized book in her lap, and began to browse through the pages. Of all the travel books and brochures she owned, *Glamorous Getaways* was her favorite. She'd purchased it with money from her first babysitting job and chosen it because the book highlighted Los Angeles, with the Hollywood sign nestled in the foothills. Within the City of

Angels were the stars and celebrities, people like her father, she thought, when she was still little enough to dream.

Buying this book had enabled her to picture the places she thought he'd go, the restaurants he'd frequent, and the people he'd meet there. She'd conjured scenarios in which he'd take her by the hand and introduce her to the beautiful people while showing her the exotic places. Later, after she'd grown up and realized he wasn't ever coming back for good, she'd substituted the dream of him taking her with him to traveling and seeing these places for herself.

But with that dream came the dreaded fear of being like the man she disdained, and Charlotte knew in her heart she'd never dare make those kinds of trips herself. Never again take the chance on being disillusioned by bitter reality. Or of turning selfish, like him.

Still, when she needed soothing, books like this one provided the distraction. She'd simply put her father and her past out of her mind, and enjoy the fantasy of travel and seeing wonderful new places. She inhaled deeply and flipped through the pages, but she wasn't able to lose herself. Not tonight.

Just then, she heard a banging on her door. She rubbed her arms, realizing goose bumps had settled on her skin. The knock sounded again and she headed back inside to see who could possibly be out there. Nearly midnight wasn't appropriate calling time by Yorkshire Falls standards.

She placed the book back on the table and walked to the door. "Who's there?"

"Roman. Open up."

Her stomach did an unsettling flip. "It's late." And she wasn't in the mood for any more push and shove between them.

He banged on the door once more. "Come on, Charlotte.

Give me five minutes." His voice was a deep, seductive rumble.

She leaned against the door—even with plasterboard between them, her body flushed with heat. "Go away."

"Not until we talk."

"Come by the shop in the morning." When Beth was around as a buffer, Charlotte thought.

His fist pounded the door in response.

"You're going to wake the neighbors."

"Then let me in."

"I wish I could," she said, too low for him to hear. No way could she allow him into her small apartment, where he'd overwhelm her with his presence, his scent, his essence. She tipped her forehead against the cool plaster but found no relief from the internal heat he inspired.

Silence descended from outside, and though it was what she'd told him she wanted and she ought to be relieved, Charlotte was disappointed he'd given up so easily. She walked back to the table, but the book, which she'd found appealing before, now just served as a reminder of pain. Suddenly a loud clatter reverberated from outside, the sound of heavy banging coming from the fire escape stairs.

Obviously the man didn't give up as easily as she'd thought. Her heart rate picked up rhythm and her pulse pounded in her dry throat. She watched as Roman reached her terrace and ducked so he could wedge his big body through the window frame. He entered her apartment and rose to his full height.

He was imposing no matter when she saw him, but in her small apartment, his size and magnetism were overwhelming. She swallowed hard, wondering what he wanted—and if she'd have the strength to resist the tug-of-war he so enjoyed.

CHAPTER SIX

Charlotte stood in her apartment, hands on her hips, and eyed Roman warily. He felt like a first-class shit—which he supposed he was, considering all that had passed between them since his return, including his current uninvited entry into her apartment.

After leaving the dance, he'd hung around her building for the better part of the night. The longer she'd been gone, the wilder his imagination had grown, until he'd been forced to face the fact that when it came to Charlotte, his emotions were out of control. That she'd finally returned, alone, hadn't made a bit of difference in calming him down. Though Rick respected brotherly boundaries, Charlotte by no means belonged to Roman.

No matter how damn proprietary he felt, he had to let go. His pacing time tonight had given him the opportunity to think, and Roman now knew exactly what he had to say to Charlotte. He just didn't know how to begin.

"You're strangely silent for a man who just broke into my apartment," she said at last.

"I didn't break in—"

"I didn't let you in the front door, so what do you call barging in through the window?"

"Visiting." Stalling. He ran a hand through his hair. "Obviously you're not in the mood to talk to me, so how about you just hear me out?"

She shrugged. "You're here. The sooner you talk, the sooner you'll leave."

Now that he'd entered the inner sanctum, leaving was the last thing he desired. Her small apartment was frilly and feminine, much like Charlotte. He took in the white walls, yellow trim, flowered furniture, and though he ought to feel out of place surrounded by so much femininity, he was intrigued and aroused instead. The journalist in him wanted to dig deeper, learn more. The man in him just wanted her.

Looking at her skimpy tank dress pumped more adrenaline through his veins. Though obviously meant for casual comfort, it was completely sensual. The snow-white shade contrasted with her tousled black hair. For a color that symbolized innocence, the white sheath conjured thoughts that were anything but pure.

But he wasn't here to indulge in the sensual dance they did so well. He was here to explain himself and his feelings—something Roman Chandler had never done before, certainly not to a woman. But Charlotte wasn't just any woman. She never had been.

And she deserved to know his pulling back had nothing to do with his feelings for her and everything to do with their differences—and the fact that he respected her needs. "I need to clear some things up."

"What things?"

"You talked about the need to get me out of your system and vice versa."

Her eyes opened wide, her vulnerability as apparent as

the sexual tension humming between them. "You rejected that offer, as I recall. You pushed me away, then ignored me in public and now you're back, barging into my private space, wanting to talk. You're interested, you're not interested, you're interested again." Her hands waved back and forth in time to her rapid-fire talk and her quick pacing in front of him. "Do I look like a pull toy to you?"

Her question confirmed Rick's claim and Roman's fears, that he was hurting her with mixed signals, and for that he owed her an explanation. But she didn't give him a chance to respond.

"Or maybe that's what you like—the chase. The forbidden. Maybe you're one of those men who doesn't want something once it's too easy." She shook her head. "And damn but I made it easy." Her face flushed crimson with the memory of what happened between them in the dressing room of her store.

He caught her wrist on one of her walk-bys and held her in place until she met his gaze, her green eyes focused solely on his.

"You think I don't want you?" he bit out through clenched teeth.

"I haven't seen any evidence to the contrary."

Her words were the equivalent of a dare, arousing his baser instincts. All good intentions aside, she'd pushed him to the edge and over. He stepped forward, backing her against the wall until their bodies aligned. No way could she miss the evidence of his desire any more than he could ignore her distended nipples, pointy and hard against his chest. Without waiting for a response, he bent his head for a kiss—a tongue-tangling, dueling kiss that was as mutual as it was hot.

Breaking the moment between them took all the resolve

he had but he lifted his head. "How's that for evidence?" He asked, still breathing heavily.

She sucked in a heavy breath, then pushed herself back. "Okay, Roman. No more games."

The last thing he intended was to play with her emotions, but every time she was near, his own feelings rampaged out of control, causing him to act contrary to common sense.

"What do you want with me?" She rubbed her hands up and down her skin, as if she could cradle herself in warmth and comfort.

He let out a groan. "What I want and what I can take are two different things." They'd finally gotten to the crux of the matter. "I'm not staying in town," he said, softer now, lowering his voice, speaking the one truth he knew would push her away. No matter how much it hurt him to do it.

"I know." She bit down on her lower lip, gnawing the plump skin between her teeth. "And I wish my father had been as honest with my mother."

Her words caught Roman off guard. He knew only what the rest of town knew—that Russell Bronson had breezed out of Yorkshire Falls, abandoning his wife and young child. He returned at intermittent intervals, stayed for a while, only to take off again. Roman also knew the abandonment caused both women much pain. Something he never wanted or intended to do.

He reached out and touched Charlotte's cheek. "It's not the same thing."

"That's because I'd know going in there's no long-term commitment involved. Otherwise it'd be exactly the same."

Her voice was husky and emotion-filled, reaching deep down and touching Roman's heart. It had been a long time since anyone or anything struck such an emotional chord inside him. Not since his father's death and the early years of his mother's grief, and Roman instinctively rebelled against the welling feelings.

Unfortunately, the chord, once struck, reverberated with intensity and truth. And he didn't like being lumped in a category that held the town's deadbeat dad and wandering husband, the man who'd hurt Charlotte badly.

"I'd never dishonor my commitments that way." But as Roman spoke, he realized that was exactly what he'd planned to do.

Get married, impregnate his wife, and get out. Exactly what Charlotte's father had done to her mother. Roman had just been too self-absorbed by the life change ahead of him to consider what his actions would or could do to the woman he involved.

He shook his head, disgusted. Even if his motives were unselfish, for his mother's good and not his own, his actions were destined to hurt someone just the same. He swallowed a curse. Seen through Charlotte's eyes, Charlotte's past, his plans were disgraceful.

But the family obligation and his mother's need remained. Roman could only hope his same plan, as selfish as he now realized it was, would be viewed differently by a woman who didn't fear abandonment, who understood the way things had to be going in, and who wanted a child but not necessarily the typical family scenario too. Charlotte wouldn't understand or accept. Another woman might. But if Roman didn't get Charlotte out from under his skin as soon as possible, his promise to his brothers was in jeopardy.

"I know you're not sticking around," she said. "I knew that when I . . . when I approached you. But getting you out of my system—that has nothing to do with long-term. I don't want a commitment from you. I wasn't asking for one."

"But you'd resent me in the end. It's not in you to accept less, and I can't give more. I'm not the kind of man you need. The stay-around-forever kind of guy." He shook his head. "Us getting involved would be foolish. And painful." For both of them. "No matter how much we wish otherwise."

She inclined her head and her cheek came to rest in the palm of his hand. "I know you wouldn't. Dishonor your commitments, I mean. You Chandlers are too forthright."

If she only knew, Roman thought. Charlotte must never ever know about the coin toss and the damn deal. "We're the town's most upstanding citizens," he said wryly.

"That's why you're here spilling your guts why you turned me down. It's more than I once did for you," she admitted softly. "You're a hell of a man, Roman. More than I ever gave you credit for."

"Don't make the mistake of painting me as a good guy," he warned her.

She tipped her head back, looking at him through thick lashes. "I wouldn't call you an angel, but you are looking out for me. I appreciate that even if I don't like what I'm hearing." A regret-filled smile tilted her lips.

"I can't say I like it either." Any of it. Despite his words of warning and protest, Roman desperately wanted to kiss those lips one last time. A final good-bye.

She must have read his mind, because she lifted up onto her tiptoes at the same time he lowered his mouth to hers. But a simple kiss wasn't enough to satisfy his craving and he held her face in his hands, cradling her for deeper access to her moist mouth.

It was meant to be a farewell kiss, strong and hot enough

to fill a lifetime of memories. He slipped his hands around her waist and began to bunch the material of her dress, pulling the soft cotton upward inch by inch until he could finally feel the bare skin on her midriff.

His fingers gripped her soft, warm flesh, and as she let out a soft sigh, his heart thudded harder in his chest.

And all of a sudden he knew—he couldn't say good-bye any more than he could choose another woman as his wife to bear his children. Before he could process that thought, a loud knock sounded at the door, startling them both.

She jumped back and reality returned along with a banging that wouldn't cease.

Roman expelled a frustrated groan. "Tell me you're not expecting company."

"I'm not." She averted her eyes, unable to meet his gaze. "I wasn't expecting you either, and there's no one else who'd come by this time of night without calling first."

"Good." He wasn't in the mood to deal with other human beings. "Go away," he called out and got one of her elbows in his ribs.

"I said I wasn't expecting anyone, but it could be important."

He let her go, shock still rippling through him at the conclusion he'd come to after that kiss.

"Open up, Roman. It's the police." Rick's voice traveled to them.

Despite the somber mood that had settled between them, Charlotte failed to stifle a laugh and Roman wasn't amused. Rick was the last person he wanted to see. Especially when just the thought of his brother and Charlotte still managed to charge him up.

As she walked to the door, she smoothed her wrinkled

dress and ran a shaking hand through her messed hair. It was impossible to hide what they'd been doing.

Nor did he want to. Her well-kissed lips branded her, and damn if Roman didn't like it that way.

So much for good intentions. He'd barged in to apologize for sending out those mixed signals. He'd intended to say good-bye and put an end to any illusions either of them held about each other. But with Charlotte, nothing was ever final or finished, no matter how hard he tried.

Realization dawned, taking him off guard. Good-bye wasn't possible. Not with Charlotte. He couldn't walk away from this woman and turn to another, no matter what his reasons.

He shook his head, knowing he'd had a shock just now. Knowing he'd give her one too. Instead of freeing himself for his potential wife hunt, Roman already had his candidate. One who didn't want to play the stay-at-home wife to the long-distance, globe-trotting husband. There'd have to be compromises there. But that was okay. Even the best-laid plans often changed along the way. And when it came to Charlotte, he'd alter accordingly. He had no choice.

But first he had to convince her to give *them* a chance after his whole speech about walking away. He let out a groan. Roman knew she wouldn't slam doors in his face. Given the chance, she'd sleep with him in an attempt to get him out of her system. And all the while she'd be trying to convince herself she could walk away in the end.

He had no choice but to convince her she was wrong. He'd have to take her there slowly, that much he knew. But this time there was no turning back.

His stomach churned with the conclusions he'd drawn, but dammit, they felt right. He rolled his shoulders, attempting to ease the tension, and before he could contemplate further, Charlotte had let Rick inside. Chase followed close behind.

Roman wondered what was up, to bring both his brothers to her apartment.

"Is Beth okay?" Charlotte met Rick's gaze, concern for her friend obvious.

"She's fine. I left her when I got an emergency call, but she was doing okay."

"Then what's going on?" She eyed Rick warily. "Roman doesn't need a chaperone, so to what do I owe this visit?"

Roman wanted an answer to that as well.

"Let's sit," Rick said.

"Let's not," Roman muttered. He didn't want to prolong their visit.

"It's the panty thief, isn't't?" Charlotte asked, her voice rising. "He's struck again?"

"She's smart," Rick said. "Did you know she was smart, Roman?"

"Smart aleck." Charlotte laughed.

Roman rolled his eyes, turned, and headed for the living area. Apparently he was in for a sit-down with his cop brother, his other sibling, and Charlotte, not his lover or even his ex-lover . . . but his future wife. He refused to consider the ramifications if she refused him. Roman's adrenaline began a steady pumping, nerves and acceptance warring for dominance. He could only imagine *her* reaction to his thoughts—but no way could he clue her in. Not yet. Not until he'd made her his in a way she couldn't deny.

He lowered himself onto the butter-soft flowered couch. "What's up?" he asked when they were all seated.

"Charlotte's right. We've had another break-in." Rick broke the silence first.

"And I'm going to press on it in the morning," Chase said.

Roman nodded. He knew his older brother couldn't keep another theft under wraps. That he'd done it at all was out of respect for the police and their need to investigate without tipping their hand.

Charlotte leaned forward. "Please tell me they didn't steal the exact same brand."

Rick nodded. "Jack Whitehall isn't too thrilled about the brand choice either."

"Frieda's pair?" Charlotte placed her head in her hands and groaned. "I only just finished making them. We mailed those to her house a few days ago."

Roman picked up on something Rick had said. "What's got Whitehall so upset, other than the obvious fact that his house was robbed?" Why would the older man give a damn what brand had been taken?

"Well, as far as Jack knew, his wife favored plain, utilitarian white," Rick said.

"Frieda's pair *was* white," Charlotte said, in obvious defense of her customer.

"White and sexy," Chase clarified. "We left them arguing over who she planned to wear the panties for."

"She bought them for her husband's seventieth birthday surprise," Charlotte muttered. "Leave it to a man to draw all sorts of wrong conclusions."

"Hey, go easy on the gender, babe," Roman said and she slugged him in the gut with her elbow. He let out a grunt. At least the pain gave his body something to focus on other than his desire. And when the pain subsided, Roman turned to taking in his surroundings as a distraction from her luscious scent. He ran his hand over a glossy coffee table book that had seen better days.

"So that's three robberies total . . ." she said.

"Five."

That number caught Roman's attention.

"*Five?*" he and Charlotte asked at the same time.

"Three occurred tonight alone. While the entire town was at the St. Patrick's Day dance, some guy was out stealing women's panties."

"Who would do something so . . . so . . ." Charlotte rose from her seat, and, sensing her frustration, Roman didn't try to stop her. "So juvenile? So stupid? So *perverted?*" she asked.

Rick snickered. Roman had no desire to relive his youth in front of Charlotte. "Well, we can narrow down the list of suspects by knowing who we all saw at the dance."

"There's one problem," Rick said.

"What's that?"

"The timing won't work. The last robbery took place around ten-thirty. Whitehall chased the guy into his backyard, but he was slick and made for the small stretch of woods. Then Whitehall's asthma kicked in and the old man collapsed."

"Damn," Roman muttered.

"Exactly. We know it's someone with good stamina. And if he hit two houses before ten-thirty, on different streets, far apart, he had plenty of time. Collectively we don't know a damn thing. I left the party around nine forty-five, Chase never made it because he was working, and according to witnesses, you, little brother, took off by nine forty-eight."

"Something Whitehall made certain we knew," Chase said.

Apprehension settled in Roman's gut. "Why?"

Charlotte stopped her pacing in front of where Chase sat in her oversized club chair. "Yes, why?"

Chase pinched the bridge of his nose and Roman knew he was in deep shit. "The old man was reminded of a certain prank Roman played a long time ago."

"A long, long time ago," Roman muttered.

"When he was juvenile and stupid," Rick said, picking up on Charlotte's chosen words.

"But not perverted," Chase said with a grin.

"The panty raid," Charlotte murmured. "It's been so long I'd forgotten."

"I wish everyone had." Roman shot his brothers a nasty look.

"Still, why would Whitehall dig up an old stunt like that now?" she asked.

Roman rubbed his hands over his eyes. "Because the sleepover was at Jeannette Barker's, but the panties I snagged—"

"And hung from the rearview mirror," Rick supplied ever so helpfully.

"Belonged to Terrie Whitehall," Chase finished. "Who came racing into her parents' home tonight just as we were leaving."

Damn, how had Roman forgotten that? All the while he'd been talking to the prissy bank teller tonight and it'd never crossed his mind that he'd once stolen her underwear. "So when Terrie heard what was taken from her mother, she decided I had to be the culprit?" Roman asked with a disbelieving shake of his head.

"No, she just mentioned she'd seen you storm out of town hall. Unfortunately, she wasn't the only one who saw you leave." Rick rose and folded his arms over his chest. "Jack Whitehall fingered you as a possible suspect."

Roman couldn't believe what he was hearing. "That's a crock of—"

"I agree, but once an accusation's been made, I have to investigate." In his best law enforcement stance, marred only by the half grin on his face, Rick turned to Roman and said, "Mind if I ask where you went after leaving town hall tonight? And if anyone can vouch for your whereabouts?"

Charlotte opened and closed her mouth in disbelief. Chase burst out laughing.

This night had been full of surprises, Charlotte thought as she walked Rick and Chase to the door. With Roman standing behind her, she had a hunch they weren't over yet. "Thanks for stopping by to let me know there'd been another robbery."

Rick paused in his tracks. "All kidding aside, we stopped by to *warn* you. There's been five break-ins with one link and one link only—*you.* Not only do you sell the items that have been stolen, you make them."

Roman's eyebrows raised in surprise, but he didn't ask questions, just took over. "Which is why I'm not leaving her alone."

She shook her head and remained silent. She'd already anticipated Roman's protective streak kicking in, but she planned to save the argument against his staying until they were alone.

She appreciated his concern, but it was unwarranted. The panty thief had struck homes of customers and no one had been hurt. She'd be careful, but she trusted she was safe. She couldn't have him staying the night. With gossip as the town's favorite pastime, she had no intention of her neighbors waking up to find him sneaking out the door—or fire escape—at the first crack of dawn.

"You're safe enough when you're home," Rick said, eyeing Roman and helpfully giving her an out if she wanted one. "With neighbors on either side of you, no one would be foolish enough to break in here—but I suggest you keep that window shut tight and locked. At this point, you don't want to take chances by giving any sleazeball who wants in an open invitation."

She met Roman's gaze out of the corner of her eye and somehow managed to stifle a laugh. They both knew he was the last sleazeball who'd climbed through her window tonight, but she saw no reason to give his brothers any more ammunition.

They were lovingly hassling him enough already—something she'd never experienced in her lifetime. She was an only child who'd matured too quickly after her father left, while despite it all, the Chandler brothers had been able to grow up in due time and still be kids. Sibling rivalry, one-upsmanship, and love were so apparent among the brothers that being with them brought a lump to Charlotte's throat. She hadn't had any kind of true family unit and realized now how much she'd missed.

She glanced back at the open window. "I'll take care of it, I promise."

"We're working overtime, but I can't promise anything until we catch the guy, so watch out."

She nodded once more.

Chase placed a brotherly hand on her shoulder. "Once I print the article, you can bet you'll have a town full of people watching your back too."

"Just what I needed, the spotlight on me and my life." She sighed. "I hope this doesn't kill my business. I can't afford for people to be afraid to buy my goods."

Rick shook his head. "The way I figure it, the worst-case scenario will mean a decline in sales in the garment of choice."

"I hope you're right." Because she couldn't afford a drop in overall sales and still pay her rent. Her savings from her days in New York wouldn't last much longer and she was just beginning to see a positive cash flow.

"We'll have someone patrolling the neighborhood, okay?"

She nodded and finally shut the door behind Rick and Chase. Then she steeled herself and turned to face Roman. He leaned one shoulder against the wall, sexy in his stance and confident in his expression.

If she didn't know better, she'd say something had shifted between them. Again.

"What's so different about the underwear that's being stolen?" he asked.

"You tell me. You saw it yourself firsthand." She swallowed hard. "In the dressing room the other day."

The memory darkened his eyes to a stormy blue hue. "You handmade those?"

She nodded. He laced his hand through hers, his callused fingertips wreaking havoc with her nerve endings and sending white-hot darts of fire throughout her body. At last he held her hands up for further inspection. "I didn't realize I was dealing with an artist."

She let out a shaky laugh, unnerved by his touch and the longing he always inspired. "Let's not get carried away."

"Sweetheart, I saw those panties and I saw you in them. I'm definitely not exaggerating. In fact, I can see why a man would go to extreme lengths to get his hands on a pair. Especially if you were wearing them." His voice lowered to a husky, seductive level.

He turned her wrist out and placed a strategic kiss, followed by a nip of his teeth on one fingertip. Her nipples hardened with the first soft bite and as he moved on to each successive fingertip, her entire body raged with burning need.

She wondered where this was headed, why he'd started seducing her now, instead of saying good-bye. She didn't understand his sudden change in mood. She had no doubt that kiss earlier had been intended as a final farewell.

"Did you know I couldn't take my eyes off you tonight?" Roman laved the inside of her wrist and blew cool air onto her dampened skin.

She stifled a delighted moan. "You could have fooled me."

"I was trying to fool us both. Even tonight when I barged in here with the deluded notion I could walk away from you, I was trying to fool us both."

Her heart caught in her throat and she listened carefully.

"Over the years I've perfected the art of watching without being caught. It's a necessity in my line of work." His mouth traveled up her arm, arousing her with the featherlight touch of his lips. "I *was* watching you."

"Mmm. Then you definitely managed to fool me."

"But I don't think I fooled Terrie Whitehall," he said when he'd reached her shoulder, then stopped to nuzzle the sensitive skin on Charlotte's neck.

Her knees buckled and she leaned back against the wall for support. "So Terrie turned on you out of jealousy?"

"Sounds like it," he said, his breath hot on Charlotte's flesh.

He braced his hands on the wall behind her and sandwiched her with his lean, hard body. She struggled for even breaths as his erection, full and solid, came to rest between her legs. She tried to remember what they'd been discussing, but words failed her. "I can't concentrate," she murmured.

"That's the point." He threaded his hands through her hair. "Let me stay tonight, Charlotte. Let me take care of you."

She'd expected this attempt to play bodyguard. "Your staying is not a good idea." Much as she would have enjoyed it. She braced both her hands against his shoulders, but instead of pushing him away, she savored the heat and strength of his body against hers.

"Then why does it feel like one?" His hips jerked forward, thrusting his hard length against her feminine mound.

Waves of sensation rose to life. Her lashes fell and she savored the feeling. "It feels good because there's nothing rational about sex. But I'm being rational now. You can't stay because you came over here to say good-bye. You said as much earlier." She recalled his words, the pain lodging in her throat.

"And then I kissed you and I realized there's no way in hell I can walk away."

"What?" Excitement and hope unlike any she'd known sizzled to life inside as she contemplated his words. "What are you saying?" she asked, because she had to be sure.

"There's always been something between us. Something that won't go away. If you've got the guts to take the risk and see where it leads, then so do I." His blue eyes stared into hers.

Her pulse began an unsteady beat. He'd taken her by surprise. Apparently he'd shocked himself too. She understood the push and pull between them as well as he did.

But despite the fact that he'd taken her off guard, she'd already thought this possibility through. An affair with Roman wasn't only what she wanted, but what she needed as well. Because by giving in to the desire that had been brewing for years, she'd give it a chance to run its course.

Without a doubt, Charlotte knew she'd be risking her heart. She'd walked away from him once before, and though she never admitted it, even to herself, she'd regretted it deep inside. She needed to experience making love with him. Needed the memories to cherish for a lifetime without him.

But she'd have closure. Unlike her mother, who subjected herself to an endless stretch of waiting ahead of her, Charlotte would be strong and come out whole.

"So can I stay?" he asked with that charming grin on his face.

"Because you think I need protection from a nonexistent threat or because you want to be with me?"

"Both reasons work for me."

"I can take care of myself. Even Rick said I'm safe. As for the other . . . it's too soon." Charlotte wasn't about to leap into bed with him no matter how hard her body protested against her decision.

She wanted time to assimilate his intentions. To know this time he wouldn't change his mind again. But most of all, she wanted to get to know him better. All of him. She needed time to get inside both his head and his heart. Because when he walked away, as she knew he would, she had no intention of being hard to forget. Heaven knew, she wouldn't forget him, even if she would be moving on.

Roman nodded, accepting her answer. He didn't want to push, not when he'd made headway and broken past her wary barriers. She was laughing at his jokes, accepting his change of heart. It was enough for now.

After all his mixed messages, he didn't expect her to open up and trust him overnight. "How about I sleep on the floor and play bodyguard?" he asked in a last-ditch effort to spend more time with her.

She shook her head and laughed. "Neither of us would get any sleep."

"Sleep's overrated. We could stay up talking." At least he'd be by her side.

"We wouldn't talk, and you know it." Her cheeks flushed a healthy shade of pink. "But the neighbors would."

Personally Roman didn't give a damn what the neighbors said, but Charlotte did, and in a small town, business was tied to reputation. He ran a frustrated hand through his hair, then he forced himself to accept what she was saying.

"You'll call if you need me? If you even think you need me?"

She met his gaze. "Oh, I need you, Roman. I just won't be calling for *that* kind of need."

He exhaled hard. He needed her too. In a way that reached past sexual desire. Like she'd wrapped a hand around his heart. He just hoped like hell she planned to release him when it was time to move on.

Roman rose to a blanket of sunshine covering his childhood room and bathing his body in heat. He'd left Charlotte's apartment, but she'd remained with him all night long, in dreams that were hot and compelling, yet strangely unfulfilled.

He shut his eyes and leaned back into his pillows, conjuring everything he'd learned last night. While she and his brothers had discussed the latest break-ins, Roman had used his talents for listening to one thing while taking in something else—and he'd discovered the glossy oversized books and magazines laid out on the table in front of him. The covers detailed distant places and glamorous locales. Some were domestic, others foreign, like castles in Scotland, or exotic, like the South Pacific. Nothing unusual for conversation pieces, Roman thought.

Many people bought similar oversized books for decorative appeal. But few people read them until they were well worn and even fewer left those dog-eared copies out for show. Charlotte had.

So as he'd glanced around, he'd been able to put a picture together in his mind, one of contradictions and enticements. Charlotte was feminine and sexy. Predictably, she liked flowers. Yet she was hesitant, uncertain of her appeal, and any bold moves didn't come easily—which made her choice of business rather unpredictable, he thought. As were the undergarments she handmade. They exposed more than they hid—baring not just the skin beneath the crocheted panties, but Charlotte and her inner self.

The books revealed much more. Although she liked hearth and home in Yorkshire Falls, there was a part of her that was intrigued by foreign locales and exotic places. The notion brought a rush of adrenaline through his veins. She was more perfect for him than she was ready to admit.

Charlotte, he thought. She enthralled him in a way no story, no woman, ever had. He needed to win her over, to convince her that they were so intricately entwined, they had no choice but to make a life together work. Only then could he fulfill his obligation to his family and satisfy his mother's desire for a grandchild. Only then could he return to life on the road, go where the stories took him, and continue to bring public awareness to important issues. And maybe one day, she'd want to travel with him.

"Oh, my God. Roman, wake up." His mother's voice traveled toward him.

There was something to be said for living alone, and

when his mother barged into his room without knocking, he remembered what it was. Privacy.

He sat up in bed and yanked the covers over himself. "Morning, Mom."

Her eyes glittered with knowledge and a touch of amusement that absolutely alarmed him. "Read this." She shoved the *Gazette* into his personal space, waving it in front of his face.

He grabbed the paper. "'PILFERED PANTIES,'" he read aloud.

"Nice alliteration," she said. "Chase always did well in English."

He glanced up at his mother and saw laugh lines creasing her cheeks. "Aren't you concerned about the thefts?" he asked her.

"Rick's got things under control. So does Chief Ellis. Besides, no one's been hurt. Read the last line, Roman."

Before he could comply, she whisked the paper out of his hands and read to him. "As of yet the police have no suspects, but Jack Whitehall chased a male, Caucasian, into his backyard before he disappeared into the woods behind the house. Although the police have yet to name a suspect, Jack Whitehall fingered Roman Chandler's return as coinciding with the first theft one week ago. According to Mr. Whitehall, Roman Chandler was behind a childhood prank involving stolen underwear. No charges were filed in the incident, which took place over a decade ago, and the police believe the incidents to be unrelated."

"Nice piece of reporting," he muttered.

"What do you have to say for yourself?"

He rolled his eyes. "Jesus, Mom, I was in high school." What did she expect him to say?

But as for his brother, Roman was pissed. Even if the

quote was attributed to Whitehall and denied by the cops, Roman couldn't believe Chase would report such bullshit. "You'd think Chase would have more sense than to—"

"Chase reports the facts, young man. Don't go blaming your brother for things coming back to haunt you."

Roman hadn't heard his mother take that no-nonsense tone with one of her sons in years. Given the soft-spoken voice she'd developed since her illness, her tone surprised him now. But she'd never put up with one brother being angry at another, and that wouldn't change just because she wasn't feeling well. She believed her boys should be a unit. Stick together no matter what.

Most times Roman agreed. Now wasn't one of them. But he didn't like her pacing or worrying because he was annoyed with Chase. "Sit down. Getting upset isn't good for your heart." He patted the bed.

She looked startled, then lowered herself slowly to the foot of the bed. "You're right. I just thought you ought to be prepared. You've been fingered as a panty pirate."

Roman could do nothing in return but scowl and fold his arms across his chest.

"The one thing I can't figure is what the women's reaction will be."

He braced himself. "What do you mean?"

His mother shrugged. "I'm not sure if they're going to throw themselves at you or run the other way. For your sake, you'd better hope it's a turn-on. *I* hope it's a turn-on, or those grandchildren I want are an even longer ways off."

Roman muttered a curse. "How about you pick on Rick or Chase?"

Raina tapped her foot against the hardwood floor, narrowly missing the braided rug she'd bought him years ago. "Unfortunately, your brothers aren't here right now." She picked up the article and seemed to skim it once more. "You know, the more I think about it, the women in this town will probably steer clear until the charges are dropped. No one wants to be involved with a convicted felon. Even a potentially convicted felon isn't someone a nice girl would bring home to Mom and Dad."

"Jesus, Mom," he said again.

"Didn't I tell you these things come back to haunt you? It's just like SAT scores or your grades in ninth grade. They affect the college you got into. But would you listen? No. You knew best." Without warning, she whacked him on the shoulder with the paper, "Didn't I tell you this would resurface one day?"

Sensing she was just getting started, Roman groaned and pulled the covers back over his head. He was too old to be living with his mother and too tired to deal with this now.

CHAPTER SEVEN

The line started forming outside Charlotte's Attic at nine forty-five A.M. Charlotte glanced at Beth, who wasn't discussing anything with her except business. Apparently she was talked out from the night before and Charlotte respected her privacy—for now. She fully intended to corner her friend by the end of the day and find out exactly what was going on.

"Did you advertise a sale and forget to tell me?" Beth gestured to the throng of waiting women outside.

"I wish." Charlotte knitted her brows in confusion.

She walked to the front and unlocked the door. The women poured in as if she were giving merchandise away, and surrounded her until Frieda Whitehall stepped forward, obviously the spokesperson. The older woman had graying hair, cut and set in the only style Lu Anne knew. Frieda typically dressed in polyester pants with matching, handwashable silk blouses, and today was no different. But Charlotte knew Frieda wanted to put the sizzle back into her marriage, and so she had purchased Charlotte's handknit bra and panty set.

"What can I do for you ladies?"

"We're interested in the . . ." Frieda cleared her throat and blushed.

"The pilfered panties," Marge Sinclair called out from the back of the crowd. "My Donna could use a pair too."

"And I need to replace mine," Frieda said. "I'd also like a pair for Terrie. Maybe they'll loosen her up a bit."

"Pilfered panties?" Charlotte blinked in surprise. "You mean the crocheted ones." Obviously the robbery had become common knowledge. News traveled fast in this town and only Rick and the police chief's pleadings had kept the situation quiet after the initial break-ins.

"We'd all like a pair."

"*All* of you?"

The murmur of assent rose, while the storefront had become a revolving door of women. Some of them were older, some younger, all of them interested in Charlotte's "pilfered panties."

"We don't keep them in stock, you understand." Beth had taken over. "These are individually made. I'll take your names, color preference, and measure you for size. Line up and we'll get started."

"What in the world is going on?" Charlotte asked. Just last night she'd been worried about losing business, and now there was this deluge of customers for the very style of panties that encouraged robbery. At this rate, she'd be busy crocheting through Christmas, nine months away.

"Have you seen the morning paper?" Lisa Burton, an old classmate of Charlotte's and now a respected schoolteacher, asked.

Charlotte shook her head. She'd overslept, thanks to a restless night with fevered dreams starring herself and Roman. "No time for paper or coffee. Why?"

Lisa's eyes glittered with excitement as she handed over a copy of the *Gazette.* "If there was one man in this town you'd *want* to break into your home and steal your panties, who would it be?"

"Well . . ."

Before Charlotte could respond further, Lisa answered her own question. "A Chandler man, of course."

Charlotte blinked. "Of course." Roman was the only Chandler who interested her, not that she'd share that truth aloud.

And she didn't need him stealing her panties, she'd willingly hand them over—so would half the women in this town, she realized. She recalled his brothers' accounting of last night's theft and the accusations surrounding Roman. Chase had said he was going to press.

"What did the paper say exactly?" she asked her friend. "Don't leave anything out."

Half an hour later, Charlotte had locked her doors, needing a break. In her possession, she had a new list of women who wanted to purchase her panties, many of whom desired luring Roman Chandler into their homes.

"I'm going to be sick." Charlotte lowered herself into the chair behind her desk. She left Beth out front, organizing and straightening the store after the morning's madness, while Charlotte made a copy of the list of names to give to the police.

Not only had they taken orders for the most expensive items in the store, but she'd sold things to the women while they waited—sachets for inside the drawers, lingerie hangers, and other items of clothing. It was the most successful day she'd had since opening, and it wasn't yet noon. But instead of feeling satisfied, Charlotte was ill at ease.

She disliked earning money because of Roman's bachelor reputation. Jealousy seared her heart as she thought of all the women who'd mentioned his name in her shop today. She resented being slapped with the reminder of what and who he was: a wanderer who loved women. And she'd agreed to be one of those women—until he left town. Charlotte shivered, yet nothing that had happened this afternoon changed her mind about the course she and Roman had chosen.

She glanced at the paper Lisa had left behind and shook her head. Roman was many things, a bachelor and a wanderer included, but he wasn't a thief. And she didn't believe for one minute he was behind the robberies. The idea was ridiculous and the fact that grown women had bought into the suggestion floored her. They were building a fantasy concept around the entire idea. Around him.

Charlotte understood the desire to do so, but she also knew better than most: Fantasies didn't come true and reality was a much harsher teacher.

Roman made certain to overexert himself with push-ups and a hard run before showering, getting dressed, and heading on over to the *Gazette* offices. He was hoping to eliminate the driving urge to put a fist through his big brother's even bigger mouth. As a reporter, Roman respected the truth, but in this case, he figured there had to be a better way to deal with town gossip than giving it more credence by putting the speculation in print. Damn people in this town had memories longer than an elephant's.

He drove down First Street, car windows open, the fresh air waking him up and calming him down. He slowed as he passed Charlotte's Attic. A small crowd had gathered out front, which surprised him, considering she'd been worried about the thefts adversely affecting her business.

He wanted to see her badly. Thanks to the morning's paper and his new notoriety, Roman needed to steer clear of Charlotte's Attic. The home of the pilfered panties was the last place Roman Chandler needed to be seen.

He pulled his car to a stop at the traffic light at the edge of town. A gray sedan squeezed alongside. He glanced over as the driver lowered the passenger window. Alice Magregor, Roman realized. Her hair no longer exploded upward, but was now puffed out like a lion's mane. Still, Roman summoned a friendly smile for Alice.

She reached down to the seat beside her, then lifted her hand and waved something in the air before honking twice and driving away.

He blinked. As the light turned green, it dawned on him—Alice had just waved a pair of panties at him. She'd issued the ultimate female challenge. *Come and get me, big boy.*

Just as he came to the conclusion that he wanted only one woman, the single females of Yorkshire Falls decided to declare open season. Roman let out a heavy sigh as he realized what was in store for him from the town's feminine population. In his younger days, he'd have appreciated the attention. Now he just wanted to be left alone.

Hell of a way to embark on his crusade to get Charlotte into his life, Roman thought, and experienced a renewed desire to pummel his oldest brother. No doubt Alice's actions had been inspired by the article in the *Gazette.* Though Roman knew Whitehall was a biased source, now everyone in town had been reminded of Roman's prank over morning coffee.

Five minutes later, Roman parked in front of the *Gazette* and walked up the long driveway. He paused at the mailboxes, each marked with a different editorial department name. The boxes weren't overloaded yet, but the Local section had more than its share, thanks to the editor's long days with his wife and new baby. Roman grabbed the local information from the box, figuring a couple hours' worth of writing would give Ty more time with his family.

Roman told himself he was getting involved with *Gazette* business as a favor to an old friend. Lord knew Roman's actions sure as hell weren't motivated by the desire to aid his older brother.

He walked inside. "Hi ya, Lucy." He nodded to the receptionist, who was as much a fixture in this place as the foundation. She'd worked first for his father and then for Chase. She had a way with people and the organizational skills no newspaperman could live without.

"Hi, there, Roman." She crooked a finger his way.

He came up beside her. "What's up?"

She crooked her finger once more and he leaned closer. "What are you doing with the pairs you pilfer?" she asked in a whisper. "You can tell me. Are you into cross-dressing now?" She winked and let loose a laugh.

He rolled his eyes, belatedly remembering she also had a wicked sense of humor. "That isn't funny," he muttered.

"If it's any consolation, Chase didn't want to print it—he just had no choice. Whitehall basically called his journalistic integrity into question if he held back because you two were related."

Roman shook his head. "Where is he, anyway?"

Lucy pointed thumbs upward. Roman stormed up the stairs and entered Chase's office without knocking.

"Mind telling me what the hell you were thinking?" Roman slammed the morning paper onto his brother's desk.

"'Bout what?"

Roman leaned forward in a threatening stance that had

no effect on his big brother. Chase merely relaxed further. He rocked backward, and the top of what was once their father's leather chair touched the windowsill, blocking a view Roman knew by heart. The pond and aging willow trees standing guard below were as much a part of him as this old Victorian house that was and always had been the *Gazette* offices.

"You're too smart to play dumb and I'm not in the mood for games. Any reason you had to use my name at all?" Roman asked Chase.

"I print the news. If I'd left out Whitehall's quote, it would have been a glaring omission."

"To who?"

"Anyone in town old man Whitehall talks to. I don't want people around here thinking we play favorites or protect family members."

"A past prank isn't news."

Chase shook his head. "As a reporter you know better." He rocked the chair forward. "You couldn't give a rat's ass what people think of you, so I can't believe the article's got you so bent out of shape. What really has you so pissed off anyway?" He rose from his seat and walked over, his gaze never leaving Roman's face.

"You go back to living with our mother and you won't need to ask that question."

"That'd drive you to drink, not want to put me through a wall. This has nothing to do with Mom. Come to think of it, you look like hell. What'd you do? Dig ditches last night, instead of getting laid?"

"It wouldn't have just been 'getting laid,' " Roman responded without thinking.

"Come again?" Chase pushed Roman into the nearest chair, then slammed the door to his office closed. "Never know when Lucy'll get bored and wander up here," he explained, then opened the cabinet in the corner.

Their father had always stored liquor in there and Chase hadn't changed things that much. He splashed two glasses of scotch and handed one to Roman. "Now talk."

No matter that it was morning, Roman kicked back in the chair and downed the drink in one burning gulp. "I needed that. And I don't have a clue what you mean."

Chase raised his gaze upward. "You're pissed as hell that you lost the coin toss. You're pissed your life has to do a one-eighty, and because you think you owe me, you weren't going to admit it."

"Damn right." There was no point in denying the obvious. Even if Charlotte made the prospect of marriage and children more appealing, his life plans had changed since his return home, and not by freedom of choice.

"Don't do it if you can't live with it." Chase braced his arms on the desk. "I told you that night, no one would blame you if you backed out."

"*I'd* blame me. Did I ever tell you how much I respect you for the decisions you made?"

"You don't have to tell me. I know how many people you're reaching with your news and your talent. And every time I read a piece you wrote, every time you send clippings home, you show me what kind of man you are. And how much you appreciate everything you have in your life."

Roman glanced at Chase and shook his head. "I'm not talking about how much I appreciate life. We both know I do. I'm talking about how much I respect you." He stood and shoved his hands into his back pockets. "It wasn't until I lost that coin toss that I fully understood the sacrifice you made. You did it young and I respect you for it."

"*Sacrifice* is too strong a word," Chase said as he inclined his head.

Roman had embarrassed his brother and Roman knew it was as much of an acknowledgment of thanks as he'd get.

"Now tell me what Charlotte Bronson has to do with things," Chase said.

Roman poured himself another drink. Because Chase had made tough choices in his lifetime, no one would understand better what Roman was going through now than his big brother. "I love my life. The travel, the stories, informing people about important things in the world."

Chase shot him a wry smile. "Even when we were kids, I always related to you best. I saw myself in you." He inhaled deeply. "When Dad died, I knew my dreams had gone with him. But if I couldn't be the one to travel, I was damn well going to make sure you had the opportunities I didn't."

A swell of emotion rose in Roman's throat. "I owe you for that."

Chase waved away the words. "I didn't do it so one day you could owe me. Payback is the last thing I want. If I still wanted to travel, I could get on a damn plane now. My life is fine. So if you can't do this thing and be satisfied," he said, speaking of the coin toss, "then don't do it."

"Hey, I have every intention of doing my duty, but damned if I can see myself tied to just any woman in this town. Not when . . ."

"Not when there's only one you want."

Roman reached for the bottle again, then shoved the liquor away instead. "Exactly," he said, facing Chase's words head-on.

He pushed himself out of the chair and walked over to the window. He gazed out at the scenery that had always given his father such great pleasure—he knew this because all three kids had taken turns sitting on their father's lap as he typed in an article, took ads on the phone, or just hung out with his children, all with this view behind him. Computers replaced the old Smith Corona typewriters now, and the trees were larger, the roots buried deeper, but otherwise things hadn't changed. Young as he'd been when his father was still alive, Roman's memories were vague. But they existed on the fringe of memory and gave him comfort, even now.

"It's obvious she's interested in you too, so what's the problem?"

Roman inhaled. "I don't want to hurt her and everything about this coin toss and my plan reeks of her dad, Russell Bronson."

"Damn." Chase pinched the bridge of his nose.

"I'll take that as an agreement."

"So who's in the running instead?" Chase asked.

Roman watched as a breeze blew through the branches on the not-yet-budding trees. Only the yellow forsythia and the newly green grass added color to the setting below. As he stared down, a distant memory came into focus, of a family picnic he'd had here, one planned by his mother in an attempt to get his workaholic father out for fresh air and time with the kids. He could almost smell the chicken sandwiches his mom had made and hear his father's voice as he coached Rick on how to hold a bat while Raina pitched the ball.

When it came to his own child, Roman couldn't imagine any woman other than Charlotte playing the role of wife and mother—but neither could he picture himself settling down into the family role at the expense of the career he'd built and loved. But a child *was* in his future. And he didn't want to make that child with any woman other than Charlotte.

"No one else is in the running."

Chase came up behind him and slapped him on the back. "Then I suggest you figure out a way to convince the lady she can accept a long-distance marriage, little brother."

Now, that was a challenge, Roman thought. Charlotte wasn't ready to hear the words *marriage* or *babies* coming from his lips. Hell, he wasn't sure he was ready to say them either. But he had to begin somewhere. "What'd you tell me when I wanted to do my first interview and I chose the mayor?" He'd been sixteen and convinced he could take on the world as a reporter.

"Start slow and learn as you go. Same words Dad told me. You impress me. I can't believe those words penetrated that thick skull of yours." Chase grinned.

"You mean since I parked outside the mayor's office until he'd answer my questions, instead of going to the president of the PTA like you suggested?" Roman laughed at the memory.

"When it comes to Charlotte, I'm going to follow your old advice," he said to Chase. "But don't let it go to your head."

Roman would start slow. Spending time and getting to know her again would be a pleasure. He didn't have to worry about seduction. The attraction handled itself whenever he and Charlotte were together. If things worked out, he'd have the career he loved, and the woman he'd always wanted, not just in his bed, but in his life.

He started for the door.

"Where are you going?"

He turned back to Chase. "To make sure I get under

Charlotte's skin and into her life—to the point where she never wants me out."

Charlotte closed the store for the day at five. Saturday night was officially upon her. She rubbed her eyes and glanced up at Beth, who was twirling a pencil between her hands. "What are you thinking?" Charlotte asked her friend.

"Nothing."

"Baloney. You've been avoiding any serious talk with me for the last two weeks. You need a friend and I'm it. So please, let me help you."

Beth shook her head. "I wish I could, Charlotte, but you wouldn't understand."

Charlotte wondered if she should be offended. "Do I look that unfeeling to you?"

"No, just set in your beliefs. Any relationship that resembles your mother and father immediately gets your stamp of disapproval. I'm just not up to hearing it."

Charlotte's heart hammered in her throat as she walked over to her best friend. "I never meant to pass judgment. I just hurt for you. If anything I said or did came off harshly, I'm sorry. But Beth, you're a beautiful woman, engaged to a man you love, and you're still miserable. Why?" Charlotte swallowed hard, not wanting to sound disapproving. "Because you're here and he's in the city?"

Beth shook her head. "Not just that."

"Please explain things to me. I promise to listen, not judge." Charlotte tugged on Beth's hand and led her to the chairs in the waiting area. "I'll get us something to drink and you can talk to me, okay?"

Seconds later, a can of soda popped for each of them, Charlotte joined Beth. She curled her legs beneath her. "So you two met over Christmas?" She brought Beth's memories back to the beginning.

"Yes. Norman had his annual party and David was in town visiting the Ramseys—Joanne is his mother's sister. Anyway, we were introduced, started talking . . . I fell for him that night. I just knew he was the one."

"What'd you talk about? How did you know he was the one?" Charlotte leaned forward, dying to hear that her suspicions about David were wrong, that he and Beth truly had more goals and interests in common than she'd seen so far.

"His job, mostly. He has famous clients, but he also had everyday women who needed a change to make the most of their potential."

"Sounds interesting," Charlotte lied. "And when he walked you home, did he kiss you under the stars?" For Beth, Charlotte wanted the happily-ever-after story she'd yet to come across on her own.

"No. Actually, he was a gentleman. He kissed me on the cheek and . . ."

Charlotte placed her hand over Beth's. "And what?"

"Gave me his card. He said if I was ever in New York, to look him up. That he was certain he could maximize my beauty."

Charlotte's stomach plummeted, her fears coming to life. "Beth—I'm going out on a limb here, so hit me if you have to—why did you feel like you had to maximize what was already beautiful? None of us are perfect, honey."

"Well, I wasn't attracting the right man as I was," she said defensively.

"Because Yorkshire Falls doesn't have all that many *right* men." Except Roman.

Charlotte shook the traitorous thought aside. He was the wrong man, right for only a few weeks, she brutally reminded herself. Then she turned her attention back to Beth. "What happened next?"

"I took a trip to New York. I'd always wanted to see a Broadway show and so I convinced my mom to go for the weekend. We stayed in a hotel, took in a show—my treat—and spent a nice weekend." She bit down on her lower lip. "I sent Mom home on Sunday and on Monday I looked David up at his office. Things took off from there. A month later, we were engaged."

"After you'd undergone implant surgery?"

Beth's glance darted away. "He was amazing. So focused on me and my needs."

On what he wanted to create, Charlotte thought. The man wasn't interested in the incredible woman Beth already was. She downed a sip of soda. "Did you make a lot of trips there?"

Beth nodded. "And he came up most weekends after that. We had such incredible plans," she said, her eyes lighting up with the memory, but the hint of sadness and reality remained. "He has this beautiful penthouse. You can see the East River and the shopping is incredible. There are baby stores galore. We agreed we wanted kids right away and he said he wanted me to stay home and raise them."

"Can I ask you a personal question?" One Charlotte knew would sound judgmental and biased based on her mother's experience, but in Beth's case, Charlotte had a hunch she was dead-on accurate.

"Go ahead," Beth said warily.

"A man with his money and your shared dreams—why didn't he suggest you move to the city to be with him now? He could certainly afford it, so why be separated?"

"Because he believes in a traditional courtship! What's so wrong with that? Not every man who doesn't stay in

Yorkshire Falls is a creep like your father." Beth's eyes opened wide, then filled with tears. "Oh, God, I'm sorry. That was an awful thing to say."

"No, it was just honest," Charlotte said softly. "I'm asking valid questions and you're defensive. What are you afraid of, Beth?"

"That he's found someone else that interests him more." Her friend swiped at her eyes. "He's been engaged before to a patient," Beth admitted.

"To a patient?" Charlotte had a feeling Dr. Implant was more of a Svengali—a man who fell in love with his creations, not with the women inside the bodies he fixed, and one who lost interest once he discovered another project.

In Beth, he'd found the ideal subject, because despite her all-natural good looks, she'd never quite felt perfect, something Charlotte knew from their teenage years. Though she never was certain why.

"So he wasn't interested until you decided to go along with his plastic surgery suggestions, was he?" Charlotte hoped she'd walked Beth through this painful realization slowly enough so as not to force the conclusion upon her.

"No," she said softly. "And I've sensed the truth for a while. Even when he was here, he was distant. If we discussed anything, it was about changing me." Beth's eyes filled again. "How could I have been so stupid? So desperate?"

Charlotte grasped her friend's hand. "You're not stupid or desperate. Sometimes we see what we want to see because we want something so much. You wanted a man to love you." She glanced down at the cola can in her hands. "We *all* want that."

"Even you?"

Charlotte let out a laugh. "Mostly me. I'm just more

aware of the pitfalls than most because I've seen what my mother went through trying to keep a man who didn't want to be tied down." She twirled the can between her palms. "Why would you think I don't want more out of life? Like someone to love me?" Feeling the heat of Beth's stare, Charlotte lifted her gaze.

"Because you're so independent. You left, went after your dreams, came back, and fulfilled them. I stayed here in a dead-end job until you pulled me into fashion, something I've always loved. But it took your guts to get me to make a move in the right direction."

"You had your reasons for staying, and they were right for you." Charlotte glanced around her and took in the store, decorated in frilly white eyelet and lace. "I couldn't have done all this alone. You're partly responsible for our success. Look at this place and be proud. I am." She settled her stare back on Beth, waiting until her friend acknowledged the truth with a small nod. "I'm not sure where the insecurity comes from, but now that you're aware of it, you can work on strengthening your self-confidence."

"The insecurity was always there. I doubt you know what that's like—"

Charlotte shook her head. How could Beth view Charlotte's less-than-perfect life through such blinders? "You are so wrong. Of course I understand insecurity. I just believe in working on it from the inside out, not the outside in. That explains the philosophy behind this shop!"

"I suppose I should take lessons." Beth forced a smile. "Is Roman a part of that *working on it* you spoke of? You won't let yourself get involved. Is it because you know what's best for you?"

Charlotte sighed. Now how to explain to Beth her

change regarding Roman? "Roman's different. Our relationship is different."

"Aha! So there is a relationship."

"Short-term," Charlotte qualified. "We both know the rules going in."

"I always *knew* there was something between you two. Do you realize he only dated me after you two had gone out that one night and things didn't work out?"

Charlotte shook her head. Now wasn't the time to add to her friend's insecurities. Besides, she'd never thought Roman turned to Beth on the rebound. Charlotte hadn't let herself believe she'd meant that much to him. But thinking of it now, her stomach began to flutter at the possibility.

But Beth's ego needed boosting right now, not Charlotte's. "Give me a break. You were the perky head cheerleader. He couldn't resist you," she said, revealing what she'd believed in her heart at the time.

Beth rolled her eyes, amusement and humor back at last. "We had fun, but that's all it was. Nothing serious or irresistible about it. I was getting over Johnny Davis, and Roman was getting over you."

"Beth . . ."

"Charlotte . . ." her friend parroted, hands on her hips. "Now it's my turn to explain some facts of life to you. There are different kind of guys and relationships. There's the forever guy, and then there's the rebound guy. Also known as the interim guy. The one you have fun with and move on. That was Roman for me, and me for him." She paused in thought. "I think it's time you figure out what Roman is for *you*."

"How did you manage to turn this conversation back to me?" Charlotte asked.

"Because we're friends, like you said. You need me as much as I need you."

"Well, I promise to explain Roman to you one day." When she could explain him to herself.

Beth glanced down at her watch. "I've got to go. Rick will be here any minute."

"That playboy is the last man you should be getting involved with! Especially while you're still engaged."

Beth laughed. "Rick and I are friends. F-R-I-E-N-D-S."

Charlotte exhaled a sharp breath of relief.

"Rick listens and he makes me laugh. I need both right now. Talking to a guy is actually giving me the confidence to face David—and my fears." Her smile faded. "Then I need to face life on my own—and figure out who I am and what I need."

"What if we've miscalculated David?" Charlotte felt compelled to ask. "What if he loves you and—"

Beth shook her head. "I'll never know if he fell for me or the woman he thinks he made me into—did I tell you he wants to fix my nose?"

Charlotte shot out of her seat. "Don't you dare—"

"I'm too smart for that—thanks to you and Rick." She hugged Charlotte tight. "You're a good friend."

"Ditto." She squeezed Beth back.

A knock sounded at the door and Charlotte ran to get it.

Samson stood outside, his graying hair damp and a stack of letters in his hands. "Don't you get your mail?" he muttered. "Leave things outside and they'll blow away or get wet in the rain. Here." He shoved his hand out and waved a stack of letters in her face.

"Thanks, Sam." She took the letters out of his hand and dug into her pocket for the money she remembered shoving in there this morning. "You know I never would have remembered to get those on my own." She held out her hand, crumpled bills in her fist. "Can you drop a bottle of soda off here if you get a chance, and keep the change, okay?"

He grumbled but took the money, a flash of gratitude in his dark eyes. "Anything else you can't remember to do yourself?" he asked.

She swallowed a laugh. "Stop by Monday morning. I'll have a package or two you can drop off at the post office for me." She'd be finished packaging some panties among other things for her customers by then.

As a special part of her service, Charlotte liked to surprise customers with their special orders when she finished them early, instead of calling and having them come to the shop to pick up their order. "How does that sound?" she asked Sam.

"Like you're lazy. I'll see you then."

Charlotte grinned and locked the door again behind him. The poor, misunderstood man. She shook her head, then began sorting through the mail when the phone rang. "I'll get it," she called out to Beth.

She grabbed the receiver. "Charlotte's Attic, Charlotte speaking."

"It's Roman."

His deep voice wrapped her in warmth and her insides twisted with longing. "Hi, there."

"Hi, yourself. How's it going?" he asked.

"I had an incredibly busy day. You should have seen the lines outside the shop."

"I did. Couldn't miss them. But I did miss you." His voice dropped a husky octave.

Tremors of awareness rippled through her. "I'm easily found."

"Can you imagine the headlines if I actually walked through the front door of your shop?"

She bit down on her lower lip. If her shop had been the beneficiary of today's headlines, Roman had probably suffered in reverse. "That bad?"

"Let me put it to you this way. I've been accused of cross-dressing by Chase's secretary, called a potentially convicted felon by my own mother, and more than one woman waved a pair of those panties you're so fond of my way."

"Oh, no." Charlotte lowered herself into a chair, her stomach in knots over the thought of other women propositioning Roman.

"What's wrong?" Beth came up from behind her.

Charlotte waved a hand to halt further conversation. "It's Roman," she mouthed and placed a fingertip over her lips.

Beth grinned and settled in to wait.

"Was it that bad?" Charlotte asked him.

"Bad enough that I was thinking of getting out of town for the rest of the weekend."

Disappointment filled her and she realized how much she'd been looking forward to seeing him. Spending time with him. Consummating their relationship. She trembled at the prospect, her body reacting to the mere thought.

"The weekend's over tomorrow night," she reminded him.

"But can you imagine how much we can do together in twenty-four hours?"

"We?" She gripped the phone harder in her hand.

"Well, we don't live in a thriving metropolis, but I wanted to take you somewhere nice."

A warmth rushed through her, a heat that had nothing to do with sexual awareness. Oh, that was there too, but the caring in his voice struck her by surprise—in the heart. "What did you have in mind?"

"I was considering the Falls." The town's one restaurant with a dress code, Charlotte thought.

"But can you imagine eating while women are slipping panties into my jacket pocket?"

She laughed. "Don't tell me they tried that too."

"Not yet."

"Your ego astounds me." She caught Beth's eager glance and swiveled her chair around so she didn't have to see her. "You're asking me—"

"To go away with me. One night, one day. You and me. What do you say?" he asked.

"A date?"

"More than that and you know it."

Charlotte sucked in a deep breath. They'd been leaning toward this for a while now. She'd already rationalized why she'd allow herself to get involved in an affair. Because being with Roman seemed the only way to get over him. If she were lucky, she'd discover he had too many bad habits to count. If not, at least she'd store memories for the future. She'd never again look back and regret the road not taken.

"He's asking you out. What are you waiting for? Say yes," Beth said from behind her.

Charlotte glanced over her shoulder. "Shut up."

"Not the answer I expected."

"Sorry. I wasn't talking to you." She waved Beth away with one hand. "Yes. I say yes," she said before she could change her mind.

Beth let out a whoop of glee,

"I'll make sure it's a time you never forget," he said in that sexy, compelling voice.

And Charlotte believed him. She knew for certain that

when this weekend was over, she'd never again wonder what she'd missed since her teenage rejection of him.

She would, however, keep in mind this was a short-term affair. And Roman was her interim guy.

CHAPTER EIGHT

Roman picked Charlotte up on time. He drove her to the outskirts of town before pulling over to the side of the road and reaching into the glove compartment for a silk scarf. He dangled it in front of her.

"What's that for?" Charlotte eyed the scarf, intrigued.

"I don't want you to see my surprise before I'm ready."

Anticipation kicked in to high gear. "I love surprises."

Roman's deep laugh wrapped around her in the confines of his small rental car. "Is that a note of appreciation I hear in your voice?"

He leaned over and tied the sheath of silk around her head. A shiver of awareness rippled along her nerve endings.

She lifted her hands to feel the blindfold covering her eyes and her stomach jolted with awareness. As quickly as she'd lost her sight, her other senses had heightened, taking over. The rasp of Roman's deep breathing and his heady, masculine cologne touched off tremors inside her. "So where are we going?"

"You should have tried a more subtle approach. If I

wanted you to know, then you wouldn't need the blindfold, now, would you?" He started the car once more and she jolted backward as they pulled onto the highway.

She wasn't sure how much time passed as they made companionable small talk. They got along well, which wasn't surprising. Neither were the things they had in common—love of history and a keen interest in foreign locales, many of which he described to her in detail as only a first-hand observer could. She envied his travels much more than she'd admit aloud.

"When I was in your apartment, I couldn't help but notice the books on the table." Not a surprising turn in conversation after the stories and descriptions he'd shared.

"Many people have those books," she said, not ready to give too much insight into her soul.

"That's what I thought. Then I looked closer. Yours were worn and well read."

Damn the man. He was still observant and dissected the littlest thing until he came up with the correct conclusion. "So call me shallow. I like picture books."

"I'd call you a lot of things." His hand came to rest on her knee, his hot palm searing her flesh through the light cotton spandex pants she wore. "Shallow isn't one of them. *I* think you harbor a secret desire to travel."

"Such a big conclusion from a few books."

He shook his head. "I'd already assumed as much, but your twenty questions about my travels and the longing in your voice pretty much told me you'd like to visit those places yourself one day."

She contemplated lying, then decided against it. She'd promised herself to release all inhibitions and enjoy to the fullest, so she'd have no regrets. That meant no lies or omissions. "I suppose a part of me wants to travel," she admitted.

"The adventurous part you hide?" Humor tinged his voice.

"The shallow part," she said, no touch of humor in return. Charlotte glanced away from Roman, where she knew the car window would be, but the same blackness awaited her any direction she looked.

"*Shallow.* There's that word again."

She felt the slowing of the engine, the jarring feel of the car being put into park, and the slide of denim against vinyl as Roman turned in his seat.

"I travel. Is that what you think of me?" he asked at last.

In her mind, she could see him, one arm propped over the headrest, as he looked at her. Only she couldn't. See him, that is. She could only guess what he was doing, what his expression revealed. His voice held the slightest hint of hurt at the possibility that she'd found him lacking. He sounded as if he cared what she thought of him and the notion set her heart beating out a rapid pulse.

Roman was intelligent and caring. He understood both of those traits enough to report the news in a way that drew a reader in. She'd read his work. Shallow wasn't what she thought of Roman, far from it.

"It's what I fear *I* am." No regrets, she reminded herself, and under the cover and protection of darkness, she admitted her greatest fear. Of all people, she wanted him to know.

"Curiosity about the unknown makes you intelligent, not shallow."

She often wondered. "What if the need to see those places or do those other things takes you far from home and keeps you there?" she asked. "Far from the people who love you."

Roman listened to her words and looked for deeper meaning. She could be talking about him, but he had a hunch she was admitting to more personal fears. "You're talking about your father, aren't you?"

"That's a rhetorical question." She still faced the window, away from him.

He reached over and touched her chin, turning her toward him. "It's not his desire to live in Los Angeles or even to act that's caused the problem. It was his unwillingness to live up to his responsibilities and the fact that he seems emotionally disconnected from his family. Those are choices he made. Yours would be different because *you're* different."

She shrugged. "My father, my genes. You never know."

"You also have your mother's genes, and she's a homebody." More of a recluse, though he didn't say it. "You're most likely a combination of both." The best of both, he thought. "So what's the other reason you're so afraid of those hidden desires?"

She didn't answer.

He had a hunch genetics wasn't what was really bothering Charlotte. It was a convenient cover. He knew her better than to think she'd turn selfish, or into any kind of replica of her father. She had to know better too. Though to fear doing so was a normal, fleeting notion for anyone who resented a parent, Roman thought. Charlotte was intelligent enough to look inside herself and see the truth. "You're no more shallow than those books on your table."

"You're biased." Her lips turned upward in a half smile.

"And that's not an answer. Come on, Charlotte. You lived in New York, you cherish the books about foreign places. You crave travel, but you refuse to acknowledge it might make you happy. Why?"

"What if the reality is a disappointment?"

And she'd had too many of those in her life, he thought. But he was about to change that. "If you could be anywhere right now, where would it be?"

"Other than here with you?"

He grinned. "Good answer." On impulse, he leaned over and grazed his mouth against her warm lips. An unmistakable tremor shook her and his body tensed in response. "I guess it's time I show you where *here* is. I'm coming around to get you." He climbed out of the front seat, walked to her side, and helped her out of the car.

A light drizzle fell around them, mist and clouds heavy in the darkness, the weather adding to the almost moody atmosphere of this spot he'd chosen. Only when he had her facing their ultimate destination did he pull the blindfold off. "Take a look."

As she refocused on her surroundings, Roman watched her. Her jet-black hair, mussed from the scarf and the weather, swirled over her shoulders and around her neck. She brushed the long strands back with one hand, leaving her neck bare and exposed. The urge to nibble the white skin was strong and overwhelming, but he managed to watch and wait instead.

She blinked and squinted, crinkling her nose as she took in her new location. "It looks like a farmhouse."

"Actually, it's a renovated dairy barn. It's pretty secluded, with an incredible view of the Adirondack Mountains. We missed the sunset, but there's no reason we can't catch the sunrise."

She took a step forward, obviously eager to see more.

"Hang on." He grabbed their bags from the trunk. She'd packed light, something that not only surprised him, but in a ridiculous way made him feel like he could relate to her better. Or she could relate to him and his lifestyle in a way he wouldn't have expected.

Unsure what to make of those feelings, he caught up with her instead. "It's not a Scottish castle, but it'll make you feel like you've left the real world behind. And I promise you won't be disappointed."

She turned to face him. "You're perceptive and intuitive. As a reporter I'm sure it comes naturally. What I can't figure out is whether this is for your benefit or mine."

He knew better than to be insulted. Because she was ruminating on her father, she felt compelled to look for Roman's ulterior motives. He understood and didn't mind answering. "Getting out of town is for our benefit, taking you with me is for mine, and choosing this particular place was all for you, sweetheart."

"You think you've got me figured out." She bit down on her lower lip.

"I don't?" He swept an arm out, gesturing to the mountain getaway. "This sudden escape doesn't please you? Doesn't this inn remind you of places you'd like to visit but haven't had the chance?"

"You know it does. That's obvious from you studying my apartment, or dissecting me with those reporter's instincts. But that doesn't mean you know everything. There's plenty that's still hidden."

"And I can't wait to uncover the rest of your secrets."

A slow smile tilted her lips until it turned into a wicked grin. "So what are you waiting for?" She tossed the parting shot. Then she pivoted and started for the inn, the effect of her regal departure diminished by her teetering, high-heeled walk on the unpaved parking lot.

* * *

Charlotte's time with Roman was, by agreement and necessity, a short-term affair. *Affair* being the operative word. As much as she liked confiding in him and listening to his comforting voice and understanding words, she didn't want to waste what little time they had—time of undetermined duration—on talk.

Not when they had many more exciting, *erotic* things they could do. Things to give her memories to cherish and a way to prove she was her own person—stronger than her mother. She could take what she desired and walk away, instead of waiting for him to come back and make her life whole. She'd be whole on her own. No matter how much she'd miss him.

By the time she made it inside the converted farmhouse, unpretentiously named The Inn, excitement had become her sole companion.

They were greeted upon entering by an older couple. "Welcome, Mr. Chandler."

"Roman, please."

The woman with streaked gray hair and bright eyes nodded. "Roman it is. Do you know you look just like your father?"

He grinned. "So I've been told."

"She knows your parents?" Charlotte asked, surprised.

"Mom and Dad came here on their honeymoon."

He spoke in a matter-of-fact tone, but Charlotte didn't find the information so cut-and-dried. He'd brought her to the place his parents had shared their post-wedding night. Wow.

"They most certainly did. I'm Marian Innsbrook and this is my husband, Harry."

Charlotte grinned. "So *that* explains the name of this place."

"Easy to remember in case folks want to come back," Harry said.

Charlotte nodded.

Roman stepped beside her and placed his hand on her lower back. He branded her with his touch and the excitement she'd felt upon entering The Inn turned to pure unadulterated arousal. Warmth flooded her, a heaviness in her breasts and a distinctive throbbing between her legs. All inappropriate for the time and place—but soon they'd be alone, and she intended to shed not just her clothing but her inhibitions.

As if oblivious to the havoc he wreaked on her body, Roman smiled at the Innsbrooks. "This is Charlotte Bronson."

She managed an easy smile while she and Roman took turns shaking hands with the older couple. She even forced herself to look around and appreciate the Old World charm and atmosphere The Inn offered. Wood-beamed ceilings and paneled walls. *Comfort* and *homey* were the words that came to mind.

Empty was another word that ran through her head. There was no one else around. "Do you run this place by yourselves?"

Marian shook her head. "But it's quiet this time of year. Though we're an hour from Saratoga, we still experience the lull between winter getaways and racing season. I'm just glad we were able to fit you in on short notice."

"And we appreciate it," Roman said.

"Our pleasure. Now let's get you settled."

A short flight of stairs and a narrow hallway later, Marian Innsbrook led them into a dimly lit room. "In here's the sitting area, up those stairs in the loft is the bedroom. There's cable television, the temperature controls are over here." She walked to the far wall and explained the in-room system. "Breakfast is served at eight and you can have a wake-up call anytime you'd like." She started to step out of the room.

"Thank you, Mrs. Innsbrook," Charlotte called after her.

"It's Marian, and you're welcome."

Roman walked her out and seconds later the door shut with a resounding click. They were alone.

He turned, his back propped against the closed door. "I thought she'd never leave."

"Or stop talking." Charlotte grinned. "I really like them, though."

"They kept in touch with my mother all these years. They even came to Dad's funeral."

"That's so sweet."

"They're good people." He shrugged. "And Mom and Dad came back every year for their anniversary."

His gaze met hers, dark and compelling, staring until she was shaken. "I'm not sure what to say next," she admitted.

He started walking toward her. "I can think of a lot better things to do than talk." He paused in front of her.

His musky scent filled her with a longing so strong her knees nearly buckled, and she swallowed hard. "Then why don't you show me?"

A rumble rose from his throat that resembled a low growl, a deep admission of desire. The next thing she knew, he'd swept her into his arms, up the stairs, and laid her down on the king-sized loft bed. Then his lips came down hard on hers.

It was what she hadn't known she'd been waiting for—this hard, demanding kiss that never ended and caused wave after wave of carnal need to rush her body at lightning speed. His lips were unforgiving, crushing hers, and the hot, moist assault on her senses brought everything inside her to life.

She cupped his face in her hands and threaded her fingers through his hair, reveling in the silky softness, such a contradiction to the hard male body poised above her. He traveled a path with his mouth, across her cheek, and down her neck, pausing to nibble at her tender flesh.

"When I picked you up and saw you in this low-cut sweater, all I could think about was tasting you," his voice rasped, a husky sound in her ear.

His need, his desire made her feel wanton and brave. She arched her back, stretching her body out against the mattress and pushing her aching breasts and tight nipples against his chest, giving him complete access to her neck. "So? Do I taste as good as you thought?"

He let out another of those groans that turned her on and nuzzled his lips harder into her skin.

The pulling sensation of his teeth against her flesh found an answering response between her legs, the place that was and had always been empty—and would be until Roman filled her.

He settled himself more completely against her, his groin nestled hot and heavy between her thighs. Denim was a restricting barrier, but she felt his weight and breadth anyway, pushing against her, seeking entry. Her body bucked beneath him, wanting more than a teasing thrust of clothed bodies. Though she'd never admit it aloud, her body reminded her of what she'd tried to forget—she'd been waiting for this man all of her life. For now he was hers.

And she was his. His large hands seemed to take possession, as he traced her shape with his palms, pausing only to cup her breasts in his hands and hold tight, feeling their weight and caressing her nipples with his thumbs. She let out a moan that surprised her.

He sat up, resting his weight back on his legs. "You have no idea what you do to me."

She let out a shaky laugh. "Trust me, I have some clue."

When he reached toward the elastic waist of her pants, she sucked in a deep breath and waited for him to tug them down. Off her body.

Instead he paused. "About protection . . ."

In most cases, the subject would be a mood killer. With Roman, it was just a delay she didn't want. "I'm on the pill," she admitted.

Surprise flickered in his eyes, replaced quickly with the unmistakable flare of desire. She wondered if his thoughts mirrored hers—all she could imagine was him inside her, flesh against flesh, no barriers, nothing between them. "But . . ." She was too smart for reality not to assert itself.

A taut muscle ticked in his jaw, evidence of what this restraint was costing him. "What?" he asked in a softer voice than she'd believed he could manage right now.

"It's been a long time for me and the few times I . . . we . . . used protection." She darted her gaze to the cream-colored wall to her left, shocked by the utter intimacy of this conversation. Then again, there wasn't anything more intimate than the step they were about to take.

He sucked in a breath and she wondered if he was shocked by her words. Wondered if she'd scared him away. Men didn't like to think a woman was investing too much into any one night. But she and Roman had had that conversation already and both knew the score.

"I'm not indiscriminate."

At the sound of his voice, she refocused on him before she could lament the end of what hadn't yet begun.

"I'm careful," he continued. "And before each trip abroad I have every blood test imaginable." A heavy silence descended between them. "And I never cared so much before what a woman was thinking, so don't leave me in suspense."

A heaviness formed in her chest and a lump rose to her throat as she grabbed his wrists in her hands. But she refused to succumb to emotion, not when desire was so strong and encompassing. "Stop talking and make love to me, Roman. Or I might have to—"

He cut her off by pulling down on her pants in one swift move, and cooler air hit her thighs.

"I like a man that listens." In fact, she liked him a whole lot. More than was prudent, she thought as she kicked the pants off her ankles.

He stood to undress and she shed her sweater next. When he returned to the bed, he was nude and he was magnificent. His tanned skin complemented his dark hair and his blue eyes had darkened with desire—for *her.*

"I like a woman who isn't afraid to tell me what she wants." He placed his hands on her thighs and spread her legs wide. "A woman who isn't afraid of her sensuality." Sparks of light glittered in his gaze as he took in the light blue bra and panty set. "Know what my favorite color is?" he asked.

She opened her mouth to answer, but with his burning touch searing her skin and liquid desire pulsing through her veins, no words would come.

"As of right now, it's blue." And with that, he dipped his head to taste her.

Charlotte thought she'd die of pleasure. She wondered if such a thing were possible. And then she couldn't think at all. His tongue worked magic, managing to ease inside the open holes of the handmade panties. With broad strokes, he laved, then alternated with insistent suckling that sent white-hot darts of fire throughout her body as every nerve she possessed begged for release.

He brought her to the edge of climaxing more than once, only to slow the loving strokes of his tongue and bring her back down. She writhed and begged until he used his tongue and teeth to graze her sensitive folds of flesh, taking her upward once more. But she refused to have her first orgasm without him being inside her. She needed to feel that emotional connection with him too badly, and when he reached up and held her hand in his, she knew he understood.

Without warning, he slid up beside her, his warm body cradling hers in heat. He made fast work of her bra and panties, before cuddling alongside her again.

"You taste good." He brushed her hair off her face and before she could respond, he closed his mouth over hers. At the same time, he pressed his hand over her aching, empty feminine mound. Waves of need began to build inside her again. She jerked her hips upward and whimpered, a sound he caught in his throat.

He broke the kiss but his lips lingered over hers. "What is it, sweetheart? Does this help?" he asked, easing his finger deep inside her.

Her body trembled in reaction. "I know what would help more."

So did Roman. This restraint wasn't easy. He was enjoying every minute, but if he didn't come inside her, he was going to damn well explode. "Tell me what you want." He needed to hear it from those well-kissed lips.

"Why don't I show you instead?" Her cheeks were

flushed pink with desire, her eyes glazed with need as she reached out and held his hard length in her hand.

He didn't need to answer, just follow her lead—and he did, easing himself over her as she spread her legs and placed the head of his penis into the damp, moist vee of her thighs. At that moment, foreplay was over.

He thrust inside her, hard and fast. She'd said it had been a while and when her smooth muscles contracted around him, he realized how long she'd actually meant. She was tight and wet, capturing him in silken heat. He broke into a sweat, not just because he was aroused and so damn close to coming he thought he would burst, because he felt like he was exactly where he belonged.

He felt like he'd come home.

Roman opened his eyes and met her startled gaze. It wasn't pain or discomfort he saw there, but awareness. She obviously felt it too.

He began a rapid thrusting meant to distract him, to separate himself from the reality of his feelings. Sex had always been a distant form of quick and easy release in the past. Not now.

Not with Charlotte. Not when her rhythm complemented his rhythm, her breaths matched his, and her body molded perfectly around him. And when he climaxed, taking her with him, Roman somehow knew—things would never be the same again.

Roman walked out of the bathroom and toward Charlotte, completely nude and not the least bit embarrassed. She supposed there wasn't much left to hide between them and she didn't mind looking at him. Not a bit.

She wasn't as ready to be that free herself. She crossed her legs and pulled the sheets up around her. "I'm starving."

Roman's eyes glittered with deliberate mischief. "I can satisfy that hunger of yours."

She grinned. "You already did. Twice. Now it's my stomach that needs filling." She patted the sheet above her belly. They'd worked up a healthy appetite and she wasn't ashamed to admit it.

She was ashamed to look too deeply into her heart, because she wasn't the same woman who'd walked into this inn. She found it too easy to be with this charming man who promised honesty as easily as he guaranteed he'd be walking out the door.

He reached over and grabbed the green leather-bound folder from the nightstand and looked through the selection of late-night snacks.

"What are my choices?" she asked.

"Would you believe not much? There's a cookie platter with assorted teas, or a vegetable platter with honey mustard or blue cheese dip, and a choice of colas. There's also fresh seasonal fruit. Can't imagine what that would be at this time of year, but one thing's clear. We're eating cold and nothing homemade." He laughed. "So am I ordering you the vegetables?"

She raised an eyebrow, surprised he'd chosen wrong. "Guess you don't know me as well as you think you do."

"Now, there's a challenge. So you want the fruit?"

She crinkled her nose. "Roman Chandler, what kind of women do you hang out with?" She shook her head. "Forget I even asked."

He settled himself next to her. "Sorry, can't do that." He lifted her hand and began a slow, steady massaging of her palm. His touch was as seductive as his eyes were mesmerizing and blue. "The Chandler reputation's way overrated."

"Oh, really? You brothers don't collect women?"

"I'm not saying they don't line up for me." His impish grin told her he was joking. "But I definitely turn them away. I'm getting too old for the revolving door."

But despite the teasing upturn of his lips, she tossed a pillow at him anyway. "Tell me something. I don't really remember your father. Did he have that same 'women love him' reputation? Is that what you three are living up to?"

He shook his head. "The only woman my father was interested in was my mother and vice versa."

"If only my dad reciprocated my mother's feelings, like yours did."

He tipped his head back in thought. "You know, our mothers aren't really that different."

Charlotte couldn't help it. She laughed. "You've got to be kidding."

"Nope. Step out of your single-minded resentment of your father and take a look at something. He took off and your mother's been waiting around ever since, yes?"

"Yes," she said, completely unsure of where he was headed.

"And my father died and my mother never got involved with another man again. Until this week, but that's another story." That darn perceptive gaze met hers. "Nothing's really different," he said. "They both put their lives on hold."

"I guess you've got a point." She blinked, surprised to realize they had something that fundamental in common.

But nothing had changed for them—even if she had become more emotionally attached. Dammit. Their long-range goals were still disparate and far apart, something she'd best keep in mind during their time together, she warned herself.

Roman's own words reverberated in his head. His mother had put her life on hold for what seemed like forever. Because she'd been so much a part of his father's life, she'd been lost without him. Until he'd spoken his conclusion aloud, he'd never realized that his mother hadn't moved forward.

"But at least Raina lived some version of happily ever after." Charlotte's voice interrupted his thoughts.

Her words gave him pause. Was that fairy-tale ending women wanted worth anything if the rest of their lives were spent in unhappy limbo? In his mother's case, short-term happiness at the expense of long-term fulfillment? In Charlotte's mother's situation, chasing a fantasy that would never come true? He shook his head, neither choice appealing to him.

He'd watched his mother after his father died, the mourning, the withdrawal, and then the small steps back into the real world. But she'd never fully been what she was with his father, and she hadn't tried to redefine herself either.

Her choice, he realized. Just as it had been his choice to take off and distance himself from not only his hometown, but his family—and the pain he saw in his mother's eyes each time he was home. Especially in the beginning.

At that moment, Roman realized he'd been running from emotional attachment—the same way Charlotte was running from him. She feared the same pain she'd grown up seeing in her mother, day in and day out.

But making love to her had shown him that when it came to some things in life, there was no alternative. *They* were meant to be. Not just because he desired her but because he wanted to give her things she'd missed in life, the family and the love. How he'd accomplish that and still maintain the freedom he needed for his job and his life, he didn't know.

He had a long road ahead of him—to prove to himself and to her that his lifestyle could satisfy them *both.* That their lives didn't have to be a repeat of their parents' mistakes but one of their own making.

And that meant commitment, he realized now. Not just the commitment he promised his family he'd make, but one he wanted to make with this woman.

He looked into her soft eyes and something inside him melted. "Is happily ever after what you want?" he asked.

"Is it what you don't want?" she shot back.

"Touché." He stroked a finger down her cheek.

Poor Charlotte. She had no idea he'd figured out both himself and her. He knew what he wanted—her. He was about to storm her defenses and she hadn't a clue. "I notice you changed the subject earlier. I wanted to talk about 'my' women."

Her face flushed a charming shade of pink. "I don't."

"So once again, you don't have to talk. But you are going to listen." In one smooth move, he had her flat on her back, straddling her hips.

She scowled up at him. "You play dirty and you forgot to order my food," she said.

"You finish this conversation and I'll get you all the cookies you can eat and *more.*" He moved his hips against hers, deliberately provocative and hot.

"That's bribery." But her eyes glazed over, letting him know she was enticed by his erotic teasing. Her stomach chose that second to grumble loudly, killing the mood. She grinned sheepishly. "I suppose I have no choice but to listen if I want to eat."

"I suppose you're right." But he wasn't above a little erotic coercion to get his way. He settled his weight so as not to crush her, but so he could feel her supple curves and smooth flesh. Damn, but she felt good. "Just hear me out," he said, refusing to be distracted. Not when so much was on the line. "Number one, my life's been so busy women rarely factored into the equation—believe it or not. And I promised you I'd never lie. Number two, I may not have gotten involved before, but I sure as hell am now."

He shocked himself and obviously shocked her by the admission, because silence descended around them.

Something akin to fear shimmered in her eyes. "You said you'd never lie."

"This time I think I should be insulted."

She shook her head. "I'm not calling you a liar."

"Then what?"

"Don't make this"—she gestured between their naked bodies—"out to be more than it really is."

"Oh, and what exactly is *this?*" he asked, because he needed to hear exactly what he was up against when it came to turning her thinking around.

"Sex," she said, deliberately trivializing what they had shared.

As much as Roman recognized the protective mechanism, he couldn't say she hadn't hurt him. He forced an easy laugh. "Good thing you never made that promise not to lie, sweetheart."

With those words, he let her know he didn't believe one word she'd uttered, and this time she sucked in a deep breath, realizing she'd been caught.

He inhaled deeply. The scent of sex did hover in the air, arousing him and making him want her despite her stubborn minimizing of what they'd shared. He'd already made his point. Together they'd experienced something much deeper than just sex.

He nudged her legs apart with his knees.

"What are you doing?" she asked.

"You said you're hungry, yes?" He didn't wait for a reply. "You also said what's between us is just sex." He nudged the head of his enlarged penis between her legs and entered her slowly, methodically, with a slick, thick stroke she couldn't help but *feel.* He sure as hell did.

Her lips parted and her eyes dilated as she took him inside.

What was he doing? she'd asked. "I'm going to make you eat your words." He was going to make her experience every taste, touch, and sensation so that he'd always be a part of her. He was going to prove to her that everything between them was deep and meaningful.

His powerful strokes inside her body elicited a response he couldn't mistake. One she couldn't either, if the arousing sounds coming from her were anything to go by.

Every moan that passed her lips settled inside him and brought a stinging sensation to his eyes, a thick lump in his throat.

And later, as she lay asleep in his arms, he knew she'd become a part of him too. Or maybe, he thought, she always had been.

The next day, the sun had long ago dipped below the horizon, an orange ball of fire in the reddened sky, when Roman drove them back into town. Charlotte's stomach plummeted. She wasn't ready to end their time together so soon.

After that one serious conversation that got them nowhere, things had lightened up. They'd made love, hand-fed each other homemade cookies, slept in each other's arms, and woke in time for the sunrise. They'd had a picnic lunch outside on the beautiful premises, then shared dinner with the Innsbrooks before returning to the room to make love one more time before they left The Inn for good.

Perhaps Roman's melancholy matched hers, because they rode home in silence. By the time he walked her to her apartment, her stomach was in twisted knots.

She wasn't ready to say good-bye. "I wonder if there were any break-ins last night," she said, looking to prolong his time with her.

"Not that I wish it on anyone, but it would definitely get me off the hook with the women in this town." His blue eyes glittered in amusement. "I have an alibi."

She smiled. "Yeah. I know what you mean. If no one knows you left town, the thief can't use you as his shield—if that was his intent after the article." She shrugged.

"Only Mom and my brothers know I was out of town, so we'll see what happens."

Her mother knew too, but since she rarely left the house to socialize, there was no chance of her disclosing the news. "Breaking into houses and stealing panties," Charlotte said with a shake of her head.

A blush stained his cheeks and she raised a hand to touch him one more time. As her fingertips lightly stroked his roughened cheek, he met and held her gaze. Knowledge glittered in those intelligent blue eyes and she pulled back, embarrassed by her simple display of affection that gave away too much of her feelings.

"This is more serious than a juvenile prank," she said, keeping things between them light. "No one in their right mind would blame you. The whole idea of panty theft is ridiculous."

He shrugged, drawing her gaze to his black T-shirt and the tight muscles beneath. "You never know what's going to turn a man on. A strange man, anyway."

She nodded, then swallowed hard. Silence surrounded them. No noises sounded from the other apartments or the street below. Nothing remained but to say so long. "So . . ."

"So."

"Will I see you again?" She mentally kicked herself as soon as the words escaped. That should have been *his* line.

"Why? Looking for more sex?" he asked, a wry smile on his lips.

She scowled, his words hitting like a punch in the stomach. She'd regretted the defensive words as soon as they'd escaped her lips. Now she knew how she'd made him feel. "I suppose I deserved that."

She'd obviously hurt him when she'd classified their relationship that way. She hadn't meant to, had merely been looking to protect herself. As a means of defense, words were too little, too late, anyway.

He reached out and cupped her chin in his hand. "I just don't want you to shut me out with remarks like that. Open your mind and see where things lead."

Charlotte already knew the outcome. She'd end up in Yorkshire Falls while he traveled abroad. End of discussion, end of relationship.

But he didn't seem in any rush to reach that inevitable conclusion, didn't seem to be leaving town anytime soon. So why borrow trouble by arguing with him? She summoned a smile. "I suppose I can manage that."

"She says too lightly."

"Come on, let's not ruin a spectacular weekend by arguing, okay?"

He stepped closer. "I was spectacular, huh?"

His masculine scent wrapped around her, became a part of her, and her heartbeat kicked into high gear. "I meant the weekend was spectacular."

His arm came to rest above her head and his lips came within kissing distance. "And I?"

"You were even better," she murmured as his mouth touched hers. The kiss was too light, too fast, and over too soon. He left her wanting more, which, she supposed, was the point he'd intended to make.

"You will see me again." He grabbed her key from her hand, opened the door, and let her inside.

By the time she turned back, he was gone.

CHAPTER NINE

Roman walked into an unlocked house and tossed his keys onto the counter. The darkened rooms and absolute silence told him his mother wasn't home. He muttered a curse. You'd think the woman had more sense than to be careless, with a thief on the loose. Then again, she probably thought the panty thief business was a joke—along with half the women in this town.

"Ridiculous." Tomorrow morning he'd touch base with Rick and find out what, if any, break-ins had occurred last night.

But for now, he needed sleep. God knew he'd gotten none last night, and the memory of why was enough to set him off once again. He made his way into his old childhood room, dumped his bag onto the floor, and headed for the bathroom.

He set the shower water on cold, but it didn't help ease the ache Charlotte inspired. He'd showered with her earlier today and he vividly remembered coming inside her, water pelting them from all sides. The spray hit his skin now, but not even this ice-cold dousing could cool him off.

He was tired and aroused all at the same time and when he walked into his room, he was so exhausted he didn't even turn on the lights. Only one thought cruised through his mind. After his time with Charlotte, his life and future had changed, and not just because of a family promise.

He had decisions to make, but first he needed sleep. He crawled into bed. His head hit the cool sheets, his back eased into the mattress, and his body came into contact with warm, soft flesh.

"Holy shit." Roman jerked back and bolted upright in the bed. "Who the hell's there?"

He jumped out of bed and started for the door, intending to hit the switch on the wall so he could shed light on the intruder.

"That's not the reaction I expected, but I suppose a girl has to start somewhere. Now get back into bed and I'll show you what I brought for you." The voice sounded more feline than female.

Considering Roman definitely felt like trapped prey, the analogy made perfect sense. The sound of a hand patting the mattress echoed around him.

He flicked on the light and was greeted by the grotesque sight of Alice Magregor, her frizzy hair overwaxed and oversprayed, and her body stuffed into Charlotte's infamous panties. It was a body Roman wouldn't touch in drunken stupor, and he was stone cold sober now. More's the pity.

"Oh, you don't sleep naked."

She pouted in a way that turned his stomach.

"Never mind. I'll take care of that. Now turn out the light and get back into bed." She arched and preened, stretching her hand across his pillow.

Damn, he'd have to change the sheets before getting

some sleep. He clenched his jaw, her invasion of his privacy unwanted and unwelcome. "I'm going to turn around and let you get decent. Then I'm going to pretend this never happened and you're going to do the same."

She didn't flinch, and before he could turn, she said, "Don't tell me you aren't interested. I flashed you a sign the other day and you smiled at me."

"You've got your facts out of order. I smiled before you flashed your panties."

"You journalists and your facts. It all means the same thing. You smiled. You showed interest. Now come to bed."

Whether she was being deliberately dense or pitifully stupid, he couldn't say. "We live in a small town, Alice. I was being neighborly. Now get dressed." He crossed his arms and turned away. He leaned against the doorframe, unable to believe Alice Magregor was naked in his bed.

Being cruel wasn't his style, but damned if he was going to humor her or give her any indication he wanted something like this to happen again. If the house had been locked, it couldn't have happened in the first place. His mother was in for one hell of a lecture on safety. She couldn't be so darn trusting any longer. Thanks to her false sense of security, she'd left the house open, her panties in danger of being stolen, and his body in danger of being violated, if Alice had her way.

He couldn't imagine how she'd known his mother wasn't home so she could come in and make herself comfortable. Not that he cared, as long as she got the hell out now. He glanced over his shoulder, but she hadn't made a move.

"I love a man who plays hard to get."

The distinct sound of laughter traveled up from the front hall. His mother's laughter and a man's rumbling chuckle.

At the sound of other people in the house, Alice's eyes had opened wide.

Just what he needed, Roman thought, an audience. He motioned for Alice to move, but she sat up in shock.

". . . see a light on upstairs. Roman, is that you?" Raina's voice grew louder and accomplished what Roman couldn't.

Alice flew out of bed. "Oh, my God." She dove for her clothes. Scrambling to pull on her pants, she danced around on one foot, attempting to get one leg inside jeans that had been turned inside out.

"Roman? If it's you, answer me."

"Don't you dare," Alice hissed.

"I thought they taught you the basics back in kindergarten," Roman commented. "If you sat down and put only one leg at a time in there, it might make things easier."

Raina's footsteps sounded louder than his pounding heart and, now that he stopped to think about it, sweeter than anything he'd heard in a long while. There was nothing like being caught to kill off interest, and if Alice's beet-red face was any indication, she wouldn't be returning here or facing him anywhere, anytime soon.

He waited until Alice had calmed down enough to get her leg into half of her jeans before calling down to his mother. "I hear you, Mom. I got back a little while ago."

A male voice spoke with Raina—Eric, probably—which explained why she hadn't made her way up the stairs. She only walked the steps once in the morning and again at night. Roman had been considering speaking to Chase about turning one of the rooms downstairs into a bedroom to accommodate Raina's health.

"I want to hear all about your weekend," Raina called and he heard her footsteps on the stairs at a quick pace that surprised him.

"Ooh, no!" This time Alice shrieked in panic.

Roman, still standing in his doorway, turned back to his bedroom in time to see her kick the pants away. She'd instead yanked up the comforter, wrapping the beige quilting around herself like a shroud.

Strange and stranger, Roman thought and shook his head. "By the way," he said to Alice. "Dr. Fallon's here too. But don't worry. Thanks to years of doctor-patient confidentiality, I'm sure he knows how to be discreet."

Besides, Roman thought, things could be worse. It could be Chase, Mr. I-Only-Report-the-Facts, pounding up the stairs behind his mother.

Raina reached the top step and walked up to him. Roman blocked her view of his room as best he could. "Hi, Mom. Feeling okay?" He glanced over her shoulder to where Eric stood behind her.

"The stairs winded me. Let's sit on your bed and talk." She started to push past him and he gently held on to her arm. "You can't go in there."

"Who's there? Is it Charlotte?" she asked, sounding excited at the prospect.

"No, it's not Charlotte, now please—this is a big enough mess without you getting involved or upset." Raina shook her head and tried to see over his shoulder.

Behind her, Dr. Fallon rolled his eyes, as if to say, *Once she's on a roll, I can't stop her,* something Roman understood too well.

"Okay, see for yourself," Roman whispered, putting a hand to his lips, silently asking his mother to keep quiet. It wasn't his job to protect Alice from her stupidity, but he'd rather Raina take a quick peek and disappear than humiliate the woman by bulldozing in.

He stepped into the room, his mother behind him, in

time to see Alice trying to open the window with shaking hands. But as Roman immediately realized, the latch was secure and Alice was in no jeopardy of height or success.

"I think we should let Eric take care of her, Roman. She's obviously disturbed and upset," Raina whispered, then grabbed his hand and pulled him out of the room.

Realizing he faced his mother in his underwear, Roman snagged his jeans, which he'd left on the floor. He'd survive the embarrassment better than Alice. "You're right. Let's go downstairs, okay?" Roman led Raina out.

He quickly detoured into the bathroom to pull on his pants, then he returned to the kitchen in time to see his mother take a spoonful of antacid liquid.

"Would you make me some tea?" Raina asked. "All this excitement's gotten to me."

He glanced at her, concerned. "Are you sure it's just heartburn? Nothing heart-related? I can get Eric—"

"No. I'm fine. Just some normal indigestion." She patted her chest. "That girl needs Eric more than I do right now."

"Just don't neglect your health if something's really wrong, okay?" He checked the teakettle for water, then turned on the burner beneath it.

"I think Alice could use a sedative and a good talking-to. What was she thinking?" Raina shook her head and settled herself into a chair.

"That reminds me. What were *you* thinking, leaving the house wide open?"

"May I remind you, in the lifetime I've been living in Yorkshire Falls there's never been a reason to use a lock?"

"Five thefts over the last week isn't enough of a reason for you?"

"I agree, and we'll discuss that later." Eric walked into the room. "Alice is waiting in the hall—fully dressed," he said in a lower voice. "I'm going to drive her home. I promised her that word of this wouldn't get out." His gaze settled not on Roman, who had every reason to keep this incident quiet, but on Raina, who Roman figured would love to burn the phone wires and share her eventful night with friends.

"I'm sensitive enough to know when to keep quiet," she said, hurt flashing in her eyes.

Roman placed his hand over hers. "I'm sure he didn't mean to insult you, Mom. He's just being cautious."

"Exactly. Thank you, Roman. Raina, I'll call you." Eric's voice softened. "I'm sorry our evening got cut short."

"I appreciate you getting me out of the house. You know the boys feel better about my health when I'm with you." She gave him a wary glance. "I'll just enjoy tea with my son. You and I can always spend time together."

"Tomorrow night works for me."

"Let's stay in tomorrow, okay?" Raina expelled a prolonged sigh.

Eric stepped forward, but she waved him away. "A cup of tea is all I need. Norman's grease is just lying in my chest. Someone ought to break into his place and steal all the lard from his cabinets."

Eric laughed, then turned to Roman. "I'm not sure whether to tell you to watch out for your mother or yourself." He chuckled and before Raina could respond, Eric walked out, leaving her without the last word.

The teakettle began to sing and Roman stood up to get it. "You know, I think Dr. Fallon's good for you."

"You aren't angry?" Her voice sounded soft and worried.

He glanced over his shoulder, surprised, then got back to work, steeping the tea bag in the water and adding her one teaspoon of sugar before rejoining her at the table. "Angry at what? The man obviously makes you happy. You're getting out with him, smiling more than you have in years, and despite your health scare—"

"Maybe that's because you're home."

"Or maybe it's because a man's finding you special and you like the attention." He set a mug down in front of her.

"Don't let your imagination run away with you. He's a lonely widower and I'm keeping him company. That's all."

"You've been a lonely widow for the last twenty or so years. It's about time you started living your life again."

She glanced down, staring into the cup. "I never stopped living, Roman."

"Yes, you did." He didn't want to have this deep conversation, yet he couldn't deny the time had come. "In some ways you stopped living—and you changed how we lived as a result. Roman, Rick, and Chase, the bachelor brothers," he said wryly.

"You're saying it's my fault you boys are still single?" His mother sounded outraged and hurt.

He steepled his fingers in thought. He wanted to tell her there was no blame involved, no fault, but he couldn't lie. "You and Dad gave us a great family life."

"And this is a bad thing? Bad enough to make you steer clear of marriage and family?"

He shook his head. "But you were devastated when he died. It was almost as if life stopped. You . . . you lived in pain—"

"That eventually dimmed," she reminded him. "I wouldn't have traded one minute with your father. Not even if it meant I wouldn't have suffered or grieved. If you don't feel pain, you haven't really lived," she said softly.

He'd already realized he hadn't been living—when he'd

connected with Charlotte this weekend. And as his mother spoke, he realized why. In an effort not to repeat the painful grieving process he'd seen his mother go through, Roman had opted to run, to travel, keeping his distance—from the town, his family, and Charlotte. Charlotte, the one woman who he'd always known, or at least sensed, could tie him to Yorkshire Falls and keep him here.

The one woman who had the power to hurt him, to make him *feel* the very pain he feared, should she die or leave him in any way. But his one night with her proved he couldn't live without her either.

She was worth any risk.

"I've lived and I've loved. Not everyone can say the same. I've been lucky," his mother said.

A wry smile twisted Roman's lips. "You could have been luckier."

A combination of sadness and happiness, of obvious memories, settled in her eyes. "I won't lie. Of course I'd rather we'd have grown old and raised you boys together, but then I wouldn't have this chance with Eric." Her concerned gaze met his. "You're sure you aren't upset about that?"

"I think he's good for you. Nothing about that upsets me."

She smiled. "You do realize you can't run away from life forever."

He wasn't surprised she'd read his thoughts. His mother had always been perceptive. He'd inherited the trait that had helped shape his career, but it was a pain in the ass when used against him. And it was that perceptiveness which left him too open to seeing and feeling his mother's hurt.

"Well, I suppose you can keep running, but think about

how much you'd be missing." She patted his hand in the motherly gesture he knew so well. "And you're too smart to continue on with something that's an escape and not a solution. So, having said all that, where does Charlotte fit into your life now? And don't tell me she doesn't."

She'd returned to her mission. "You know me better than to think I'd tell," Roman said.

She raised her gaze toward the heavens. "Girls. Why couldn't God have given me one girl with my boys, so I could understand what just one of you were thinking?"

"Come on, Mom. You know you like to be kept guessing. It keeps you young."

"I'd rather drink from the Fountain of Youth," she muttered. "Speaking of girls, *you* told me you were going to visit an old friend who'd moved to Albany last night, but Samson tells me he saw Charlotte leaving in your car."

"For a man who's the town recluse, he's too full of information." Roman wondered who else had seen them leave. Not that it mattered. He intended to make an honest woman out of her, no harm to her reputation involved. Unless marrying a Chandler who had a rumored fetish for women's panties was a problem.

As amazing as it seemed, even to him, he was ready to make a commitment now—one that offered more than he'd envisioned after losing the coin toss. But before he approached Charlotte with the idea, he needed to convince her that he could and would make a good father and husband, that he wanted more than a long-distance marriage of convenience. Exactly how much more, how much he was willing to sacrifice in his career, his travel, he still had to think through. He had commitments, people relying on him, and a real enjoyment of his job he didn't want to lose when this leave of absence was through.

But his goal now was personal. His mother's grandchildren would be the by-product of that goal, but not the reason for Roman's marriage. He felt light-headed and dizzy, much like the day of his first AP assignment.

"You could have told me you were going away with Charlotte," his mother said, interrupting his thoughts.

"And have you questioning the poor woman? I figured I'd spare her."

An amused gleam lit her gaze. "Well, I can still do that despite your intent to keep me in the dark. But I won't. She has enough on her hands now."

His inner alarm went off. If Alice had been crazy enough to crawl into his bed, who knows what else was going on in this town? "Why's that? Another panty theft?"

His mother shook her head. "No, and Rick's plenty annoyed that no one got you off the hook last night, that much I can tell you. Not that the police consider you a suspect, but with Alice and the ladies in town still in an uproar—"

"Mom, what's wrong with Charlotte?" He interrupted her rambling.

"Sorry. I got carried away." She flushed.

He didn't like the sound of her voice or the frown on her lips. "What's going on?"

She sighed. "Russell Bronson's back in town."

Roman muttered a curse.

"Behave yourself," his mother said, but the sympathetic look on her face told him she understood just why he was upset.

The timing of Charlotte's father's return couldn't be worse. Just because Roman had come to terms with himself, his past, and his future didn't mean Charlotte had. He'd been struggling with himself from the moment he'd come back to town and lost the coin toss. Despite his attempts to stay away, Charlotte was the only woman he wanted in his life. The only woman he wanted to sleep with, the only one to have his children.

Originally he'd made that choice due to losing the coin toss. It'd been a selfish, unemotional decision because he'd still been running. Still thinking of himself more than Charlotte, no matter how much he'd attempted to convince himself otherwise. He'd had a need. She'd been the one he'd chosen to fill it. So simple. So stupid. She deserved so much more—a man who loved her, who'd be there for her, and who would give her the family life she'd been denied as a child. Roman wanted to be the man to provide her with all those things. But she'd never believe him, especially not now.

Raina rested her chin on one hand. "Do you have a plan?"

If he did, he wouldn't share it with his mother. But as things stood now, his mind was as blank as his laptop screen on a bad day.

"Well, I suggest you come up with something," she said in the wake of his silence.

He shot his mother an annoyed look. "That much I already figured out. But unless Russell's not the scum of the earth the town thinks he is, I'm in trouble."

"I don't know what Russell is." His mother shrugged. "He's been gone too long. You're the reporter, you ferret out the facts. Just remember, there are three sides to every story: his, hers, and the truth."

Roman nodded. He just hoped the truth was enough to secure their future.

Charlotte floated into work Monday morning, light on her feet and happier than she'd been in ages. For as long as the euphoria lasted, she intended to enjoy it and not dissect all the reasons why she shouldn't get too used to Roman or his attention. He'd asked her to keep an open mind and he made her feel too good to argue. He made her think anything was possible after all. Even them. She shocked herself with her new, enlightened attitude, but he'd given her no reason to doubt him.

"I smell coffee," Beth said, coming out of the back room.

"You smell chai tea. Norman hasn't progressed to iced lattes, but he has gotten this tea in and it's delicious. Hot, cold, doesn't matter. I went for hot today. Here, taste." Charlotte handed Beth her own cup. "It's very sweet," she warned Beth in case she was expecting a more bitter taste.

Beth took an experimental sip. Her eyes opened wide. "It's like a mix of honey and vanilla. Yum."

"It's originally from India. First time I had it was in New York last year."

"I don't even want to know calorie count."

Charlotte shook her head. "Me neither, but this is pure indulgence and I refuse to do anything but enjoy." A motto she seemed to have adopted since reuniting with Roman. "I'll just eat a light salad for lunch." Charlotte closed her eyes and inhaled the fragrant spiced tea before drinking some more. "Mmm." She drew out the sound.

"Uh-oh." Beth's voice disturbed her satisfaction.

Charlotte opened her eyes and met her friend's knowing grin. "Uh-oh, what?"

"I recognize that look, that sound. It's pure rapture. Ecstasy."

"So?" Charlotte shook her head. "I told you I love this stuff."

"Your cheeks are flushed and you're sounding practically orgasmic. Don't tell me it's all about tea."

"What else could it be about?"

Beth settled herself into a chair across from Charlotte's cluttered desk. "What else could it be, she asks. As if I wouldn't find out you and Roman were both out of town Saturday night. Coincidence? I think not." Beth tapped her fingers on a stack of invoices. "You see, Rick and I spent Saturday night hanging out. We played darts with my most recent picture of the good doctor as the target—"

"Did he call?"

Beth's eyes filled with tears. "I called him and when he rushed me off, I called back and ended things—and you're interrupting." She abruptly changed the subject.

Charlotte recognized the avoidance technique but couldn't remain silent. "You ended it?" She rushed around her desk to hug her friend. "I know it couldn't have been easy for you."

"No choice." Beth shook her head, obviously choked up.

Charlotte stepped back and sat on the corner of her desk, dangling her legs off the side. Now that she knew to look, she realized Beth no longer wore the sparkling diamond on her left hand. "And he just let you break up with him?"

"I think he was relieved."

"The schmuck."

Beth laughed, but tears filled her eyes. "Well, I agree, but I'm the one with the bigger problem, you know? I let myself get involved. I never looked deep enough or admitted this was a tendency he had." She shivered. "Let's change the subject, okay?"

Charlotte nodded. She didn't want to add to her friend's pain.

Beth leaned forward, resting her elbows on the arms of the chair. "So let's get back to my original point."

"Which was?"

"You, and how those flushed cheeks and sounds of pleasure have nothing to do with the chai tea." Charlotte rolled her eyes, but Beth ignored her.

Leave it to Beth to turn the tables and put Charlotte in the hot seat. She held up both hands in front of her. "I take the Fifth." Anything involving herself and Roman was too personal to discuss. Even with Beth.

"Aha!" She sat upright in her seat.

Charlotte narrowed her gaze. "What?"

"Taking the Fifth means you have something to protect. Something private." Interest sparkled in the depth of Beth's eyes as she leaned forward. "Come on, fill me in. You had more than a date, right? Please let me revel in your good news. I have so little of my own."

Though Charlotte felt badly about Beth's current problems, she also recognized when she was being played, and Beth did it well. "How about this?" Charlotte offered as a compromise. "When I have news, I promise to share. Right now all I have is . . . hope." Hope she held close to her heart, too afraid to let it into daylight for fear her dreams would be just that—and she'd be left alone, like her mother.

She met her friend's concerned gaze. "If I had something to tell, you'd be the only person I'd talk to." She leaned forward and squeezed Beth's hand. "That's a promise."

Beth exhaled hard. "I know. I just hate being the only one revealing all her problems and weaknesses."

"You are not weak. You're human."

Beth shrugged. "Let's drink up." She raised her Styrofoam cup. "Cheers."

"Cheers." Charlotte finished her now lukewarm tea in a

few satisfying sips. "So. Do you mind tending shop today? I'm going to hole up in my apartment and knit."

"Oooh, sounds exciting."

"Not really." She laughed. "But the money that'll come in when we deliver the finished goods is definitely worth the hours of television watching I'll have to endure."

Beth rose. "Better you than me."

"I'll meet up with you at the Little League game later, okay?" Charlotte's Attic had sponsored a team and Charlotte tried to get out and cheer the kids on as often as possible. Though the season was barely under way, they'd already played twice and were going into tonight's game with a winning record. She thought of them as her team and was proud of every hit and catch made.

Beth shrugged. "Why not? It's not like I have anything more exciting to do."

"Gee, thanks," Charlotte said wryly.

"Actually, I'm serious. Watching the game beats an evening of solitaire."

Charlotte tossed her empty cup into the garbage can. "Sad as it is, the game is the highlight of my day too." Unless Roman stopped by. *You will be seeing me,* he'd said, and her stomach twisted in coiled knots of anticipation. She couldn't wait.

"My heart bleeds for you." Beth eyed her with a complete lack of pity.

Charlotte laughed, "Yeah, yeah. Just bring dinner, because after a day of hard work, I'll be starving." By agreement, Charlotte and Beth alternated supplying food. Last week they'd frozen over fried chicken, and with the temperature dropping, tonight would be no different. "Don't forget your jacket."

"Yes, Mom."

At Beth's words, an odd flutter took up residence in her chest. Maybe it was her biological clock that caused the accompanying lump in her throat because it certainly couldn't be a sudden desire for children. Roman's children.

Keep an open mind. But the man was still a traveler, by choice and by occupation. No way could she open her mind that wide.

Or could she?

Later that day, Charlotte's hands were tired, her shoulders stiff, yet she had a sense of accomplishment running through her veins. She'd crocheted, sewn, and put in a full day's work. Then she'd painstakingly hand-wrapped a light blue pair of panties and delivered them to the next person on her customer list before stopping by the general store for some staple items for her refrigerator.

She'd returned home to find an odd message from her mother on her answering machine, promising to meet up with Charlotte tonight at the baseball game. Little League games were a town event, but her mother never made an appearance. Charlotte wondered if the local vet had anything to do with her mother's sudden willingness to go out. If so, Charlotte was heading over to Harrington, the next town over, to pick out a dog from the shelter as added incentive for Annie to visit with the man.

Though her mother had called, Roman hadn't. Of course, he hadn't made any promises, which meant he hadn't broken any either. Still, she was disappointed their time together hadn't left him panting for more of whatever she had to offer. So much for her charm. Skill. Erotic proficiency, she thought wryly.

She couldn't completely shake off the dismay, but she

knew she'd be fine. She wasn't her mother's daughter, at least in that respect.

She straightened her spine, held her shoulders back, and approached the school. A chilly breeze floated in the air around her. As promised, the temperatures had taken a bizarre drop throughout the day and she hugged her arms closer around her. But, lucky for the kids and the bleacher bums like herself, they had perfect softball weather in which to enjoy the game. Charlotte's Attic sponsored the Rockets, and she wanted to see them kick some more butt.

As she walked through the full parking lot, the baseball diamond came into view in the distance, located beyond the football field and bleachers. Her stomach growled and she placed a hand over her empty belly. She hoped Beth was waiting with something good to eat, because she was starving.

As she reached the rows of makeshift stadium seats, a place where she'd spent a lot of time as a teenager, she quickened her pace. Without warning, she was grabbed from behind. A strong hand anchored her waist, locking her arms at her sides.

Fear lodged in her throat—for all of two seconds—before familiar cologne assaulted her senses and a sexy voice muttered in her ear. "I always wanted to make out with you under the bleachers."

Fear turned to excitement, excitement to arousal. She'd missed Roman today. And if she let herself think about just how much, the fear might well return. Instead she chose to relax in his arms and enjoy now.

As soon as he spoke, Roman felt Charlotte's muscles ease against him. He didn't know how he'd managed to stay away from her all day. Hell, he didn't know how he'd stayed away from her for the last ten years. A humbling admission, for a man who made traveling his MO. He buried his face between her neck and shoulders, inhaling her fragrant scent. "You know I'd have killed to get you behind the bleachers back in high school."

"And what would you have done with me?"

From her playful tone, Roman figured she was in a good mood. Obviously she hadn't yet heard about her father's return, which gave him this small window of opportunity to cement everything they'd shared. He grabbed her hand and pulled her around the benches until they were well hidden from view. He ought to know. He'd specialized in hanging out here in high school. With the wrong girls.

Now he had the right one. She was dressed in blue jeans and a Little League jersey beneath an open denim jacket with a fuzzy lining. But what drew his attention most was her mouth—her lips were as red as her snakeskin boots.

He grabbed the white fleece collar and pulled her within kissing distance. "You never wore such hot-looking makeup back in high school."

She grinned. "I wasn't looking to attract attention back in high school."

Unexpected relief washed over him. "Missed me today, did you?" He'd wanted to give her time to do just that before seeing her again. But he hadn't stayed away easily.

She rolled her eyes. "I didn't say I was looking to attract *your* attention."

He wasn't fooled. She'd missed him as much as he'd missed her. "Well, you've got it anyway. Now shut up and kiss me."

She did. Her lips were chilled and he warmed them, slipping his tongue inside her mouth. She wrapped her arms around his waist and pulled him close, deepening the kiss and letting out a sigh of satisfaction he could relate to. She slid her hands into the back pocket of his jeans, her palms flat against his behind. Her tongue met his thrust for thrust, the same way their bodies, now aligned, sought to mimic the erotic motion. Unfortunately, too many layers of clothing stood between them.

Cheers sounded in the distance and she broke the kiss. "I can't do this now," she said through dampened lips.

He stared at her dazed expression. "Sure you can. And you want to." Having already experienced slick heaven inside her, so did he.

She cocked her head to one side. "Okay, then, I'll rephrase. I want to, but I can't."

He still gripped her forearms with both hands and the desire to make love to her—hard, cold ground be damned—was overwhelming. "Give me one reason why not, and make it a good one."

"Because my mother left a message on my answering machine. She said she'd meet me at the baseball field. She almost never comes to town events and now we're talking two in one week. I have to be there."

The regret in her eyes was enough to satisfy him. For now. "I didn't think you could come up with anything compelling enough. You did." He released his grasp. His body wasn't thrilled, but his heart won out. He wanted to give her what she desired, in this case seeing her mother. He just wished it wouldn't cause her pain. "You haven't spoken to her since you've been back?"

Charlotte shook her head. "We played phone tag."

Then she definitely didn't know about her father. "Charlotte . . ."

"Come." She grabbed his hand. "Let's go find my mother, catch the game, and if you're lucky, I'll let you catch me afterward." She laughed, and before he could say another word, she took off running.

With a groan, he ran after her, figuring he could just be there to minimize the damage when the shock came.

Charlotte glanced over her shoulder and laughed. Thanks to her quick dash, she was light-headed. Of course, Roman's kiss had much to do with her dizzy state, but her escape had been born of pure self-preservation. She didn't care how far from the baseball field they were, everyone would take one look at her and figure out what they'd been doing. So the less she did under the bleachers, the better as far as she was concerned. Until later. Then they could pick up where they left off and do whatever they wanted.

The thought sent tingles of anticipation up her spine, arousing every nerve ending she possessed, bringing a stinging flush to her cheeks. A quick glance over her shoulder, and she realized Roman was walking behind her at a leisurely pace. He grinned and waved, then got sidetracked by Rick, who grabbed him on the shoulder.

Charlotte slowed her steps, and turned back to walk right into her mother. A glowing version of her mother, from her made-up face to her bright smile and twinkling eyes.

"Mom!"

"Where are you coming from in such a hurry?" Annie steadied her with a hug before letting go.

"I'm . . . I was . . ."

"Making out under the bleachers with Roman." Her mother reached a hand up and brushed her knuckle over Charlotte's cheek. "I recognize the signs. Your father and I used to do it all the time."

A protest rose to her lips. Charlotte didn't want to accept that anything about her feelings for Roman was similar to

Annie and Russell. Not even something as light and fun as acting like teenagers.

"So what brings you out tonight?" Charlotte asked.

She glanced around, looking for Dennis Sterling, then eyed her mother with curiosity. "Or maybe I should ask, who brings you out tonight?"

From the corner of her eye, Charlotte noticed Beth waving wildly in the distance. If Beth was that hungry, she should just eat without waiting. Charlotte signaled back with one finger, indicating she'd be another minute or so.

Annie sighed. "I should have known I couldn't keep a secret in this town."

Charlotte turned back to her mother. "Apparently you can, because I haven't a clue what you're talking about." The only thing Charlotte did know was that her mother had a high-wattage smile and an easy laugh she hadn't seen in way too long. When Charlotte ran into Dennis, she'd plant a huge kiss on him herself.

She pulled her mother into a tight hug. As she inhaled, a beautiful scent Charlotte didn't recognize teased her senses. "Perfume and makeup," she murmured.

"I hope you'll greet me with the same enthusiasm, Charlie."

That voice, using that name. Charlotte stiffened and dropped her arms, backing slowly away from her mother. Betrayal settled like lead in her stomach. Charlotte should have known better than to think her mother had allowed herself to be interested in anyone other than her absentee husband, Russell Bronson.

She turned and faced the man who casually walked in and out of her life on his own schedule. He was as good-looking as ever, dressed in khakis and a navy pullover sweater. His hair was neatly combed, with more gray than she remembered. His face offered a few more lines, but he'd aged well. And looked happy.

Unlike her mother, Charlotte had no doubt his moods didn't change depending upon whether or not he was with Annie. But her mother's mood, actions, and even how she looked hinged on whether Russell was in town. And when he took off again.

Charlotte's anger grew, not just at the man who made Yorkshire Falls and his family into a revolving door—but at her mother, for allowing herself to be manipulated so easily. And for so long.

"Charlie?"

Charlotte wrapped her arms tightly around her waist. "So the prodigal father's returned."

He stepped forward and she stepped back.

Disappointment flickered in his eyes—or maybe that was what she wanted to see. That darn kernel of hope she'd always held in her heart wouldn't be extinguished, but she refused to act on it.

The baseball game continued, but Charlotte had lost interest. And apparently so had the rest of the crowd. Unless she was paranoid, she felt dozens of pairs of eyes trained on the dysfunctional Bronson family. Small-town curiosity at its finest. She braced herself against the stares and chatter, and stood in silence, waiting for her parents to speak.

Russell sighed. "Not the reception I was hoping for," he said finally.

"But the one you expected, I'm sure."

Roman strode to her side and placed an arm around her shoulder. More fodder for gossip at Norman's, she thought wryly. "Am I interrupting a family reunion?"

She shook her head. "Roman, you remember my . . ."

She cleared her throat. “You remember Russell, don’t you?”

“Of course.” He extended his hand. “Nice to see you again.”

Sweet Raina had instilled perfect manners into all three of her sons. Too bad she hadn’t given them her sense of stability and roots.

Russell shook Roman’s hand. “It’s been a while.”

“It certainly has,” Roman said.

She gritted her teeth, forced a smile, and aimed her next comments Roman’s way. “True. And considering you’ve been in town for a few days, you’re more up on what’s new around here. So why don’t you catch Russell up on what he’s missed during this last absence?”

Roman’s sharp intake of breath sliced into her heart, but she refused to let it change her intentions. In her mind, she saw herself as she’d been when she’d run out from behind the bleachers, laughing, happy, and excited from her run-in with Roman. Looking forward with aroused anticipation to the night ahead, when she could get him alone. And before her now, she saw her mother, with similarly flushed cheeks and a carefree expression—all because Russell Bronson had deigned to return.

The parallels between herself and her mother were strong. So strong, she could begin to see how Annie’s life began and ended with Russell. A lifetime in limbo. No way would Charlotte allow herself to end up like her. She looked back and forth between the two men with the power to rip her heart to pieces if she let them. She couldn’t afford to soften toward either one right now.

Much as she didn’t want to hurt Roman, he represented everything she feared. How had she let herself forget that?

"You know, now that I think about it, you two have so much in common it's uncanny."

Russell glanced at Roman, or, more accurately, Charlotte thought, Roman's hand on her shoulder. "I'm not sure that's true."

"Oh, I am. How long are you in town for this time? A day? A weekend? Or maybe longer, since you have a few months before pilot season starts."

"Charlotte!" Her mother spoke up, giving her daughter a warning touch on the arm.

Charlotte covered her mother's chilled hand with her own. The last person she wanted to hurt was Annie. "See? He doesn't have an answer, Mom. He'll leave when he gets bored."

Charlotte glanced up at Roman, then turned away when a lump rose to her throat. "How about you?" she asked without meeting his gaze. "Raina looks healthier by the day, thank God." She pointed to where his mother sat on a beach blanket with Eric Fallon, watching them. So were Fred Aames, Marianne Diamond, Pearl Robinson, Eldin Wingate, and everyone else in town. Charlotte hated being the center of notoriety. "You can take off anytime now too. I told you, you both had a lot in common."

Before she could lose control of herself or what remained of her composure, she pivoted and took off. Away from her mother, her father, but most of all, away from Roman.

CHAPTER TEN

Roman watched Charlotte go. Away from the field, her father, and away from him. Her pain was his pain, and he shoved his hands in his pockets and groaned in frustration. He couldn't let her run off alone. Not when she was so upset. He'd just seen firsthand the devastation her father's return had caused.

"Someone ought to go after her," Annie said. Clearly she wasn't referring to herself, since she gripped Russell's arm more firmly.

"Someone should," Russell added. "But she won't listen to anything I have to say."

"Is it any wonder?" Roman raised an eyebrow at her parents. "I'm not here to pass judgment"—Lord knew he didn't live a blameless life—"but did either one of you consider talking to her privately instead of making a public spectacle of this family reunion?" Feeling precious minutes slipping away, Roman glanced out toward the field. Relief passed through him when he realized Charlotte was taking the long route home, on foot.

Russell shrugged helplessly, regret obvious in the green

eyes that looked so much like Charlotte's. "Annie felt sure she wouldn't come over if we told her on the phone and thought she wouldn't walk out on us in a crowd."

"And you don't know her well enough to say differently."

Russell shook his head. "But I want to. I always have."

Roman's mother and Eric chose that moment to join them. Roman had been surprised to see his mother at the baseball game, but since she'd been with Eric again, and sitting on a blanket the whole time, he figured she was feeling up to it. And maybe even feeling a bit better.

"I hope we're not interrupting," Eric said.

"Apparently, in this group, the more the merrier," Roman muttered. He had little time left before he'd have to break down Charlotte's door if he wanted to get her alone. "Russell, can I have a word with you?" he asked, shooting his mother a pointed, knowing glance.

"Annie, come have some lemonade. I made it myself and it's delicious."

"But . . ." Panic flared in Annie's eyes, as if she were afraid in the five minutes she'd be gone, Russell would disappear again.

Watching Annie gave Roman better insight into Charlotte's fears. She wasn't anything like her insecure mother, yet he could see how she'd instilled a fear in Charlotte—the fear of becoming as needy and sadly pathetic and isolated as her own mother.

He wanted to shield her from pain and take care of her forever, but Charlotte would freeze him out before she'd let him close enough to hurt her. And the thought shook him straight to the core.

Because he loved her.

He loved her. The truth settled in his heart, warming places that had always been cold.

He admired her fierce desire to maintain herself and her individuality, to not end up like her mother. He admired the business she'd built on her own, in a town that hadn't been prepared, yet she'd won the people over anyway. He loved how she saw the best in him even when he didn't deserve it. He loved everything about her.

Viewing her deepest pain up close forced him to acknowledge his feelings. Feelings that had to come second to Charlotte's needs or he'd risk losing her forever. He'd tell her, but the timing had to be right.

It was beyond him how he'd know when that was. Roman's family was hardly setting an example of functional relationships. Chase was hanging out with the single guys from the paper, drinking beer, talking sports, and sleeping with the occasional good-time woman and never getting involved. Rick rescued women, and right now he was playing Prince Charming to Beth Hansen until she got over her broken engagement and was ready to move on. Then he'd move on as well to the next woman in his life.

Roman shook his head, knowing he didn't have the role models to look to for answers. He was on his own.

"No buts," Eric cut in, speaking to Annie, his voice somehow soothing yet authoritative at the same time. "I have to insist you taste Raina's drink. Besides, Raina isn't supposed to spend too much time on her feet, and I'd appreciate you taking her back to the blanket until I can get there."

"Go on, Annie." Russell patted her arm and eased himself out of her grasp.

Once the trio had disappeared, Roman faced Charlotte's father. "I don't have much time."

"I realize that. But you should know life is more complicated than any of you"—Russell swept his arm around, gesturing to the ball field and hence the people of the town—"can understand."

In his pained expression, Roman didn't see the self-absorbed actor who'd abandoned his family for fame and fortune. Instead he saw an aging man who'd lost much. Roman let out a groan. "It's not any of us who needs to understand. It's your daughter." He pinned Russell with a steady gaze. "If you really care, I hope you'll take the time during this trip to prove it."

"She'd have to be willing to listen."

Roman shrugged. "*Make* her listen." After a last glare, Roman took off for the parking lot at a run, intending to take his own advice.

"It's time, Annie." Russell Bronson sat on the picnic blanket loaned to him by Raina Chandler. After the four of them had talked, Eric had taken Raina home, leaving Russell and Annie alone. Russell remembered Raina as a kind neighbor, a good mother to her three boys, and a friend to his wife. Obviously things hadn't changed.

And that was the problem, Russ thought. Nothing had changed. From the day he married Annie Wilson, the girl he'd fallen in love with in fifth grade, until now, everything in Annie's world had stayed the same.

She curled her legs beneath her and stared out at the players on the field. "I'm not sure it will make a difference," she said at last.

Neither was he, but all they could do was try. Russell patted his pocket and felt for the paper he'd taken from Dr. Eric Fallon. Before taking his leave, Eric had spoken to both Russell and Annie as her doctor. Annie was depressed, he'd said. Clinically, most probably.

Why hadn't Russell realized it before? He'd like to think it was because he wasn't a doctor, but he was man enough to acknowledge his own faults. He was selfish and self-centered. His desires had always come first. He'd never slowed down long enough to consider why Annie spoke and acted the way she did. He'd just accepted Annie, same as she'd accepted him.

Depression, he thought once more. Something Charlotte had picked up on and called Dr. Fallon about. Now it was up to Russell to ask Annie to get herself help. He shook his head and silently thanked his beautiful, headstrong daughter for realizing what he hadn't.

His daughter. A woman with a combination of disdain, fear, and vulnerability in her eyes. He'd caused each emotion. And he despised himself for it. But he had a chance now to correct many wrongs. Starting with Annie and ending with his daughter.

Annie hadn't responded to his declaration. It was time. And he'd lead her there any way he had to, Russell thought. "How does Charlotte feel about Roman Chandler?"

Annie tipped her head to the side. Her soft hair fell to her shoulders and the urge to run his fingers through the jet-black strands was strong. Always had been.

"Same as I feel about you. Charlotte's destined to repeat the pattern. He'll go, he'll return. And she'll be here when he does. It's in our genes." She spoke matter-of-factly, as if that possibility didn't bother her at all. She was too complacent, too accepting—and he'd taken advantage of that, he realized now.

Whether he'd known she was clinically depressed or not, he'd used her complacency as an excuse to come and go as he pleased. He shook his head, disgusted with himself.

He couldn't change the past, but he didn't want the same future for his daughter. "I disagree," he said, fighting Annie's description of Charlotte and Roman. "But she is destined to end up alone, pushing away any man who doesn't choose to settle in Yorkshire Falls."

Annie shook her head. "If you're right, at least she won't spend her life waiting for him to come back. Feeling alive only during visits."

Russell looked at his wife, seeing her, their past, and their future all together now. He'd thought that by remaining in her hometown, Annie would be happy, but instead she was miserable. By choice, he admitted. "Whether she waits for Roman's sporadic returns or she turns her back on him and ends up alone, either way it will be cold and lonely. And you damn well know it."

She rested her head on his shoulder. "I'm not cold or lonely now." She sighed, her breath warm against his neck.

No, Russell thought, she was accepting and he was coming to hate that word. Annie accepted. Whatever he did and whatever life threw her way. He'd once believed he could make them both happy, but that notion had shattered quickly. Nothing would make Annie truly happy unless he gave up on himself and settled in Yorkshire Falls. And even then, a part of Russell had always suspected that wasn't the answer. Not that it mattered.

He hadn't been able to forfeit his life for her, any more than he could get Annie to leave this town behind. He'd committed himself to her. They'd each chosen their way of life. He couldn't say they lived full or happy lives; still, they carried on. He loved her as much now as he had way back when. But he'd done no one a favor by letting her have her way.

Least of all his daughter.

Charlotte deserved to choose her destiny as well. But she deserved to make an educated decision. "She needs to know, Annie. She needs to understand the choices we made."

"What if she hates me?"

He held her close. "You raised her well and she loves you. In time she'll come to understand." And if she didn't, well, at least he and Annie would free her from repeating the past. He hoped.

Roman caught up with Charlotte walking down First Street. He beeped once, then slowed his car alongside her. She glanced over and kept walking.

"Come on, Charlotte. Get in the car."

"You don't want to deal with my mood right now, Roman."

"Any woman who admits to being in a mood is all right by me." He kept the car at a slow crawl. "Where are you going?"

She tilted her head his way. "Home."

"Is your fridge as empty as mine?"

"Go away."

He wasn't taking no for an answer. In fact, he had three things guaranteed to change her mind. "I'll take you for Chinese food, I'll get you out of town, and I won't discuss your father."

She paused.

"And in case those promises don't sway you, I'll start honking the horn, making a scene, and I won't stop until you're buckled in next to me. The choice is yours."

She swung around, yanked open the door, and flung herself into the seat beside him. "It was the Chinese food that got to me."

He grinned. "I wouldn't presume anything else."

"Good. Because I wouldn't, for one second, want you to think it had anything to do with your charm."

He hit the gas pedal and headed on out of town. "You think I'm charming?" he asked.

Arms folded, she eyed him warily.

In the wake of her silence, he said, "I'll take that as a yes."

She shrugged. "Suit yourself."

Obviously she wasn't in the mood for verbal games. That was okay. As long as she was within two feet of him and he could keep an eye on her, he was happy.

Twenty minutes later, they were seated in a typical Chinese restaurant—red velvet brocade wallpaper and dark sconce lighting added to the ambience.

A waiter led them to a corner table, half booth, half with chairs. A family of four, two adults and two young boys, were noisily eating beside them on the right. A fish tank sat in one corner and an indoor pond full of tropical fish was located to their right.

"Okay with you?" Roman asked Charlotte, of the table. He didn't mind the kids, but he couldn't gauge her mood.

A smile pulled at her lips. "As long as I don't order fish, this is fine." She slid into the booth.

He could have sat across from her and kept his distance. Instead he chose to join her, trapping her between himself and the wall.

She greeted him with an obviously fake pout. "You don't play fair."

"Did I say I would?" He recognized the verbal sparring

as a means of avoiding anything serious. He wondered how long it would last.

Charlotte shook her head. She couldn't focus on Roman now. Instead she looked past him to the family of four. The two blond-haired boys had trouble gleaming in their eyes as one brother lifted a crispy noodle, held it between his thumb and forefinger. He narrowed his gaze, getting ready to flick it. His brother whispered something in his ear and when he shifted for a different angle, Charlotte figured he was egging him on. Their parents, engaged in serious conversation, seemed not to notice.

"He wouldn't," Roman leaned back and whispered.

"I wouldn't bet the ranch." She used the old cliché. "Actually, in your case, I wouldn't bet the suitcase."

"Ouch."

She ignored him, watching the kids instead. "Ready, aim, fire," she whispered in time to the boy's actions.

As if on cue, the kid sent the hard noodle, which had broken in two, soaring into the air before it took a less-than-graceful plop into the goldfish-strewn water.

"Can a fish die from being hit with a fried wonton?" she asked.

"What about swallowing a fried wonton? If he were my kid, I'd grab him by the collar and dunk him headfirst. After I silently applauded his aim."

"Spoken like a man who's seen his share of trouble as a kid."

He shot her the incredible smile that melted her insides and made her want to crawl into his lap and never leave. Dangerous thought. She bit down on the inside of her cheek.

"I can relate to him. My brothers and I caused plenty of trouble when we were young."

She turned toward him and leaned forward in her seat, resting her chin on her hands. "Such as?" She needed to get lost in happy times. Other people's happy times.

"Let's see." He paused in thought. "I've got one. There was the time Mom attended back-to-school night and left Chase to watch me and Rick."

"Chase ruled like a dictator?"

"When he was awake, yes. But that night he fell asleep." Laugh lines touched the corners of his eyes as he recalled the memory.

"Please don't tell me you tied him up."

"Hell, no!" He sounded offended. "Give us some credit for imagination. Let's just say Mom's makeup case offered a wealth of possibilities."

She felt her eyes opening wide. "He didn't wake up?"

"The only benefit to having Chase as a pseudo-dad was that he slept like a dead one. We made him look mighty purty," Roman said with a deliberate southern drawl. "His date thought so too."

Charlotte let out a whoop of laughter. "No kidding?"

Roman shook his head. "He was eighteen, dating a college freshman, and she'd offered to meet him at our house so they could leave as soon as Mom got home. Doorbell rang, we woke him to answer it . . ."

Charlotte didn't hear the rest; she was laughing too hard, tears running own her face at the absurdity. "Oh, I wish I could have seen that."

He leaned closer. "I have pictures."

She wiped at her eyes with a linen napkin. "I have to see."

"Marry me and I'll show you."

Charlotte blinked and sat up straighter in her seat. The boys were joking nearby, the scent of egg rolls drifted toward her, and Roman was proposing marriage? She had to have heard wrong. Had to. "What?"

He grabbed for her hand, holding it close and tight within his strong, heated grasp. "I said, marry me." His eyes grew wide and he seemed stunned he'd spoken the words, but he obviously wasn't too stunned to repeat them.

She was floored. "You don't . . . I can't . . . you can't mean that," she managed to sputter. Her heart beat frantically in her chest and she had trouble catching her breath. Two surprises in one day. First her father, now this. She reached for the water, but her hands shook so badly she had to put the glass down before she dropped it.

He raised the glass and held it to her lips. She took a long, cold sip, then licked the droplets off her mouth. "Thank you."

He nodded. "I didn't mean to blurt it out that way, but I did mean every word."

She wondered when the room would stop spinning. "Roman, you can't possibly want to get married."

"Why not?"

She wished he'd look away, anything to break the connection, because those mesmerizing blue eyes were begging her to say yes, and to hell with the hows and whys. But her father's timely return had shown her exactly why she couldn't follow her heart. "Because . . ." She shut her eyes and attempted to formulate the best answer. The one that made the most rational sense. The one that explained their differences.

"I love you."

Her eyelids fluttered open wide. "You can't . . ."

He leaned forward, one arm propped over the back of the booth, and he shut her up with a kiss. A warm, heart-melting kiss. "You need to stop using that word—*can't,*" he murmured, his mouth still lingering over hers. Then he locked his lips with hers again and swept his tongue deep inside, consuming her, until a low growl rose in her throat.

"Hey, Ma, look! They're *French* kissing."

"Eew, tongues and all. Can they do that in public?"

Charlotte and Roman broke apart. The heat from an embarrassed blush rose to her cheeks. She shook her head and laughed. "This from the kid who was using fish for target practice."

"I asked you a question," Roman said, all too serious.

"And you have to know my answer." Her heart beat painfully in her chest. "I . . ." She licked her damp lips. "You've seen my parents, you know my mom's life. How can you ask me to repeat it?" She hung her head, wishing with everything in her she could sustain the righteous anger she'd summoned at the baseball game, even if she had transferred her feelings from her father to Roman.

"I'm not asking you to relive their lives." He held her face in his hands. Gently. Reverently.

The lump returned to her throat. "Are you planning on living in Yorkshire Falls?" She already knew the answer and prepared herself accordingly.

He shook his head. "But"—his fingers tightened around her face—"I'm looking into possibilities. I don't want to lose you and I'm willing to work out a compromise. All I'm asking you to do is keep an open mind. Give me time to work out something we'll both be comfortable with."

She swallowed hard, unable to believe what she was hearing, unsure if she could trust in the intangible and not get hurt. Then again, she'd be hurt losing him any way things played out. She wanted more time with him before the inevitable happened.

If the inevitable happened. She shoved all thoughts of

her parents from her mind. She'd have to deal with them soon enough. Roman had used the word *compromise,* which meant he was taking her needs into consideration. Unexpected adrenaline flowed through her system. "You said you loved me?"

He nodded. Swallowed. She watched his throat move convulsively up and down.

"I've never said that to anyone else."

She blinked back moisture. "Me neither."

His hands fell from her face to her shoulders. "What are you saying?"

"I love you too."

"He's gonna do it again," one of the kids at the other table yelled.

"Eww," his brother repeated, twice as loud.

Roman laughed and she felt his pleasure as strong and intense as her own.

"Can you imagine having a houseful of boys?" he asked.

"Don't even joke about something so serious."

He ignored her and merely grinned. "Boys run in my family and we both know it's my genes that determine sex. And think about how much fun we could have making those babies." His fingertips began a rhythmic massage of her shoulder muscles that turned into erotic foreplay.

Roman's children. She trembled from the inside out, wanting more than she ever believed possible and knowing it was probably out of reach. They still had much to work out before she could let herself think about that kind of future.

But he'd touched her heart—owned it, actually. He always had, from the night he'd shared his deepest dreams and she'd had no choice but to push him away in response.

She hadn't made any concrete decisions, but she knew she wouldn't push him away now.

"Ready to order?" a tall, dark-haired waiter asked.

"No," they both said at the same time.

Charlotte didn't know how, but minutes later, stomach still empty and a twenty-dollar bill left on the table, they were back on the road, headed home, and half an hour after that, she let them into her dark apartment.

She hit the switch in the hall and the overhead lamp came on, bathing them in muted light. He kicked the door closed behind him and pulled her into his arms. Standing, she leaned against the wall as his lips came down hard on hers. His need was blatant, apparent, and as deep as her own. She shed her jacket, dropping it to the floor, and Roman made even faster work of her jersey, until she was wearing only her red boots, blue jeans, and white lace bra.

He sucked in a shallow breath as he traced the floral pattern with roughened fingertips. Her nipples pebbled beneath his touch and her body coiled tight, desire spiraling through her at a rapid pace.

"You've got to be hot in all those clothes." She reached for the collar of his jacket and pulled it down, letting it join hers in a heap.

His blue eyes glittered with anticipation and desire. "What I'm feeling goes way beyond hot." He pulled his navy shirt over his head and tossed it aside. It hit the wall behind them and dropped with a muted thump. "Your turn."

A steady rhythm took up residence between her legs, and moisture accompanied his seductive words. Excitement was her companion as she bent over and pulled at her boots to get them off, but her hands shook and the leather seemed to mold tighter to her foot.

"Let me." He knelt down and pulled first one red snakeskin boot off, then the next, before turning his attention to the button on her jeans. He worked it like a pro, his strong hands lowering the zipper, then easing the waistband over her hips.

Her legs shook and only the wall supported her as he brought the heavy denim around her ankles. And stopped. She tried to wiggle one foot free, but the darn jeans were too narrow at the bottom.

"Don't bother. I've got you right where I want you." He knelt on the floor at her feet and looked up at her. A wicked grin tugged at his lips and a satisfied expression settled on his handsome face.

She was held captive by more than confining clothing. She was imprisoned by desire and bound by love. Love he reciprocated. And when he bent over, his hair dark against her white skin, white-hot arrows of desire shot through her body, a distinct combination of erotic craving and emotional need.

She wanted nothing more than for him to satisfy the divergent desires, but knew nothing less than him being inside her would do. He met her gaze and must have read her mind, because instead of pleasuring her with his mouth as he'd seemed intent on doing, he worked her pants off and rose to his feet. In seconds, he was as undressed as she was, gloriously naked and as aroused as she.

He stepped toward her and held out his arms. "Come."

She did as he asked and soon he'd lifted her into his arms, her legs wrapped around his waist, her hands looped around his neck, and, once again, her back against the wall. His body heat and strength seeped into her, cocooning her in warmth and arousing her even more.

"I need you inside me," Charlotte said.

Roman groaned. "I need the same thing."

It took some jockeying, but she finally felt his erection, large and full, ready to enter her. And when he thrust inside her, her heart opened to all possibilities. How could it not, when he was full to bursting inside her?

As he moved, every hard ridge of his arousal caused a glorious friction inside her that built stronger with each successive thrust of his penis higher and deeper than before. She couldn't catch her breath, didn't need to, as sensation after sensation washed over her, carrying her up and over the edge and into the most explosive climax she'd ever experienced—because it was marked by love.

His shuddering groan told her he'd felt it too. She loved him. And later, as she fell asleep in his arms, she wondered why she'd denied herself the admission for so long.

Charlotte awoke and stretched, feeling the cool sheets on her bare skin. The sensation of waking up alone was normal and alien at the same time. No different than most mornings of her life, and yet because she'd slept through the night snuggled against Roman's body, the chill was unwelcome and disturbing. So were the emotions that buffeted her still-dream-fogged brain.

She understood his reasons for kissing her and slipping out in the dead of night and she appreciated the respect he showed her in front of a gossipy small town. But she missed him, wanted to make love to him again. She loved him. Each thought frightened her beyond belief.

Rising, she went about her morning routine, attempting to pretend everything was still the same. Hot shower, hotter coffee, and a quick jump down the steps to work. Yup, Charlotte thought, same routine. But there was no getting around the fact that she was different.

Because she'd committed herself to Roman with those

three little words. *I love you.* And now that the words were spoken, she feared her life was about to change forever. If history was anything to go by—her mother's, her father's, and even Roman's—it wouldn't change for the better.

On that disturbing thought, she entered the unlocked shop, hoping the familiarity of the ruffles and lace and the vanilla potpourri she freshened daily would soothe her nerves. She stepped inside and the unexpected smell of lavender assaulted her senses, jarring her and destroying any sense of soothing sameness she hoped to find here.

"Beth?" she called out.

"Back here." Her friend strode out of the back room, a bottle of sachet air freshener in her hand, spraying as she walked. "The cleaning people were here last night and they must've spilled a bottle of ammonia in the office." She waved her hand in front of her face. "You could die from asphyxiation back there. I've been spraying from the front on back trying to cover it."

Charlotte crinkled her nose in disgust. "Yuck. Is it really that bad?" Because the lavender was enough to make her gag too. Charlotte walked farther into the store, dropping her purse by the counter, and when she reached the dressing area, she reared back from the horrific odor. "Whew." The idea of closing herself in her office and losing her thoughts in paperwork had just been shot to hell.

Beth nodded. "I shut the door from the office to stop the worst of the odor from getting into the changing rooms, and I opened the windows all the way, hoping to air the place out."

"Thanks. At least it's not too bad up front."

"Let's hope it stays that way."

"Well, we'll have to close off the dressing area and mark the receipts—you can take returns on any item bought today." Normally on-sale items, bathing suits, and underwear were exchange only, but it wasn't a fair policy if a buyer couldn't try on the merchandise first. "If the smell gets worse, we'll just close for the day. No sense poisoning ourselves."

Beth sprayed a few more shots of lavender.

"Couldn't you have picked any other scent?"

"The general store was out of everything else."

"Never mind. Just please, quit spraying and let's see what happens."

After placing the can down on a shelf, Beth followed Charlotte to the front end, where Charlotte wedged open the front door for fresh air.

"So." Beth perched herself on the counter by the register. "I'm glad to see you here and smiling. How are you after . . . you know?" She lowered her voice to a hushed whisper on the last two words, obviously referring to the spectacle Charlotte and her family had made at the baseball game yesterday.

Once Charlotte had climbed into Roman's car, she'd forgotten all about Beth, dinner, and everything else. "I'm fine," she said in equally hushed tones before catching herself. She glanced around the empty shop and rolled her eyes. "Why are we whispering?" she asked loudly.

Beth shrugged. "Beats me."

"Well, I am fine. I didn't appreciate being ambushed in public, though. If Dad—I mean, Russell—wanted to talk to me, he should have called. Or come over. Or gotten me somewhere alone. It was humiliating."

Beth glanced down at her nails, not meeting Charlotte's gaze as she asked, "Would you have given him the time of day if he had?"

Charlotte rolled her shoulders, where tension courtesy of

this conversation had lodged. "I don't know. Would you give Dr. Implant the time of day?" She immediately sucked in a sharp breath, disgusted with her comeback. "Good God, I'm sorry, Beth. I don't know why I'm taking things out on you." Charlotte ran to the counter and gave Beth into an apologetic hug. "Forgive me?"

"Of course. You don't have a sister to torture and your mother's too fragile. Who else is there but poor me?" Despite the harsh words, when Beth pulled back, she had a smile on her face.

"Actually, you asked an interesting question. I would give Dr. Implant the time—long enough to thank him for opening my eyes to my insecurities. Then I'd dump ice water on his lap."

"You're really feeling better?" Charlotte asked.

"How do I explain it?" Beth glanced upward, as if searching for answers. "I'm feeling aware," she said. "All I do lately is think, and I can see a pattern in my past relationships now. All the men I've been involved with wanted to change me, and I let them. I easily adapted to whatever they wanted me to be. David was the most extreme case. But no more. And I have you and Rick to thank for helping me on the road to recovery."

"Me?" Charlotte asked, surprised. "What did I do?"

"I told you the other day. You offered me this job because you knew better than me where my talents and interests lay. Now I know it too. And that's just for starters."

"Well, I'm glad to be of service. And what about Rick?"

"He talked and he listened. Most men don't talk. They watch television, grunt, maybe burp a few times before nodding their heads and pretending to pay attention. Rick listened to the stories about my past and he helped me draw the right conclusions."

"The man's born to rescue damsels in distress. Maybe he should've been a shrink, not a cop."

"Nah, the law-and-order thing makes him sexy," Beth said with a laugh.

"Please don't tell me you're falling for him."

Beth shook her head. "Nohow, no way. I'm on my own for a good long while."

Charlotte nodded. And she believed her friend. Beth's eyes didn't take on a dreamy cast when she spoke about Rick. She didn't seem to swoon over the sexy officer. Not the way Charlotte swooned when she thought about Roman. Her insides churned with anticipation and excitement at just the idea of seeing him again.

"I need to learn more about myself," Beth said, interrupting Charlotte's thoughts, and not a minute too soon. "I want to figure out what I like and what I don't. Not what's expected of me. So for now all I need is my friends."

"You've got us, hon." Charlotte clasped Beth's hand tightly and Beth returned the gesture. Charlotte only hoped *she* wouldn't be the one needing her friend's shoulder next.

"So what are you going to do now that you can't hole up in your office and do paperwork? Crochet again upstairs?"

She cringed at the thought. "No. My hands hurt. I need to spread out that kind of work. First I'll stop by the *Gazette* offices and talk to Chase about an Easter sale ad. I can't believe the holiday's only two and a half weeks away."

"Know what the best part of the holiday is?"

Charlotte tapped one finger against her forehead. "Hmm. Let me think. Could it be the chocolate Cadbury Bunny commercials?" she asked, referring to her best friend's weakness.

"How'd you know?"

"Are you forgetting I sent you wrapped chocolate every

holiday? I know you like I know the back of my hand." Charlotte picked her bag up off the floor where she'd left it earlier.

"We get to pig out together this year." Beth licked her lips in chocolate-heaven anticipation.

Charlotte laughed. "I'll stop by when I leave the *Gazette.* If it's quiet, I may just take the paperwork and bills upstairs."

"I knew this would happen." Beth shook her head sadly. "One day at home crocheting, and you're hooked on the soaps."

"Untrue."

"Are you denying you're going to watch *General Hospital* while you work?"

Charlotte gestured as if she were zipping her lips. She refused to confirm or deny. Of course she'd watch *General Hospital.* Because one certain sexy actor reminded her of Roman.

Man, oh, man, she was in deeper trouble than she thought. "See ya later." She waved and walked out the front door into the fresh air and inhaled deeply. "Much better," she said aloud. She hiked her purse onto her shoulder and started down the road.

As she passed the outskirts of town and the final median of grass, daffodils, and other assorted flowers, she saw Samson weeding the flower beds and called out to him. He didn't hear her, or chose to pretend he hadn't.

"Oh, well." She shrugged and continued on, grateful for the fresh spring air. As she walked, her thoughts drifted to Roman. Tingling anticipation mixed with trepidation over the words they'd exchanged and the level of commitment those words implied.

She wondered not only what Roman meant by working

out a compromise, but whether she could trust in the love he'd given and the marriage he claimed he desired.

Roman let himself into the *Gazette* offices, using his key. The place was still quiet. It was too early for Lucy's arrival, and from the look of things, even Chase hadn't made it downstairs yet. Roman needed fresh-brewed coffee and fresher air than the stuffy office provided, so he left the door to the street open, then headed for the kitchen to make something strong and caffeinated to drink.

Daybreak had forced him out of Charlotte's bed. He'd left her asleep. Only a kiss on her cheek and then he was gone. The town was talking enough about Charlotte and her family. He didn't need to add to the gossip by walking out of her apartment in broad daylight. Leaving in the early morning was chancy, but he hadn't been able to resist the opportunity to spend the night in her bed, her warm, naked body snuggled tight against his. As it would be for the rest of his life.

A tremor shook him hard. He might have acknowledged difficult truths—that he wanted to stop running, wanted to settle down, and that he did love Charlotte—but he'd be a liar if he said he wasn't scared shitless. Not enough to change his mind. Just enough to make him human, Roman thought. He was on the verge of a major life change and it had him on edge.

He still couldn't believe the words had came out of his mouth. Not that the words had been difficult. For a writer, they never were. But Roman always thought things through first, then spoke with precision. He'd never before let emotion overrule common sense. But his feelings for Charlotte were over ten years in the making. He wanted to marry her and he did love her. He hadn't planned on either declaration, but spontaneity was good. It kept a relationship fresh, Roman thought wryly.

But his hand shook as he worked on the coffee, counting scoops and filling the machine with water. His timing could have been better. He'd proposed in public, when she was coming off an emotional confrontation with her father, and before he'd had the chance to make decisions crucial to their future. Given all that, he had to admit she'd taken his words better than he could have imagined.

But now that he was alone in the office he'd spent so much time in as a kid, he realized his escape from Charlotte's bed was a good thing. He needed time alone, to figure out how to balance his life now, and he had no idea what came next. Though he figured contacting the *Washington Post* about that job offer would be a good start. The notion of picking up the phone didn't instill in him the urge to run. He decided that was a good sign.

"Hey, little brother. You're up early." Chase walked into the main room of the offices. "What are you doing here? Mom run out of Cocoa Puffs?"

Roman shrugged. "I wouldn't know." Because he hadn't been home long enough to eat breakfast. He glanced at his oldest sibling. "You know, I just realized we've done nothing but talk about me since I hit town. What's going on with you these days?"

Chase shrugged. "Same old thing."

"Any new women?" Roman hadn't seen Chase with anyone in particular since he'd been home.

Chase shook his head.

"So what do you do for company? What takes care of the loneliness?" Roman asked. And he wasn't talking about just sex. The brothers never divulged that kind of information. Chase knew what Roman meant. They both experienced that damn loneliness that came from their choices. The kind Charlotte had taken care of for him.

With a shrug, Chase said, "If I need company, I have some friends in Harrington. You know Yorkshire Falls is too damn small to get involved without anyone knowing. But I'm not lacking for company. Now back to you."

Roman laughed. Chase never could sustain a conversation about himself for too long. "What would you say if I told you the *Washington Post* offered me an editorial job?" he asked his oldest brother.

Chase padded across the room in socks, no shoes—one of the benefits of living upstairs—and joined Roman in the small kitchen area, where he poured himself a cup of coffee. He raised the mug. "Thanks, by the way."

Roman leaned against the refrigerator. "No sweat."

"I'd say don't take a desk job because of the coin toss."

He ran a hand through his hair. "I can't pretend it didn't happen." The irony was, Roman was now grateful he'd lost the coin toss, glad he was forced to stick around Yorkshire Falls, glad he'd been forced to consider marriage. Because the circumstances had conspired to give him a second chance with Charlotte, the woman he loved.

The woman he'd always loved.

"That coin toss is the reason my entire life is about to change." He shook his head. That hadn't come out right. Actually, the coin toss had provided the impetus to begin a new life. But love was the reason he was marrying Charlotte. Not family obligation.

"Marriage is a huge step. So's a baby. I know how bad Mom wants grandkids, but you have to admit, since Eric, she's calmed down a little."

"That's because he's keeping her too busy to bother us, but trust the one who sees her most mornings—she hasn't forgotten she wants grandchildren and she's still swigging Maalox." Though sometimes Roman thought she seemed more active when she thought he wasn't around, he figured he was imagining things. "So if you ask me, nothing's changed as far as that goes." But Roman's feelings about his mother's needs *had* changed.

"I still say make sure you can live with any decision you make." Chase paused for a gulp of coffee. "Rick and I will understand if you don't want to be the sacrificial lamb in Mom's quest for grandchildren just because you lost the coin toss. You can still back out of the deal."

Chase's words were ones Roman had used himself a short time ago. But things had changed from the time Roman had returned, exhausted, from London.

Until recently, he hadn't taken the time to examine the hows and whys of his actions during his short time home. Jet-lagged and exhausted, he'd just known the family had a need and it was his turn to fill it. Charlotte's presence in town had changed things. And he wondered how to explain his change of heart to Chase, the brother who prized his solitude and bachelor status most.

Charlotte walked up the path to the *Gazette*, only to find the door wide open. She knocked lightly, but no one answered. Since the *Gazette* had always been a relaxed place, one where you could stop by, hang out, talk to Lucy, Ty Turner, or even Chase, depending on his mood and schedule, she let herself inside. Expecting to see Lucy on the phone at her desk, Charlotte was surprised to see the large room was empty.

She glanced at her watch and realized it was earlier than she'd thought. But voices came from the kitchen and Charlotte followed the low-pitched tones. The closer she came, the stronger the smell of coffee, and her stomach began a steady rumble, reminding her she hadn't had anything to eat yet today.

A masculine voice sounded like Roman and her insides twisted into coiled knots. Would it always be like this? she wondered. Pure enjoyment at the thought of seeing him? His voice exciting her, turning her on? An overwhelming desire to look into those deep blue eyes and have them stare back at her with equal longing? If so, she hoped like hell he felt the same way, because she didn't see her affliction going away anytime soon.

She reached the doorway to the kitchen. Roman stood eyeing the ceiling, as if searching for answers, while Chase guzzled coffee. Neither brother realized she was there.

She was about to clear her throat and speak when Chase beat her to it.

"I still say make sure you can live with any decision you make." He paused for a gulp of coffee. "Rick and I will understand if you don't want to be the sacrificial lamb in Mom's quest for grandchildren just because you lost the coin toss. You can still back out of the deal."

Charlotte heard Chase's words and stars danced before her eyes. Her mind quickly interpreted what she'd heard. Raina wanted grandchildren and Roman had promised to give them to her? Was that why the self-proclaimed wanderer and bachelor had suddenly started talking marriage? Love and marriage? *Oh, God.*

Her stomach clenched in pain, but she reminded herself that eavesdroppers never heard anything correctly. She'd listened to part of a conversation only. But it didn't look or sound good. Not for her.

Good manners dictated she announce her presence now, before she overheard anything else that wasn't meant for her ears. But that didn't mean she could ignore what she had heard. "What coin toss?" she asked.

The sound of her voice obviously startled both men, because Chase whirled around and Roman's body jerked as if she'd shot at him from across the room. He turned toward where she stood in the doorway.

"How'd you get in?" Chase asked, with his usual flair for bluntness and no tact.

"I knocked, but no one answered. The door was wide open, so I walked in." She tossed her bag onto the kitchen counter and strode past Chase to face Roman. "What coin toss?" she asked again pointedly. With determination, fire, and . . . trepidation all locked in her throat.

"This is where I excuse myself," Chase said.

"Coward," Roman muttered.

"Somehow I don't think he has anything to do with this." Her heart pounded hard in her chest as Chase spilled his coffee into the sink and strode out of the kitchen, leaving her alone with Roman.

A man with secrets she was afraid to hear.

CHAPTER ELEVEN

Roman walked toward Charlotte, grasped her elbow and led her to a small table in the corner of the *Gazette* kitchen area. White Formica, white chairs, furniture she knew came from Raina's original set. She shook her head at the bizarre way the mind sought to avoid painful truths.

"Sit," he said.

"I have a feeling I'll take this better standing."

"And I'd rather know it wasn't so easy for you to turn and walk out. Now sit."

She folded her arms across her chest and lowered herself into the chair. She wasn't in the mood for games or beating around the bush. "Please tell me you didn't ask me to marry you because your mother wants grandchildren."

His steely blue eyes met hers. "I didn't ask you for that reason."

Her heart beat rapidly in her chest. "Then what deal did you make with your brothers?"

"Come on, didn't I just tell you last night how ridiculous brothers can be?" He reached out and grabbed for her hand. "Whatever went on between the three of us doesn't matter."

If she'd had any doubts about how serious this revelation was going to be, he'd just confirmed it. "It matters, or you wouldn't be trying to avoid telling me." One look into his serious expression and she knew she was right.

"I came home because Mom was rushed to the hospital with chest pains, remember?"

She nodded.

"She told us that the doctors said she had to avoid stress on her heart. And she had one wish that we all knew we had to make come true."

Charlotte swallowed hard. "A grandchild."

"Right. But since none of us were in a serious relationship with a woman—"

"Or planned to ever marry," she added.

He gave her a sheepish grin. "Since none of us were in the position to make it happen, we had to decide who would take that next step."

"So you flipped a coin to see who would give Raina a grandchild, and you lost." Bile rose in her throat.

"I know it sounds bad—"

"You don't want to know what it sounds like," she said bitterly. "What happened next? I threw myself at you and became the lucky candidate?"

"If you think back, I pulled away. I tried like hell to stay away. Because you were the one woman I couldn't do it to." He ran a frustrated hand through his hair.

"You couldn't do what to me?"

"It's going to get worse before it gets better," he warned her.

"I don't see how."

"I said I'd never outright lie to you and I won't start now. But you need to hear the whole truth before passing judgment." He glanced downward, then spoke again without meeting her gaze. "I thought I could find a woman who wanted kids. Get married, get her pregnant, and head on back abroad. I figured I'd honor my commitments financially and come home whenever possible, but not change my lifestyle much at all."

"Just like my father." He was more like Russell than Charlotte had ever imagined Roman Chandler could be. A true wave of nausea rushed over her, but before she could catch her breath or speak, he rushed on.

"Yes, and because of that, I immediately ruled you out, no matter how strong the attraction. I couldn't do that to you. Even then, I cared too much to hurt you. But I figured with any other woman, if we were both in agreement on things, no one would get hurt."

"Another woman." Charlotte could barely get the words past her lips. "Just like that. You could go from saying you care about me to accepting the idea of sleeping with another woman. So easily." She blinked back tears.

"No." He held onto her hand and squeezed tight. "No. I was a mess when I came home. I haven't even thought all this through until now. But I was jet-lagged, worried about my mother, and I'd agreed to this life change all in one night. I wasn't thinking clearly about anything except about not wanting to hurt you. So I pulled away."

"How noble."

He paused. Only the clock ticking loudly from the wall behind them broke the silence, but she wasn't about to make it easier.

He cleared his throat. "But I couldn't keep my distance. Every time we went near each other, things exploded. Not just sexually but emotionally. In here." He pointed to his chest. "And I knew I couldn't be with anyone else." He raised his head and his stare locked on hers. "Not ever again."

"Don't." She shook her head, finding it hard to speak, the pain lodged in her throat and chest, overwhelming. "Don't say all the right things in an attempt to make this okay when it isn't. It can't be. So you chose me," she said, trying to regain the thread of conversation without emotion getting in the way. "Because the attraction was so strong. And what happened to that caring you spoke about?"

"It turned into love."

Her breath caught in her throat. But as badly as she wanted to believe, she also was facing the truth. "The perfect words to convince me to marry you and give your mother the grandchild she wants."

"The words I've never said to anyone before. Words I wouldn't say unless I meant them." And he did. But Roman knew she wouldn't believe him. She'd heard him out; however her conclusions weren't based on his emotions, but the cold, hard facts.

What irony, he thought. As a journalist, he lived and died by the facts. Now he wanted Charlotte to throw away those facts and invest her future happiness on the intangible. He wanted her to believe in him. In his word. No matter that the *facts* pointed in the opposite direction.

She pulled her hand back and held her head in her hands. He waited, giving her time to think and regain her composure. When she glanced up, he didn't like the cool look in her eyes or the taut expression on her face.

"Tell me something. Did you plan to leave me behind in Yorkshire Falls while you went back to your beloved job?"

He shook his head. "I don't know what I planned except that I want like hell to make it work. I've had a job offer from the *Washington Post* that would keep me based in

D.C. I thought I could go check it out—we could go check it out," he said, inspired by the sudden idea. "And together we'd come up with a livable working arrangement." His heart pounded in his chest as he realized just how much he wanted that.

The fear he'd experienced earlier over changing his lifestyle was gone, replaced by a new and much more credible fear—of losing Charlotte forever. At the thought, he broke into a cold sweat.

Sad green eyes met his. "A livable working arrangement," she repeated. "In the name of love or in the name of the lost coin toss?"

He narrowed his gaze, hurt despite it all. "You shouldn't have to ask."

"Well, forgive me, but I do." She leaned back and folded her hands in her lap.

He leaned closer, getting into her personal space, inhaling her scent. He was irrationally angry at Charlotte for not trusting him, though he hadn't done anything to earn her trust. He was also furious at himself and ridiculously aroused all at the same time.

"I'm going to say this once." He'd already thought it through in his head when talking to Chase. "The coin toss led me to you. It was the catalyst for everything that's happened since. But the only reason I'm here with you now is love."

She blinked. A lone tear trickled down her face. On impulse, he caught it with the tip of his finger and tasted the salty water with his tongue. He'd tasted her pain. Now he wanted to make it go away. She was softening. He could feel it and he held his breath while he waited for her reply.

"How will I ever know?" she asked, taking him off guard. "How will I ever know if you're with me because you want to be, or you're with me because you promised your brothers you'd be the one who gave your mother a grandchild?" She shook her head. "This whole town knows Chandler family loyalty is strong. Chase is the prime example, and you're following his lead."

"I'm proud of my big brother. It's not a bad lead to follow. Especially if it takes me in the right direction." There wasn't anything more he could say. He'd already told her he was only going to state his case once. Nothing he said now would change her mind unless she wanted to believe.

"Take a chance on me, Charlotte. Take a chance *with* me." He held out his hand. His future stretched before him—would it be full or as empty as his palm was now?

His guts shook with real fear as he watched her clench her fists tight. She couldn't even meet him halfway.

"I . . . I can't. You want me to trust while I know damn well you Chandlers are confirmed bachelors. None of you wanted commitment. You had to toss a coin to decide who'd have to give up his life for the family this time." She rose to her feet. "And I can't even claim to be a prize you won, but a penalty for losing everything you held dear."

She'd put up walls he doubted he could breach. At least not now. He stood and grabbed her hand one last time. "I'm not your father."

"From where I stand, I don't see much difference."

And that was the problem, he thought. She couldn't see past her family's troubled history. She was obviously afraid. Afraid of repeating her mother's life, her mother's mistakes. He'd damn Annie and Russell to hell and back, only he couldn't blame them any longer. Charlotte was a grown woman capable of seeing the truth and making her own decisions.

The urge to pull her into his arms was strong, but he

doubted it would do any good. "I never figured you for a coward."

She narrowed her gaze and glared at him. "You're an equal disappointment." She pivoted and ran from the kitchen, leaving him behind.

"Son of a bitch." Roman walked into the outer room and kicked the first garbage can he saw across the room. The heavy metal clunked across the floor and hit the wall with a dull bang.

"I take it things didn't go well." Chase met him at the bottom of the steps that led to his upstairs office.

"That's an understatement." He let out a groan. "This isn't the way it was supposed to be."

Chase swung the door shut. "That'll keep out any more stragglers. So whoever told you life would go easy? You've just been lucky for a while. But no more coasting, little brother. You're going to have to work for this." He turned and leaned against the doorframe. "If it's what you want."

Roman should want to get the hell out of this town and away from the pain and aggravation. From his mother's heart condition to Charlotte's broken heart. Unfortunately there was nowhere left to run. The emotions dredged up would follow him wherever he went. This trip back had taught him Yorkshire Falls wasn't just a place to visit, it was home, with all the baggage that word entailed. All the baggage he'd been running from his entire life.

"You're damn right it's what I want. *She's* what I want." Yet after avoiding burden and responsibility for years, now that he was ready to shoulder all the ups and downs of a committed relationship, the woman he desired wanted nothing more to do with him.

"So what do you plan to do about it?"

He had no idea. "I do need to look into D.C.," Roman

told Chase, at the exact moment Rick let himself into the front office, keys dangling from his hand.

"What about D.C.?" Rick asked.

"Roman's going to look into a desk job." Chase's tone held surprise and he pinched the bridge of his nose as he obviously digested the information.

"Don't get carried away," Roman muttered. "I've been offered a senior editor position at the *Post.*"

"You're leaving town?" Rick shoved his hands into his front pockets.

"He might as well. No one here's going to miss him," Chase said with a grin. He slapped Roman on the back.

"Shut the hell up."

Rick laughed. "Charlotte problems? Then I guess she can't vouch for your whereabouts last night?"

Roman's head began a steady, dull throb. "Don't tell me."

His middle brother nodded. "Panty theft number six. So once again, I have to ask. Just where were you last night?"

Chase and Rick chuckled aloud, always enjoying a laugh at Roman's expense. He didn't answer, knew he didn't need to. But despite the ribbing and laughter, Roman wasn't fooled. Like him, neither of his brothers were thrilled to know they still had an unsolved crime spree in Yorkshire Falls.

Charlotte left the *Gazette* at a run, slowed when she got winded, and began a slow walk back to town. A twisting pain in her stomach made the pickup truck bumping down the road a welcome sight.

Charlotte stuck out her thumb and hitched her first ride ever. Fred Aames, the town's only plumber, offered to drop her off at her doorstep. She was halfway back to her shop and away from Roman when she realized she hadn't taken an ad in the paper. She'd just have to call Chase later. No way in hell was she going back to face the Chandler brothers and their stinking coin toss. She wondered if they were laughing about it, then shook her head.

Roman wouldn't be laughing. He was out a candidate and would have to start over. Find another woman he could screw and leave behind, pregnant.

Her stomach churned and it took all her willpower not to ask Fred to pull over so she could puke in someone's rhododendrons.

"So did you hear?" Fred asked. Before she could respond, he continued, obviously used to talking from beneath cabinets as he worked on plumbing, oblivious to the outside world. "Marge Sinclair had her panties stolen."

Not again. She began a steady massage of her temples. "Marge? I just delivered those myself yesterday."

He shrugged. "You know what they say. Here today, gone tomorrow." He let out a laugh that was interrupted by his old pickup truck hitting a pothole and jarring her shoulder into the door. "I don't put any stock in old man Whitehall's comments about Roman Chandler, though."

At the mention of Roman's name, Charlotte's stomach twisted in pain. Small-town life, she thought. She loved it, but sometimes it meant she couldn't escape no matter how badly she wanted to. "No, I don't suppose Roman Chandler would steal panties," she said, holding up her end of conversation.

"Or, he'd steal panties if it were a prank, but he wouldn't pilfer 'em the way the papers are saying."

"Mmm." Maybe, if she didn't outright respond, Fred would catch on and change the subject.

"He's got too much character."

"He's got character, all right," she muttered. She'd rather not get into Roman's character right now or she'd give Fred an earful that would quickly travel through the town's grapevine. She didn't want that any more than Roman would.

"He stood up for me back in high school. I'll never forget it and I won't let anyone 'round here either. You can bet I'm telling everyone I meet Roman Chandler's no thief." He slammed on the brakes in front of her shop.

She rubbed the bruised skin on her shoulder and gathered her bag. Who could be stealing the underwear? She mentally ticked off the victims so far. Whitehall, Sinclair . . . all over fifty, she realized and wondered if Rick or anyone else on Yorkshire Falls' police force had come to that same conclusion and whether it meant anything at all. Odd, Charlotte thought. To say the least.

"Did you say something?" he asked, rising in his seat.

"I said I wonder if you realize that you're a life saver. Thank you for driving me back here."

"My pleasure." He leaned over and placed a hand behind her seat. "There is a way you can repay me, though."

"What would that be?" she asked warily.

"Move my Marianne up on your panty list." His full cheeks colored a furious shade of red. "At least in time for our wedding night."

She grinned and nodded her head. "I think that could be arranged." Charlotte hopped out of the pickup before she could laugh out loud and embarrass the man further. "Thanks again, Fred."

"You're welcome. And when your customers come in discussing these thefts, remember to tell 'em Roman Chandler wouldn't steal anything."

Except her heart, she thought, sadly.

Fred drove off, leaving her standing on the sidewalk. She stared first at her business, then at the upstairs window leading to her apartment. Neither place beckoned to her right now. Since Roman had spent the night, her small apartment was no longer a safe haven to which she could escape. Her office smelled too vile for words, and in her shop, Beth's chatty presence would have Charlotte revealing painful secrets in no time. And her mother's house was off limits because Russell was home.

She felt like a displaced person with nowhere to go—until she realized there was one place she could curl up and be alone in peace. She stopped by the shop only long enough to tell Beth she was taking the day off, detoured into Norman's for a sandwich and soda to go, before going up to her apartment, changing her clothes, and ducking out onto the fire-escape-cum-terrace, her treasured book, *Glamorous Getaways,* in hand.

Some people chose comfort food. Charlotte chose comfort books. One in particular. A breeze fluttered the pages and she turned to the one she studied most, the famous HOLLYWOOD sign. She sat back against the wall, legs out in front of her, book resting on her knees. She sighed and traced the letters she knew by heart, then propped her chin in her hands and stared at the glossy pages.

Ironic, that this same book that gave her peace also represented her greatest pain. Charlotte understood why. *Glamorous Getaways* brought her back to a simpler time. A time when she still believed in Prince Charmings and happily ever afters. A time when she thought her father would come home and sweep Charlotte and her mother off their feet and onto an airplane to Los Angeles. To join him and give her back the security she'd lost. He never had.

So this book should be unsettling, yet it soothed her in a

way only innocent childhood beliefs could. Charlotte didn't delve deeper. Life was complicated enough. And the Chandler brothers' coin toss had certainly mixed up her life and emotions in a way she'd never imagined possible.

Charlotte wasn't into pity, nor did she believe she'd done anything to deserve this twist of fate. But, all things considered, she couldn't say she was surprised. Psychiatrists had a field day with the notion that girls fell in love with men who reminded them of their fathers. A statement she'd once have disputed with a vengeance, but of which now she was living proof.

The Chandler brothers were many things: dedicated bachelors, devoted sons, and intensely loyal men. She knew Roman had never set out to hurt her. She believed he'd discounted her from his list of available women because of her family history. But she'd certainly simplified his life by falling into his baby-needing arms.

After finishing with his brothers, Roman locked himself in Chase's office and got lost in what he did best. Writing. He tuned out everything and everyone else and spent the late morning and better part of the afternoon typing up an article on small-town life. Slice-of-life articles weren't his thing, but somehow, this time the words poured from his gut.

Big cities, bigger stories. Large continents, even larger human interest stories. But at the heart of each of those broader pieces, Roman realized he could find the essence of people—their ties to each other, their community, their land. Just like the people of Yorkshire Falls.

When Roman wrote a news piece—whether he was driving home the inequities of poverty or famine, the brutal truth of ethnic cleansing in foreign lands, or the need for a variance or new zoning laws so someone with degenerative arthritis could own a pet and walk him without pain—the stories centered on people and what they needed and did to survive.

As a journalist and as a man, the objective view had been easier for Roman, and so he'd chosen to tackle the outside world while putting up blocks against his feelings for those people and stories back home. Because home represented Roman's greatest fear—pain, rejection, loss. The kind he'd seen his mother experience.

The kind he was experiencing now because of what he'd done to Charlotte. This story was a catharsis. He'd never sell it, but he'd always have it as proof of what his mother had told him: If you haven't loved, you haven't lived. For all his extensive traveling and experience, Roman realized, he hadn't really lived. Now, how to convince Charlotte?

After trying the shop, he'd stopped in Norman's, who said he'd packed a sandwich and sent Charlotte on her way. Without trying her apartment first, gut instinct told Roman exactly where to find her. He never discounted his gut.

It was that same gut feeling that had insisted should Charlotte find out about the coin toss, he'd be in deep shit, and he'd been right. Same gut that now let him know she'd never get out of his system completely. He knew that was correct as well. He rounded the corner that led to the back of her apartment.

The sun shone low in the sky. In broad daylight, he knew he was risking being seen lurking around her apartment. He didn't care. He wanted to make sure she was okay, though he knew better than to try to talk reason with her so soon.

He stood in the shadow of the trees and looked up at her sitting on the fire escape. Alone by choice, not answering her doorbell or phone. He shook his head, hating that he'd caused her pain. Stray tendrils of hair escaped the confinement of her ponytail and blew around her pale face. She was reverently touching the pages of a book. He figured it was one of her damn travelogues. She was a dreamer and longed for things she thought were out of reach. Travel. Excitement. Her father. And Roman.

She had the nerve to start a cosmopolitan business in a sleepy upstate town, but lacked the guts to take a gamble on life. On him.

What if reality is a disappointment? she'd asked when he'd questioned her about her books, her dreams. He hadn't answered her then, so certain he could make her fantasies come true. But a weekend getaway was a far cry from fulfilling a lifelong dream. He'd been sure he could do both.

Right now he wanted to kick himself in the ass for being so damn arrogant, so sure of himself, when Charlotte's feelings were at stake. Thanks to her father, Charlotte expected life to let her down. Instead of proving her wrong, Roman had fulfilled every negative expectation she'd had of men.

He muttered a curse. One last glance, and he headed on home.

Raina gathered her purse and waited as Dr. Leslie Gaines jotted notes in her chart. With Raina seeing Eric outside of work, she had begun using Dr. Gaines as her primary doctor. She had two reasons. She didn't want to put Eric in the uncomfortable position of lying to her sons, and she wanted some mystery to remain for them as a couple. Silly as it sounded. If he listened to her chest with a stethoscope and viewed her as a patient through his doctor's eyes, how could he look at her as a man would a woman?

"So your cardiogram is fine, no change." Dr. Gaines flipped the manila folder closed. "You're healthy, Raina.

All I can say is keep up the exercise and watch the rich food."

"Yes, Doctor." But Raina knew the words were easy. Keeping up the charade of sickness with her boys was not. Though her little *fraud*, as she'd begun to think about it, still gave her fits of guilt, she believed in her cause. She wanted her boys settled and happy with families of their own.

Dr. Gaines smiled. "I wish all my patients were so cooperative."

Raina merely nodded in return. "Thanks for everything." She left the office without seeing Eric. She preferred to save that treat for later, when the subject of her "illness" couldn't cause an argument.

With Roman spending the day at the paper with Chase, and Rick on duty, Raina headed straight for home. She changed into sweatpants for a quick treadmill run. Only a twenty-year-old or Superman could keep up this routine without getting caught. As she began her brisk walk, she kept one eye trained out the basement window onto the driveway in case her sons came home early. She'd flop onto the couch quickly if they did.

Twenty minutes later, she stepped off the treadmill and took a quick shower, the relief at not being caught overwhelming. By the time she finished and had a quick bite to eat, she was ready to tackle her primary concern.

Roman's love life.

The road to romance had taken a dangerous detour with Roman's sour mood and sudden refusal to discuss anything related to Charlotte. He'd deal with his own problems, he said. But as his mother, Raina had changed his diapers, dried the tears he'd been embarrassed to shed, and she knew his every expression. No matter how hard he tried to hide his feelings, she read them anyway. And her baby boy was hurting.

This problem with Charlotte, whatever it was, couldn't be anything more than a bump on the road. No romance ran smooth, after all. Look at the good she'd done her youngest son so far; her "illness" had brought Roman home and had kept him in Yorkshire Falls, where he'd more than reacquainted himself with his first love. A little nudge, and they'd be back together in no time.

Hoping nobody noticed she'd been in town twice today and reported back to the boys, Raina walked into Charlotte's Attic later that afternoon. Thank goodness the shop appeared empty. "Hello?"

"Be right there," Charlotte's lilting voice called from the back of the store.

"Take your time." Raina walked over to the lingerie section and fingered a beautiful, pure silk Natori gown with a matching robe.

"It suits you," Charlotte said, coming up behind her. "The light ivory will bring out the green in your eyes."

Raina turned and faced the raven-haired beauty, who, like her son, had pain lurking in the depths of her soul. "I'm not sure I belong in something so white."

Charlotte smiled. "Light, not white. It's more of an antiquey color. Nothing wrong with indulging. There's no significance attached to hue. That's an old-fashioned premise, I assure you." She folded her arms across the metal rack. "I can see how much you want this. You're still fingering the lace edge."

"Caught in the act." Raina laughed. "Okay, you can package this up for me." She wondered if it would sit in the drawer or if—

"I'm glad to see you feeling well enough to be out and about."

Charlotte cut off Raina's thoughts, and not a moment too soon. Raina was too afraid to even think about such intimacies. It had been so long since anyone had seen her that way.

"I know I'm supposed to take it easy, but I needed to come here." For reasons Raina hadn't yet divulged. "Besides, isn't shopping supposed to be a stress reliever?"

Charlotte laughed. "If you say so." She perused the rack, flipping through the long silken garments. The young woman remembered each customer's size without having to ask again, something that impressed Raina from the first. Every customer who entered the shop received personal treatment from Charlotte or Beth, and each customer left with the feeling that she was the most important customer Charlotte had. Her business was thriving and she'd earned the professional success.

She deserved private success as well. Raina couldn't stand to see two people so obviously in love let themselves drift apart. As Charlotte unhooked the hanger and walked over to the register, Raina hadn't yet decided whether or how to broach the subject.

"Anything else I can get you?" Charlotte asked with a strained smile.

Talk about an opening! Raina shook her head. Surely this was a sign that questioning Charlotte was okay. Roman wouldn't hold it against her. Not once he was happily settled with Charlotte by his side. Raina leaned forward on the counter. "You can tell me why you look so unhappy."

"I don't know what you mean." Charlotte immediately began fussing with the lingerie, ripping off the bottom of the price tag and wrapping the luxurious silk in light pink tissue paper.

Raina placed a stilling hand over hers. "I think you do. Roman's as miserable as you."

"Not possible." Charlotte began tabulating the bill. "One hundred and fifteen dollars and ninety-three cents."

Whipping her credit card out of her purse, Raina placed it on the counter. "I assure you it's very possible. I know my son. He's hurting."

Charlotte slid the card through the register and went through the charging process. "I'm not certain there's anything you can do to make it better for him or me. You should leave it alone."

Raina swallowed hard. Something in Charlotte's tone warned Raina to stop now, but she couldn't. "I can't."

For the first time since Raina had brought up the subject, Charlotte met her gaze. "Because you feel responsible?" the younger woman asked softly. With no malice, but with the certainty of someone who knew everything.

Even if Raina did not. Her heart began a thready beat, one caused by apprehension and anxiety. "Why should I feel responsible?" she asked warily.

"You really don't know, do you?" Charlotte shook her head, abandoned her rigid stance, and walked around to where Raina stood. "Come sit."

Raina followed into Charlotte's office, wondering how this conversation had become about *her* and not Roman and Charlotte's romance.

"When you got sick, your sons were worried."

Raina lowered her eyes, unable to meet Charlotte's sincere and concerned gaze, that darn guilt resurfacing once more.

"And together they decided to give you your fondest, dearest wish."

"Which is?" Raina asked, unsure what Charlotte meant.

"Grandchildren, of course."

"Oh!" Raina expressed a sigh of relief at Charlotte's obviously mistaken belief. She waved her hand in the air. "No way would my boys want to give me grandchildren, no matter how much I may wish otherwise."

"You're right. They didn't want to. But they felt they had to." Charlotte raised her eyes and met Raina's gaze. "They flipped a coin. Loser would ante up—get married and have a baby. Roman lost." She shrugged, but the pain floated in the air, hovering between them, obvious and tangible. "I was the nearest candidate."

Outrage filled Raina, but her heart clenched, twisting with more than guilt. She'd meant to coerce her boys into their own happily ever after, but she'd never meant for people to get hurt in the process. "Charlotte, you don't believe Roman chose you because he lost a coin toss. You two had a history, after all."

Charlotte glanced away. "Roman admitted to losing the coin toss. The rest is painfully obvious."

"But he didn't choose you because you were the nearest candidate!" Raina addressed Charlotte's hurt first. She'd deal with the coin toss and her role in it later. Oh, yes, she would deal with her boys.

She'd lived under the illusion that she and John had set the example of a happy family and a good, loving marriage. Obviously not, but what in heaven's name had happened to convince her boys otherwise? True, Rick had that painful fiasco caused by his good-natured attempt to help, but the right woman would break through the walls he'd put up since. And Roman—Raina remembered her youngest saying that he thought she'd given up on life. Had that been enough to scare him off marriage forever?

"I really don't know why Roman chose me, now, do I?" Charlotte's voice shook with uncertainty. A good omen, Raina hoped.

"I think you know more than you want to admit." Raina leaned forward and squeezed Charlotte's hand. "I realize I'm probably the last person you want advice from, but please let me say one thing."

Charlotte inclined her head. "I don't blame you, Raina."

Perhaps the young woman should. Maybe then she and Roman wouldn't be miserable. "If you've found true love, don't let anything stand in your way. One day, just twenty-four hours, could be one day lost in a lifetime that's way too short."

Raina thought she heard a strangled sound come from Charlotte, and she rose quickly, not wanting to intrude a minute longer. Besides, she needed to be alone to deal with herself and decide what she intended to do about the pain and havoc she hadn't meant to cause.

"Take care." Leaving Charlotte sitting in silence, Raina walked out. She exited the store and stepped into the sunshine, feeling anything but warm and happy. She was at a complete loss, not knowing how to fix things.

Considering what a disaster her great plan had been so far, she was probably better off staying out of everyone's lives and concentrating on living her own. Eric had been right all along, but he wouldn't be pleased to know Raina's enlightenment had come at everyone else's expense.

Still, as much as she'd like to withdraw and take the hands-off route, she and her sons had some serious business to discuss. She sighed. What happened to Roman and Charlotte after that was anyone's guess.

* * *

Roman pounded nails into the garage shelving. If he was going to stick around, he might as well make himself useful. For the most part, Chase and Rick handled the upkeep on the house, but when he was home, Roman liked to do his share. And right now, the ability to pound a hammer was a damn good way to release frustration.

Charlotte hadn't called. Hadn't returned his calls, to be accurate. At this point he wasn't sure the distinction mattered.

He raised the hammer and swung at the same moment his mother's shrill voice reached his ears. "Front and center, Roman."

The hammer smacked his fingers dead-on. "Son of a bitch." He stalked out of the garage, shaking his hand to ease the throbbing pain. He met his mother on the driveway, where she was pacing back and forth. "What's wrong?" he asked.

"Everything. And as much as I blame myself, I still need answers."

He wiped his arm across his sweaty forehead. "I don't know what the hell you're talking about, but you look upset and it can't be good for your heart."

"Forget my heart. It's yours I'm worried about. A coin toss? *Loser* gets married and has children? What in heaven's name did your father and I do wrong that turned you boys against marriage?" His mother's hazel eyes filled with moisture.

"Dammit, Mom, don't cry." He was a sucker for her tears. Always had been, which he thought now was a partial answer to her question. "Who told you?" He put an arm around her and led her to the patio chairs out back.

She narrowed her gaze. "That's not the point, is it? Now answer me."

"I don't want you to end up back in the hospital. That's the point."

"It won't happen. Now talk."

He let out a groan but noticed she seemed stronger than she'd been since his arrival back home.

"The coin toss, Roman. I'm waiting," she said when he didn't respond fast enough for her. She tapped one foot against the patio.

He shrugged. "What can I say? It seemed like the best solution at the time."

"Idiots. I raised idiots." She rolled her eyes heavenwards. "Nix that. I just raised real men."

She was right. He was a typical man, and as a proud, card-carrying member of the species, he wasn't comfortable discussing his feelings or emotions. But he owed it to the woman who raised him the best she could on her own to explain. He had a hunch he'd have to do the same with Charlotte—if he wanted a second chance.

And he did.

"You and I started talking about this the other day." Roman leaned forward in his seat. "I was eleven when Dad died. And watching you in so much pain, well, I realized this trip home, it made me want to withdraw from anything that close to me. Being a journalist, by nature of the job, let me remain detached. I couldn't be detached here at home. Not with you and not with Charlotte."

Raina expelled some of the obvious anger, fears, and frustration with one long breath. "I'm sorry. For everything."

"You can't hold yourself responsible for fate. Or someone else's reaction to it."

She met his gaze. “You really don’t understand.”

“I do. And I love you for your concern, but don’t stress over it.” He rose. “If you do, I’ll report straight back to your doctor.” Eric or his associate would give his mother a good talking-to if she risked her health in any way.

Roman narrowed his gaze and took a good look at his mother. Dark rings circled her eyes, little makeup coated her cheeks. She’d put less time into her appearance. Because she tired more easily? he wondered. Worry about him and Charlotte couldn’t help the situation and he tried to set her mind at ease. “You’ve done your job incredibly well. Chase, Rick, and I can take care of ourselves. I promise.” He brushed a kiss over her cheek.

She stood and walked along with him back to the garage. “I love you, son.”

“Same here, Mom. You’ve got a good heart and—”

“Roman, speaking of my heart . . .”

He shook his head. “No more talk,” he said in a drill-sergeant, no-nonsense tone. “I want you upstairs and resting. Draw the shades and take a nap. Watch *Oprah.* Something, anything as long as you’re off your feet and not overthinking about your sons.”

“Is it me or did you put a fast end to this conversation about your stupid coin toss?”

He laughed. “Never could put one over on you, but no, I’m not trying to distract you, just keep you healthy. I answered your question about why we got into the coin toss. Now I’ll tell you another truth that’ll help you sleep well. I’m grateful for it. I no longer look at marriage as punishment. Not to the right woman, anyway.” A woman who wanted nothing to do with him, but, Roman decided, it was time he forced the issue.

His mother’s face lit up, her eyes sparkling and green. “I

knew something had changed since you got home. But what about your recent . . . how do I say this delicately? Your bad mood?"

"I'll solve my problems, you take a nap."

She scowled at him. "Just make sure you fix things with Charlotte."

"I never said—"

She patted his cheek as she so often did when he was a child. "You didn't have to say. Mothers know these things."

He rolled his eyes and pointed toward the house. "Into bed."

She saluted and walked inside. He stared after her, thinking of all the advice she'd given him through the years and of the happy marriage she'd shared with his father. He didn't blame her for wanting the same for her sons. With hindsight, like his mother, he couldn't believe he, Rick, and Chase had stooped to tossing a coin to decide their fate.

Roman debated, wondering if he should try to explain to Charlotte one more time, but decided against it. She wasn't willing to discuss things again and she had good reason. All he could do in conversation was reiterate the past. And the fact that he had no plan in mind for the future.

The next time he faced Charlotte, he had to possess proof of his feelings and intentions. Only then could he lay his heart in her hands and dare her to walk away.

He grabbed the portable phone he'd left in the garage and dialed his brothers. Ten minutes later, they gathered back in the garage where this whole nightmare had begun. Roman started by explaining the situation up to and including the extent of their mother's knowledge about their agreement.

"Now that you're up to speed, you two need to look out

for Mom. Make sure she gets rest and doesn't stay up trying to figure out ways to fix my life. I can do that myself."

"How?" Chase folded his arms across his chest.

"By going to D.C." He needed to prove to Charlotte he could handle settling down. He'd come back with a steady job and a plan of action. One that would make them *both* happy.

He wouldn't be giving up the news or his passion for imparting the truth to the unsuspecting world. He'd just be changing which news he covered and the place from which he covered it. After the time he'd just spent in Yorkshire Falls with his family, including the people of his hometown, Roman realized not only could he handle settling down, he wanted to.

"Well?" he asked in the face of stunned silence. "No wisecracks?"

Rick shrugged. "We wish you well."

"You can do better than that."

"I joke about a lot of things, but not when so much is at stake. This is huge for you, Roman. I wish you the best."

Rick held out his hand and Roman took it, pulling him into a brotherly hug. "You can do me one favor. Keep an eye on Charlotte while I'm gone."

"Now, that's no hardship." Rick smacked him on the back. He grinned, reverting to his old teasing self.

Roman narrowed his gaze. "Just keep your goddamn hands to yourself," he said for the sake of brotherly argument. Not because he worried about Rick making a move on his woman. Having calmed down a bit, he knew he trusted his brothers with his life—and that included Charlotte.

"He's possessive," Rick said, hands folded across his chest.

Chase snickered.

Roman groaned. "Just don't screw this up. Watch out for her until I get back. I have to go do laundry and then pack." Roman started for the short flight of wooden stairs that led to the house.

"What makes this one so special?" Rick called out.

"Other than the fact that she's his alibi?" Chase's laugh followed him to the door.

Roman shook his head. He grabbed for the doorknob, then turned back, "I can't wait for the day when the joke's on the two of you."

Charlotte ran into her apartment and dashed for the phone. She'd heard it ring from the hallway, her arms filled with dry cleaning, and by the time she'd found her keys and made it inside, whoever was there had hung up without leaving a message.

She dropped her cleaning onto the couch. "Let's see if anyone called before that." Her stomach clenched in tight knots as she prayed neither her father nor Roman had chosen to call. She couldn't avoid both men forever, but until she understood what *she* needed out of life, she was giving avoidance her best shot.

She hit the play button and listened to the first and only message. "Hi, Charlotte. It's me." Roman's voice hit her like a punch in the stomach, sucking all the air out of her lungs. She lowered herself into the nearest chair.

"I just called to say . . ."

Silence followed, and she held her breath, waiting for him to continue. Wanting to hear she didn't know what.

"I called to say good-bye."

The hurt overflowed in her veins, seeping into every part of her being. She waited for him to say more, but all that followed was the click of being disconnected. She sat in mute silence, the lump in her throat huge, the squeezing sensation that brought a pain to her chest intense.

So that was it. He'd taken off again for parts unknown, just as she'd always known he would.

Her insides churned and she thought she might be sick. But why? Why should she be upset Roman had followed the pattern he'd set? The one she'd expected? Unable to stand the stifling apartment and questions that dogged her, she grabbed her keys and ran out the door without looking back.

CHAPTER TWELVE

Charlotte walked into the general store at seven A.M, the same time Herb Cooper opened the doors.

"Third time this week you're here this early. New schedule?" he asked.

She smiled. "You could say that." A week after Roman's departure, she was amazed at the amount of avoidance a creative person could manage. No one else shopped this early and she found she could get in and out without having to make small talk with anyone other than Herb or Roxanne, his wife.

"Well, the fresh bread's not even unpacked yet, but I'll grab you a loaf and have it waiting at the register for when you're ready to check out."

"Thanks, Herb."

"Just doing my job. You keep the womenfolk happy and us men in town decided we'd best keep you happy too."

Charlotte laughed. "I wouldn't turn down fresh bread, but I think you're overestimating my importance around here."

The older man turned the color of his tomatoes in the

corner. "No, ma'am. You are definitely keeping the women happy. It's that panty thief that's driving 'em insane. The women who had theirs pilfered can't replace them fast enough and the younger ones hope that Chandler boy will wake them out of their sleep."

Charlotte lifted her gaze skyward. So much for avoidance.

"Living fairy tales, I tell you. A man like Roman Chandler has more important things to do than steal panties. But try telling that to the women." He shook his head, just as the telephone rang, interrupting him. "Well, least with him gone, we've had some quiet. Whoever is stealing those panties knows he's got no alibi now, so it's been quiet." He reached for the phone. "General store. What can I do for you?"

Charlotte escaped into the aisles while she had the chance and breathed a sigh of relief. In the seven days Roman had been gone, she had developed an odd sort of respect for her mother's ability to stay disconnected from life in a small town. It wasn't easy.

Aside from the general chit-chat with neighbors, everyone in Charlotte's life wanted something from her. Beth wanted to know what was wrong, why Roman had left so suddenly. Her mother wanted to know when she'd come for dinner with her family. Rick wanted an updated list of customers and any hunches she had, and those customers wanted the panties they'd ordered.

Since Beth was running the shop, Charlotte was able to spend her days crocheting. Another word for avoiding, she admitted, but at least her customers would be satisfied, even if the rest of the people pulling pieces from her were not.

The only person not asking a damn thing from her was

the one she'd turned away. Her throat constricted and hurt from the ever-present lump that had settled there. She blamed herself for falling into Roman's trap as much as she blamed him for unintentionally drawing her in. Though she knew he'd never meant to hurt her, the fact remained, he had.

She still had the taped message he'd left on her answering machine. Not that she intended to torture herself by replaying it, and she refused to analyze why she hadn't just let the next call tape over his seductive voice.

Half an hour later, she'd returned to her apartment to unpack the groceries and straighten up before going to work. She'd spent the last week hiding from the world. Charlotte figured everyone with a broken heart was entitled to healing time. Unlike her mother, she didn't plan to make it a lifetime.

She looked out the window into the bright sunshine. It was time to get back into her routine, starting with tonight's baseball game.

When the game ended, the Rockets had continued their winning streak, and though she'd shown her face, Charlotte had continued parental avoidance. She was ready for many things. Dealing with her father wasn't one of them. He was too much a reminder of all that hurt, past and present. She had no doubt if she stalled long enough, he'd leave too. And leave was something she had to do, before Russell could attempt to corner her again. As he'd done in the general store and outside her apartment. She'd ducked out on him those times as well.

"Here. Toss this for me, will you?" Charlotte handed Beth her soda can. "And don't forget to recycle." She hopped down off the bottom bleacher. "I'll see you at work tomorrow."

"Coward," Beth called after her.

Charlotte kept walking, though she couldn't deny her friend's words cut deep, partly because Roman had called her the same thing, and mostly because Charlotte knew Beth was right. Eventually she would have to face everything she was avoiding, including her parents. She just wasn't ready.

Halfway back to town, she decided to cut across the Sullivan Subdivision, through George and Rose Carlton's yard. The Carltons were still at the baseball game, as were most of the other townspeople, so when Charlotte heard a rustle near the front hedges, she turned around, surprised.

"Hello?" she called out.

A lanky man in forest-green pants, button-down top, and a baseball cap was skulking around the bushes. When he heard her voice, he ducked down, but not before she caught a glimpse of his face.

"Samson?" Her surprise turned to complete shock. She ran up the bluestone walk. "Get out of the bushes now." She pulled on the green shirt that blended with the foliage. "Just what do you think you're doing?"

He rose to his full height. "You don't belong here."

"Neither do you. What's going on?" Her gaze dropped to his gloved right hand, full with what looked like her panties in his fist. The crocheted panties she sold, Charlotte mentally amended. Of all the bizarre things . . . "Hand them over." She extended her hand.

He muttered a growl. "None of your concern."

"If you were just cross-dressing and not theft, it wouldn't be my concern. But since you're stealing, I'm making it my business. And I intend to find out why. But first, you get inside and put those panties back."

"No." He folded his arms like a sulking child.

"The Carltons will be back from the game any minute, so you're going to return those and then we're going to talk." She glanced toward the front door, which she assumed had been left unlocked.

This darn town was still living in an age when everyone trusted everyone else. Even with this panty thief business, no one took the threat seriously enough to lock their doors. In George and Rose's case, they probably figured they had Mick as lookout, though what the aging, slightly arthritic beagle could do to an intruder was beyond her.

Speaking of the dog . . . "Where's Mick?" she asked warily.

"Eatin' steak."

She let out a sharp exhale.

Samson's dark eyes clouded. "What was that for? You don't think I'd hurt him, do you?"

Charlotte shook her head. No, she didn't, and not just because no one had been harmed during the course of the other robberies. In her heart, she trusted the gruff older man and thought even this strange turn of events would have some kind of explanation she could understand. She hoped.

Before she could ponder what his motives were, the beagle in question came barging out of his new doggie door, baying and circling around Sam. Charlotte sighed. "You don't have any more steak in your pockets, do you?"

He shook his head, "Wasn't supposed to need any. If you hadn't stopped me, I'd be long gone by now."

She rolled her eyes and leaned down, hefting the heavy dog into her arms. She didn't want him to decide to attack if he caught Samson inside, not that Mick had a surly reputation. That distinction belonged to Samson.

Mick wasn't only heavy, he was wet as he slobbered and drooled on her arm. "I've got him, now get inside and put those panties back before I get a hernia," she hissed. "I'll stand guard."

Samson glared at her, but thankfully he turned, stomped up the steps, and let himself back into the house. Gloved hands, no fingerprints, she realized now, and shook her head. She grunted and shifted position. Mick's front paws touched her shoulder, his warm, chubby body aligned against her. "Care to dance?" she asked him.

He licked her cheek in response.

"Oh, brother. Well, at least you know how to kiss up to a lady." She twirled around the front hedges until she realized exactly how mentally disturbed she looked, then ducked behind a tree. If she was ever asked about this, she'd have to cop to a sudden love for dogs and buy herself a pet. All in the name of cover-up.

Thankfully Samson returned before the Carltons got home and she had to explain why she was holding their two-ton dog in her arms. She let Mick down and he bounded back inside. She was quickly forgotten. "Typical male," she muttered.

Without another word, she grabbed Samson's arm and dragged him with her across the rest of the yard and down the street, waiting until they were out of the subdivision before starting in on him. "Talk to me, and don't give me any of that *it's none of your business* crap. Why are you stealing women's panties? Panties I made?" she asked him.

"Can't a man have privacy?"

"Unless you want me to head straight on over to Rick Chandler, you'd better start explaining." They continued their walk to town, but he remained stubbornly silent. Frustrated, Charlotte stopped in her tracks and yanked on his sleeve. "Samson, there's nothing good that's going to come of this if you force my hand. Rick will have to prosecute and they'll probably throw you in jail for a little while, or have you tested by a psychiatrist, and then—"

"I did it for you."

That was the last answer she'd been expecting. "I don't understand."

"I always liked you." He looked down and kicked at the ground with his worn sneaker. "You were such a friendly kid. All the others ran from me, but you always waved hello. Just like your mother. Then when you moved back after your time away, you didn't change none. You still made time for a strange man."

"So you stole the panties because . . . ?"

"I wanted your business to work so's you'd stay in town."

Charlotte was oddly touched by his words. He cared, even if he had a strange way of showing it. "What made you think panty raids would help my business?"

"At first I thought it'd just give you some attention."

"I think my advertising has done the same thing."

"Not on as grand a scale. And I only planned one theft. The next morning I found out that the youngest Chandler boy came home the same night. I remembered his panty raid." Samson tapped his head. "Picture-perfect memory."

"You mean photographic memory?" Charlotte asked.

"I mean I don't forget a thing. And when I realized everyone else remembered it too and I saw the lines outside your shop, I knew I'd done good. Plus, with the Chandler boy in town, I knew I had a good cover going."

Her mind boggled at the way the older man's brain

worked. "Weren't you worried about Roman getting blamed for your . . . uh, crime?"

He waved away her concerns. "Couldn't see Officer Rick arresting his own brother without evidence, and since Roman wasn't guilty, there weren't evidence to find." He waved his gloved hands in the air and grinned, obviously pleased with himself.

She wasn't. "Shame on you for setting yourself up like that! I don't care how harmless the theft or how good your motives, you shouldn't have done something illegal at all. Especially not for me."

"That's gratitude for you," he muttered, back to his moody self.

She eyed him carefully. "Roman's been gone a week. Care to tell me what tonight's theft was about?"

He shook his head from side to side and exhaled an exaggerated sigh, as if to say she was dense and he knew it. "I got the boy into trouble. Had to get him out, didn't I?"

"You took this last risk for Roman?" Was there no end to the surprises Samson had inside him?

"Haven't you been listening?" he asked, sounding annoyed. "I did this for *you.* Because you smile at me when no one else does, except your mother the few times she comes to town. And because you give me errands for money, instead of charity. How else do you think I knew who bought the darn panties? I mailed 'em for you, didn't I? Besides, Ms. Chandler's good to me, too."

"Raina?"

Samson nodded, looking at the pavement once more. "Pretty lady. Reminds me of someone I used to . . . never mind. But the two of you seem to care about Roman. What kind of name is that anyway?"

"No more unusual than yours. Now stop stalling."

"Women are so damned impatient." He sighed. "Isn't it obvious? With Roman out of town, one more pair of panties gone would clear his name."

She blinked. "That's very commendable of you. I think." Charlotte didn't know what to make of this tale. Though things made more sense now. She understood how the thief knew which houses to target—Samson did many of her mailings and hung around town, listening without being noticed. "Just tell me you're through. No more stealing."

"'Course not. It's getting too hard, with busybodies like you snooping around. Now, if you're finished with the third degree, I have some business to take care of back home."

She didn't question what. As he said, his life was none of her concern. "I'm finished. But I want you to know . . ." How did she thank a man for committing unwanted panty thefts on her behalf? "I appreciate the thought behind your acts." She nodded. That sounded right.

"Then you can do me a favor in return."

His words held echoes of Fred Aames. "I'm not making you your own pair of panties," she said. She meant she wasn't making him a pair for the girlfriend she doubted he had, but thought better of correcting herself.

"'Course not. I ain't no sissy. Besides, I got six other pairs I don't know what to do with."

She sucked in a breath. "I suggest you burn them," she said through clenched teeth.

"There's still that favor I want."

Was he moving on to extortion now? She figured he wanted her promise of silence about his escapade tonight and all the other nights he'd broken into homes to steal panties. "I won't turn you in to the police," she said, taking another stab at what was on his mind. Though she couldn't leave Rick with an unsolved crime and hadn't a clue what she was going to tell him.

Samson waved his hand in the air as if he couldn't care less. She knew better. "You realize people don't pay much attention to me unless they're running the other way or ignoring me. I can sit beside someone and hear all 'bout their sex life because they think I'm too dumb to know what they're talking about."

She held out her hand, intending to offer comfort, but he scowled and she immediately pulled back.

"But I hear other things too. And I heard your mother and father talking the other day. They're hurting."

She stiffened her shoulders. "This time it's none of your concern," she said, turning his words back on him.

"True enough. But seeing as how you always give an old man you barely know a break . . . I think you oughta do the same thing for your folks." He started across the street, in the opposite direction of town, toward the ramshackle shack where he lived. Without warning, he pivoted back to her. "You know, some of us don't have parents or kin." He turned back and resumed his lonely walk home.

"Sam?" Charlotte called after him.

He didn't turn around again.

"You've got friends," she said loudly.

He continued his journey home and didn't acknowledge her words, though she knew he'd heard them.

He left her alone, touched as well as confused by his actions. She already knew she'd have to deal with Russell, as much as she didn't look forward to that day. But right now it was Samson who concerned her. What in the world would she tell Rick?

A laundry list of words collided in her brain: *obstruction of justice* and *accessory to a crime* being just some of them.

But she couldn't bring herself to turn Samson in. And her role as lookout tonight had nothing to do with it. His crimes were harmless, the thefts were over. She believed him when he said tonight was the end. She owed the police department some kind of explanation that would let them close the case, yet she needed to keep Samson safe.

Charlotte bit down on her lower lip. The sun had set and night had fallen around her. The evening chilled her to the core and she started a brisk walk for home, all the while wondering what to do.

She wished Roman were here to advise her. The thought rose unbidden, without warning. Roman, the journalist, the advocate for truth. Yet were he here, she'd trust him with her secret, knowing he wouldn't let Samson get hurt either. Her heart began a rapid pounding in her chest.

How could she trust him with such a huge secret and not believe the words he'd uttered? *I love you. I've never said that to anyone else. I don't want to lose you.* And then there was the pained look in his eyes as he'd revealed the truth—at a time when he could have covered or lied in order to keep her in the dark. To ensure marriage and children and the family promise.

He hadn't lied. He'd revealed all about the coin toss. Yet he'd had to know he risked losing her in the process.

What was she willing to risk in return?

The morning sun shone in the storefront window as Charlotte ran through her to-do list. "So remember to put out a dish of these chocolate eggs next week," she said to Beth, checking off item six on her list. "But keep them at the register. We don't want chocolate ruining the merchandise." She chewed on the cap of her pen. "What do you think of renting an Easter Bunny costume from the place over in

Harrington for Easter week? Maybe we can get all the shop owners on First to split the cost?"

Charlotte glanced at Beth, who stared at the storefront window, oblivious to everything, including Charlotte's brilliant ideas. "I've got a better idea. We'll undress you and send you naked down First with a sign on your back reading, COME SHOP AT CHARLOTTE'S. Sound good to you?"

"Mmm-hmm."

Charlotte grinned and slammed her notebook down on the desk loudly enough to get a rise out of her friend. Beth jumped in her seat. "What was that for?"

"No reason. By the way, you can start streaking down First around noon. That's prime traffic time."

Beth turned a bright shade of red. "Guess I was distracted."

Charlotte laughed. "Guess so. Care to share why?"

With a not-so-nonchalant gesture, Beth pointed to the window where an unfamiliar chestnut-haired man stood out front talking to Norman.

"Who is he?"

"A carpenter. Sort of a do-it-all kind of guy. He moved here from Albany. Joined the firemen too." Beth sighed and absently lifted up a wrapped chocolate egg. "Isn't he gorgeous?" Beth asked.

In Charlotte's eyes he couldn't compare to a certain dark-haired reporter, but for Beth, Charlotte saw potential. "He's hot," she agreed. However, Beth was coming off tremendous emotional pain. "But isn't it too soon after . . . well, you know?"

"I'm not rushing into anything, but I can look, can't I?"

Charlotte laughed. "You looking is a positive sign."

Her friend nodded. "Besides, anything I do or don't do now is with eyes wide open."

Her eyes glittered in a way Charlotte hadn't seen—ever. A lesson learned, she thought. A woman *could,* in fact, get over a man. Yet despite Beth's ability to bounce back, Charlotte had her doubts it was as easy as Beth pretended. Still, she smiled, glad to hear her friend was thinking clearly, even as she was mooning over the hunk du jour. "Does *he* have a name?"

"Thomas Scalia. Exotic-sounding, isn't it?" As Beth spoke, the man in question turned and faced the window, seeming to meet her steady stare. "He came up to me after the last baseball game. After you ditched me and ran."

Charlotte didn't reply to that dig. She'd already left a message on her mother's answering machine that she wanted to meet with both her parents. Her insides had been churning nervously all day because they hadn't called back and she was anxiously anticipating the moment.

As surprising as it seemed, Samson's words had had an effect on her. So did Roman's absence. She still wasn't sure how to reconcile the coin toss with his real desires, but she knew in her heart she didn't want *them* to be over.

The time had come to deal with her parents and her past. Otherwise she had no future.

"Oh, my God." Beth's squeal jarred Charlotte out of her self-absorbed thoughts, "He's coming inside."

Sure enough, the door opened and Thomas Scalia strode inside. He had the cocky, confident swagger she associated with a male in charge and Charlotte crossed her fingers. She didn't want Beth to fall into the same trap with another dominating man who wanted to take control and change the beautiful person she was inside and out.

The bells above the door jingled behind him as he walked to the desk. "Afternoon, ladies." He inclined his head in greeting. "Beth I already know." He smiled, revealing dimples that had no effect on Charlotte, but obviously had Beth squirming in her seat. "But I don't think I've had the pleasure." He glanced at Charlotte only briefly.

"Charlotte Bronson," she said, extending her hand.

He shook it. "Thomas Scalia. But you can call me Tom." He spoke to Charlotte, but his admiring gaze never left Beth's flushed face.

Charlotte watched their wordless exchange with a combination of amusement and longing for Roman. She missed him with a desperation she hadn't known she could feel, making their last meeting and all the hurtful words that had passed between them seem trivial. But there was nothing trivial about the coin toss and his feelings regarding commitment. Once Charlotte made peace with her own ghosts, there was still no guarantee he'd want to settle down. Especially now that he'd gone back on the road.

"So what can I get for you?" Beth's voice resonated with a husky quality and brought Charlotte back to the present.

"Now, that's a loaded question." Thomas leaned closer.

Beth fingered the bowl of chocolates on the counter. Her hand shook as she lifted a wrapped chocolate egg in one hand. Charlotte watched in disbelief as Beth, the poised, accomplished flirt, popped a silver-wrapped chocolate Easter egg into her mouth with trembling hands.

"I admire a woman who'll eat anything without regard to calories or weight," Thomas said with a grin.

Beth spit the candy out and dropped her face into her palms.

Charlotte swallowed a giggle. Apparently even the most accomplished seductress got nervous around the right man. "I'm mortified," Beth wailed, her voice muffled through her closed hands.

This time Charlotte did chuckle. Thomas whispered

something low and obviously personal in Beth's ear. As far as the two of them were concerned, no one else in the world existed. Time to make herself scarce, Charlotte thought.

She glanced at her watch. Four-thirty P.M. "You know what? It's quiet today. Why don't we lock up and leave early?"

"Perfect," Thomas said to Beth. "I was hoping to entice you to join me for dinner. You're more than welcome too, Charlotte," he added politely, but she sensed the reluctance in his tone and grinned.

Beth shot her a pleading glance. Oh, no. No way would Charlotte be the third wheel at the start of a new romance. She'd let these two muddle through the embarrassing beginning on their own. Charlotte touched Beth's hand for encouragement. Beth could handle this dinner with ease. As long as she unwrapped the butter pats first.

Charlotte forced a regretful shake of her head and began to gather her things. "Thanks anyway, but I have plans," she lied. "But Beth is free. She told me as much this afternoon." Charlotte felt Beth's gaze shooting daggers at her, but she didn't mind. Charlotte had more pressing problems. "I'll lock up."

"I won't hear of it. You go on upstairs," Beth said. "I'll lock up behind me."

Stalling. Charlotte recognized the tactic well. Beth obviously figured she and Romeo were safer in the shop than alone somewhere else. Little did Beth know all the erotic things that could happen in this shop. Charlotte and Roman did. Firsthand.

She swallowed over the lump in her throat caused by the memory. "It was nice meeting you, Thomas."

"Same here."

Less than a minute later, Charlotte had departed and ran

up the stairs to her apartment. The clatter of pans and sounds of chatter greeted her as she put the key in the lock and stepped inside. So did the delicious aroma of fried chicken and mashed potatoes, which brought back surprisingly good childhood memories.

Her stomach grumbled, a combination of hunger and fear, because she had no doubt her parents awaited her.

"Honey, she's home." Her mother's next words proved Charlotte right.

Inside her usually solitary apartment, Charlotte found her family and a table set for three, fresh flowers and a pitcher of iced tea in the center. Her parents met her in the small family room. Stilted hellos followed and Charlotte quickly excused herself to wash up, needing a splash of cold water on her face for bravery and fortitude.

On the way to her room, she heard the whispering sounds of two people who knew each other well. A shiver passed through her. This wasn't how she envisioned her family at all. Yet they'd gone to a lot of trouble for this meeting, obviously taking her phone call as an overture—which it was. Now she just had to find a way to make peace with her personal ghosts.

Dinner was a silent affair. Not because Charlotte intended to treat her parents to an uncomfortable meal, but because she didn't know what to say. It was years too late for anyone to ask how her father's day at work had been, or how Charlotte had enjoyed her job. She wondered if it was too late for everything. If so, it was too late for her and Roman, a notion Charlotte refused to accept.

With the main meal over, Charlotte stared into her coffee cup and twirled her spoon around and around, mustering her courage. "So." She cleared her throat.

"So." Annie looked up at Charlotte, so much hope and

expectation in her eyes, Charlotte thought she might choke on it.

Her mother wanted a reconciliation of sorts and Charlotte could think of only one way. "Why haven't you two gotten divorced?" she asked over her mother's fresh-baked apple pie. Her parents' forks clattered to the table in unison. But she wouldn't apologize for asking what had been on her mind for years.

She needed to understand how they'd gotten to this point. It was time.

CHAPTER THIRTEEN

Russell stared at his daughter, deliberately not looking at his wife. If he let Annie sway him, he'd continue to take the blame for their separations, but no more. And not just because he wanted a relationship with Charlotte, but because he had a hunch her future depended on his answers.

His truthful answers. "Your mother and I never got divorced because we love each other."

Charlotte lowered her fork and tossed the napkin on the table. "Forgive me, but you have a funny way of showing it."

And that was the problem, Russell thought. "People have many ways of expressing their feelings. Sometimes they even hide things to protect the ones they love."

"Is that an excuse for being absent all these years?" She shook her head. "I'm sorry. I thought I could do this. I can't."

She rose and Russell stood, grabbing her arm. "Yes, you can. That's why you called me. If you want to yell, scream, throw a tantrum, go ahead. I'm sure I deserve it. But if you want to listen and then go on with your life, I think you'll accomplish much more."

Silence followed and he let Charlotte take stock, decide where to go from here. It didn't escape his notice that Annie had remained in her seat, quietly watching. Dr. Fallon had said any antidepressant medication took a while to work, so Russell didn't expect miracles overnight. If she didn't feel ready to take part in the conversation, at least she was here, and he knew what a huge step that was for her.

Charlotte folded her arms across her chest and exhaled a sigh of acceptance. "Okay, I'm listening."

"Your mother always knew I wanted to act and I couldn't make a living at it in Yorkshire Falls."

Charlotte glanced at Annie for confirmation and she nodded.

"To make things one hundred percent clear, we got married before she ever got pregnant with you, and we got married because we wanted to," her father said.

"Then why'd you . . ." Charlotte paused and swallowed hard.

Watching his daughter's pain, his heart nearly ripped in two, but there'd be no healing without tearing each other apart first. He knew that now. "Why'd I what?"

"Leave?"

He gestured to the couch in the other room and they settled into the flowered fabric. Annie followed and sat on the other side of their daughter. She grabbed Charlotte's hand and held on tight.

"Why'd you go to California without us?" Charlotte asked. "If you loved Mom as much as you say, why not stay here or take us with you? Would having a wife and a child have been such a huge burden? Would it have cramped your lifestyle?"

"No," he said, clearly upset she'd think such a thing. "Don't ever believe that. I couldn't stay because being an actor is who I am. I couldn't sacrifice myself. Selfish, I suppose, but true. I needed to act and I needed to be in the best place to follow my dreams."

"And I always knew that." Annie spoke for the first time, then brushed a tear off Charlotte's cheek.

Charlotte rose and walked to the window, grasping on to the windowsill as she looked out. "Did you know I used to dream you'd take us all to California with you? I kept a packed suitcase under my bed just in case. I don't know how many years I held on to that fantasy. Eventually I realized that being an actor was more important to you than we were." She shrugged. "I can't say I ever accepted it, though."

"I'm glad. Maybe somewhere in here . . ." He pointed to his heart. "Maybe you realized it wasn't true that I didn't care more about my career than you."

"Then why don't you tell me how things really were?"

Russell wished the explanation were as concise and compact as she seemed to think it was. But emotions were involved. His, Annie's . . . it wasn't simple. All this time Russell had thought by nurturing Annie's need for familiarity and a child's need to be with her mother, he was helping them both. But as his daughter stared at him with huge, accusing eyes, he knew what a huge mistake he'd made.

He drew a deep breath, knowing his next words were going to hurt her as much as or more than his long absences. "Every time I came back, including this one, I asked your mother to come back to California with me."

Charlotte took a step back, reeling from that piece of information. Her entire life had been built on the premise that her father didn't care enough to take them with her. Annie had fostered that belief. She'd never once said Russell had asked them to join him.

Charlotte trembled, shaking in her denial. "No. No. Mom would have gone to California. She wouldn't have chosen to stay here alone, pining for you. Letting people talk about us. Letting the kids make fun of me because I didn't have a daddy who loved me." She looked to her mother for confirmation.

Because to learn otherwise now would mean she'd unnecessarily lost out on years of having a father. Even if he wasn't in town, if she'd known he loved her, known he wanted her, her emotional foundation would have been more solid.

Surely her mother would have known that. "Mom?" Charlotte hated the little-girl sound to her voice and straightened her shoulders. She'd handle whatever happened next.

Unbelievably, Annie nodded. "It's . . . it's true. I couldn't leave town and everything that was familiar. And I couldn't bear to be separated from you, so we stayed here."

"But why didn't you at least tell me Dad wanted us? You knew he wanted *you.* You had that thought to keep you warm and comforted at night. Why didn't you want the same for me?"

"I wanted what was best for you. But I'm ashamed to admit I did only what was best for me. The way you reacted when your father left and the way you kept reading up on all those Hollywood books, I was afraid of losing you if you knew. You always were more like your father than like me." She sniffed, wiping at her eyes with the back of her hand. "I thought you'd go to him and leave me behind. Alone."

Charlotte blinked. Feeling numb, she lowered herself

onto the couch. "All these years, I blamed you." She met her father's gaze.

"I let you, honey."

And he had. While her mother had allowed her child to suffer, her father had perpetuated the lie that he'd abandoned them both. "Why?"

He let out a groan. "At first, it was out of love and respect for your mother's wishes. She was so afraid of losing you, I couldn't help feeling she needed you more than I did. And how do you explain all this to a little girl?"

"And later?"

"You became an angry teen." He wrapped his hand around the back of his neck, shook his head, and began massaging. "On my trips home you wouldn't have a civil conversation with me about the weather. Then you went to college, moved to New York, and were old enough to schedule your trips home so you could avoid mine."

That was true enough, she acknowledged with sudden, unexpected sadness and guilt. Maybe there was enough blame to go around, she thought.

"I suppose I just didn't try hard enough."

Charlotte exhaled hard. "And I didn't try at all." The admission didn't come easily.

"It's my fault, but there's an explanation. I'm not looking to pass the blame, but look. . . ." With shaking hands, Annie reached for her purse and pulled out a small vial of prescription medication. "Dr. Fallon said it sounds like I've had a severe case of depression."

Hadn't Charlotte approached the doctor sensing just such a possibility?

Annie blinked back tears. "Maybe I should have taken these before, but I didn't realize I needed help. Your father said . . . he said Dr. Fallon had spoken with you and you thought there might be a problem. I didn't know. I thought I had to feel this way. I thought it was normal. I mean, I've always felt this way." Her voice broke, but she continued, "And I couldn't bear to lose you too. I know I caused you pain because of my . . . illness, and I'm sorry." Annie hugged Charlotte tight. "I'm so sorry."

Her mother smelled like her mother—warm and soft and comforting. But there'd always been something childlike about Annie. She'd always seemed so fragile, Charlotte realized now. Even the librarian job was so perfect for her because of the silence and soft words spoken there.

"I'm not mad at you, Mom." She was just off kilter and confused. The lump in her throat was so large it hurt, and she wasn't sure how to absorb the truth.

Looking back, so much made sense, but only recently had Charlotte realized there was a more serious problem. She still had a hunch they were dealing with something more deeply rooted than mild depression, something akin to mental illness. Why else would a person keep her shades drawn and windows closed, preferring loneliness to other people's company, including the husband she loved?

Why hadn't any of them picked up on the signs before? Perhaps they'd all been too self-absorbed, Charlotte thought sadly.

"I think we should leave you alone to think about all this," he said in the wake of Charlotte's silence. He grabbed her mother's hand. "Annie?"

She nodded. "I'm coming," she said, before looking at Charlotte. "And again, I'm sorry."

They started for the door together and Charlotte let them go.

She hoped and prayed that with the truth would come understanding and peace. But she needed time alone to understand the things she'd heard and decide how she felt now. How she'd feel when the numbness wore off.

Hours later, Charlotte settled herself in her bed, but kept her window shades open so she could stare out at the inky night sky. She was too wound up to sleep and thought maybe counting stars would help her relax. Unfortunately, her thoughts were running through her mind at a rapid pace. Talk about living an illusion, she thought. The father she thought hadn't cared about her did.

Yet for a lifetime, Charlotte had modeled her behavior and treatment of men—men like Russell and travelers like Roman Chandler—on the abandonment lie perpetuated by her parents. But Russell Bronson wasn't who Charlotte thought he was. He was selfish and had his faults, but he loved her mother. Charlotte had to give him some credit for that. Even if he could have done more to help both Annie and his daughter, he couldn't sacrifice his entire life in the name of love.

Charlotte wouldn't even ask that of Roman. Not anymore. Asking him to stay in Yorkshire Falls was as selfish as Russell had been in his own way. Roman deserved better from her.

It was ironic, really. Roman wasn't the man she'd needed him to be. Charlotte had needed Roman to be the wanderer with no feelings, the love 'em and leave 'em bachelor who cared for no one but himself. She'd needed Roman to be all those things because it gave her an excuse to keep him at an emotional distance. To prevent herself from being hurt the way she thought her mother had been.

Now she just needed *him*.

She curled more deeply into the mattress, pulled up her covers, and yawned. Love had a way of casting aside all safety nets, Charlotte thought. And tomorrow she would make her own leap of faith with no guarantees of where she'd land.

At some point Charlotte must have dozed off, because the sun shining through the window woke her at dawn. She'd slept well for the first time in ages and opened her eyes to a rush of adrenaline she hadn't expected. She showered, ate a cup of peach yogurt, then decided it was late enough to call Rick.

He picked up after one ring. "Rick Chandler at your service."

"Someone's in a good mood," Charlotte mused.

"Yeah, well, a good run will do that for you. What's up, Charlotte? Everything okay?"

"Yes," she said, thinking of her decision to go after Roman. "And no," she muttered, knowing she also had to tell Rick about Samson yet elicit his promise to protect and not turn the harmless older man in. "I need to talk to you."

"You know I always have time for you. But I'm on my way out the door. I've got meetings scheduled in Albany and I won't be back until later."

Her disappointment was strong. Now that she'd made up her mind, she was ready to take action.

"How 'bout I come by on the way home?" he asked. "Probably around seven."

She tucked the phone beneath her ear and rinsed off her spoon as she figured her schedule. "It's Sponsors Night. I'm supposed to throw out the ceremonial first pitch at the Rockets' game tonight." As much as she'd rather ditch her entire day and get to Roman as quickly as possible, she couldn't let the kids down. And she didn't want to.

What she had to say to Rick couldn't be done in public

and would have to wait until tonight, "Why don't you come by my place after the game?" she suggested.

"Sounds like a plan. Are you sure you're okay?"

She rolled her eyes. "Would you quit asking me? You're beginning to sound like the big brother I never had."

"Yeah, well, I promised."

"You promised what?" Butterflies began a steady flutter inside her stomach. And to who?

Silence extended over the phone line. "Come on, Rick. What did you mean?"

He cleared his throat. "Nothing. Just that it's my job to make sure you're okay."

His job as a cop or his job as a brother? she wondered. Had Roman made Rick promise something before he'd taken off?

"Well, I'm fine." As curious as she was, she accepted Rick's vague answer. She knew better than to think she'd get one Chandler brother to snitch on another.

"I'll see you tonight."

"Right. Drive safe." Charlotte hung up the phone and exhaled hard. One long workday and seven innings of baseball to go, and then she'd find out where Roman had gone. Charlotte had twelve hours to get up the nerve to make the trip to wherever. To leave Yorkshire Falls and land uninvited on Roman's doorstep, completely uncertain of the reception she'd receive.

The day was longer than Charlotte could have envisioned, each hour feeling like several. Listening to Beth go on and on about Thomas Scalia had brought out mixed feelings, happiness for her friend and envy because she was alone, her future unsure.

But the day passed and Charlotte finally threw the ceremonial first pitch while her parents sat in the stands watching her. Together. She shook her head in amazement. Not that she held any illusions. Russell would be back in California by early next week. Alone this time, but maybe not for long.

Annie had agreed to meet with a therapist. Harrington had a wonderful mental health clinic and her mother had decided, with her father's encouragement, to see a psychiatrist Dr. Fallon had recommended there. Meanwhile, her father had decided to tie up some loose ends in L.A. and come home for a while, at least long enough for Annie to begin therapy and see if she could wrap her mind around the possibility of moving west.

Would wonders never cease? Charlotte mused, happier and more hopeful about life than she'd been in a while. As if they knew, Charlotte's Rockets beat the competition again, despite their star pitcher being out with a broken wrist and some other assorted player injuries. Though it was still early in the season, they'd designated Charlotte their good luck charm, going so far as to give her an honorary spaceship locket to hang on a chain around her neck in appreciation of her sponsorship and perfect attendance record so far. The gesture brought a lump to her throat and made her glad she hadn't ditched the kids in favor of her personal life.

"What personal life?" she asked aloud as she let herself back into her apartment, the night over at last.

The joke seemed to be on her. Even her mother had a private life, whereas right now Charlotte had none. But once she saw Rick and got information on Roman, she'd be on her way—to what, she didn't know, but at least she'd be taking positive steps forward.

Charlotte dropped her keys on the kitchen table, walked over to the blinking answering machine, and hit play. "Hi,

Charlotte. It's me, Rick. I got hung up in Albany and then was called out on a case as soon as I hit town again. We have to talk, so sit tight."

As if she had anywhere else to go. Not tired and still wound up from the game, she headed into the kitchen and dug through the freezer for the pint of vanilla butterscotch ice cream she kept stashed in the back. Spoon in hand, she decided she'd hang out in her bedroom. Ever since splurging on a small thirteen-inch color television for nights in bed, she found she enjoyed lounging in her room better than hanging out alone in the living area of the small apartment. With luck, she'd find something on television to kill more time until Rick finally arrived.

She approached her room, scarfing spoonfuls of ice cream on the way. The dim lighting from the doorway took her by surprise. She didn't remember leaving her bedside lamp on when she'd left for work this morning. She shrugged, then entered her private sanctuary at the same time she licked sticky butterscotch off her lips.

"I could help you do that. If you're willing to talk to me."

Charlotte halted in her tracks. Her heart stopped beating for a second before beginning again, more erratic and quickly than before. "Roman?" Stupid question. Of course that deep, husky voice belonged to Roman.

And it was Roman, sexily lounging in gray sweats, a navy T-shirt, and bare feet on her frilly white bedspread and assorted pillows. Only a man of his stature and build could look even more masculine when leaning into feminine frills and eyelets. Only a woman in love could want to toss caution out the window and run into his arms.

She let out a frustrated puff of air. She'd missed him and was desperately glad to see him, but they had issues that remained unsettled. And until they'd discussed those problems and came to an understanding that fulfilled them both, too much remained uncertain between them. Though at this moment Charlotte felt like she could live solely on love and the air he breathed, she was smarter than that.

At least she hoped she was. Because her resolve to wait was crumbling quickly.

Roman forced himself to remain calm and relaxed. Hard to do when cushioned in Charlotte's soft bed and surrounded by her feminine scent, a scent he'd missed while he'd been gone. And even harder to do with her staring at him, a mixture of longing and wariness in her gorgeous green eyes.

He'd gotten into town, and with everyone at dinner or the Little League game, he'd remained undetected, which was good, since he'd counted on the element of surprise.

Wanting her alone, and the sooner the better, he'd planned to grab her and run—back to his house, her apartment, he didn't care. He had much to share about his trip to Washington, D.C., and a future that he hoped included her.

But no matter how anxious he was to bridge the physical distance between them, he wouldn't rush things. She had to trust him first.

"Did you miss me?" he asked.

"Did you miss *me?*" she retorted.

He grinned. Well, at least she hadn't lost her spunk, and besides, he hadn't expected her to jump into his arms. "Of course I missed you."

Instead of finding Charlotte at home or in her shop, he'd discovered her on the field, throwing out the ceremonial first pitch. Then she was embraced by her father. *Her father.* Seeing her forgiving heart, Roman had fallen in love all over again.

He'd watched her smile at Russell, and Roman instantly knew she'd made peace with that part of her life. He hoped it would allow her to make peace with him.

He patted the seat beside him. "Join me."

"How'd you get in?" she asked instead.

"The fire escape. I knew you'd go back to leaving your window unlocked without me around to look after you." And she had. So he'd climbed in through the fire escape and settled himself in her bed to wait. "You need a keeper, Charlotte." He recalled her telling him that on the day of their first reunion in Norman's back hall. He'd never envisioned they'd end up at this juncture, his heart and future hinging on this beautiful woman's choices.

"Are you applying for the job?" she asked.

He shrugged, trying not to let his emotions show. Not yet. "I thought I already did."

"Because you called heads when Chase chose tails?" she asked a little too casually.

Her lightly tossed barb stung, because it meant she was still hurting and he was the cause. "Actually, Chase was never involved."

She raised an eyebrow. "Let me guess. Because he already paid his dues."

"Rick did say you were smart."

She rolled her eyes.

"And you are. Smart enough to come after me?" He asked her, taking in the open suitcase across the room that had been taunting him with that exact possibility since he'd let himself in. Just the fact that she was brave enough to make the trip told him what he already knew. She was more her father's daughter than she'd ever realized, and *he* realized now that that wasn't a bad thing. He had a hunch she knew it too.

She was Roman's perfect soul mate. And for a man who'd never thought in such terms before, the admission was huge—and one he wanted to share with her.

"Come on, Charlotte. Could it be I saved you a trip?" He heard the hope in his voice, but didn't care. If laying his heart out for her to trample was the solution to getting her back, he'd do it.

"Damn you, Roman." She reached for a crocheted pillow on her dresser and tossed it at him hard, whacking him on the head. "You're too arrogant for your own good."

"But not for yours, I hope? Forgive me, Charlotte."

She swallowed and tapped her foot on the floor, making him wait. "You are arrogant," she muttered, but a grin tugged at her lips, one she couldn't hide, no matter how angry she was, no matter how hard she obviously tried.

"It's one of my more charming qualities. Now quit stalling and put me out of my misery."

That got to her, and she lifted an eyebrow in wonder. She was obviously surprised he'd been unhappy. That stunned him. How could she not know he was only half a man without her by his side? "Tell me where you planned to go."

She shook her head. "Oh, no. You first. Where did you disappear to, and better yet, why are you back?"

"Come sit next to me and I'll tell you."

"You're inviting me to sit on my own bed with you, the uninvited guest. What's wrong with this picture?"

He glanced around, his gaze settling on the large oval mirror across the room. The reflective glass gave him a perfect view of himself lying in her bed. He shrugged. "Not a thing, as far as I can see."

With a groan, she stalked across the room and settled herself beside him, a melting bowl of ice cream her only physical barrier. "Now talk."

"Only if you promise to feed me later."

"Roman—"

"I'm not stalling. I'm serious, I haven't eaten in hours. I flew in and came straight here to see you." With a slight detour to the baseball game that they'd get to once she opened up to him about her new relationship with her father. "So if you like what you hear, you have to promise to feed me."

"Next thing I know, you'll be asking me to feed you by hand."

"By mouth would work just as well," he teased.

Her lips tugged upward in a hesitant smile.

At least he could still affect her, he thought. "I've been in Washington, D.C."

"Fair enough," she murmured and placed the bowl on the nightstand. "I promise to feed you."

"Good. Remember I told you about a job offer in D.C.?" His next thought was interrupted by loud banging on Charlotte's door. The steady ringing of her buzzer followed.

She jumped up from the bed. "It's Rick. I asked him to come over so I could find out—" She stopped herself before she could finish.

"Find out what, Charlotte?" But he already knew. Just as he thought. She'd been looking for him.

"Nothing you need to worry about." She blushed, but before he could respond, Rick pounded on the door once more. "I need to see Rick about something else, too. You'll find it interesting, I promise."

More interesting than them? Roman doubted it. "Okay, let the pain in the ass in."

He rose from the comfortable bed and followed Charlotte into the living area, greeting his brother with a practiced glare.

"I didn't know he was back." Rick gestured to Roman. "Welcome home . . . oh, shit."

"Not the greeting I was expecting."

"You two aren't going to believe this." Rick shook his head. "Hell, *I* don't believe this."

"Well, before you launch into any story, I've got something to tell you," Charlotte said.

Roman shook his head. "You've both got me curious." Rick exhaled hard.

"Okay, then, ladies first."

"Right." She wrung her hands before her in a gesture so un-Charlotte-like, Roman grew concerned.

"No," she said, changing her mind. "Wrong. You go first."

Rick shrugged. "I got home planning to come straight here, but we got some calls at the station. Several in fact. It seems the panty thief struck again."

"What?" Roman and Charlotte said at once.

"In reverse, actually. The panties were returned."

Roman started to laugh. "You've got to be kidding."

"Nope. Every last one of them was left either inside the house or on the front porch. Even though we never officially considered Roman a suspect, I'd planned on telling Charlotte that the ladies around town were going to have to give up their notion of Roman as a panty thief." Rick ran a hand through his hair.

"Why? Did you catch the guy?" Charlotte asked warily.

"No, dammit."

Was it Roman's imagination, or did she just heave a giant sigh of relief?

"But with Roman out of town, they'd have to give up their fantasies regarding my baby brother," Rick continued.

"What's the matter? Jealous they weren't flashing their undies at you?" Roman grinned.

"Funny." Rick shook his head. "But it's just occurred to me here that with you back in town, looks like you're going to have to live with the stigma." He chuckled at the thought.

To Roman's complete astonishment, Charlotte came up beside him and slipped her warm, soft hand in his. She stood by his side as she looked at Rick and said, "No, he won't."

"You know something about this, don't you?" Roman asked.

"I might." She squeezed his hand tighter. Although he didn't need her looking out for him, he liked this protective side of her. Especially since they hadn't come close to straightening things out between them, yet she was defending him anyway.

"Come on, Charlotte. You can't withhold information from me," Rick said.

"Oh, I don't know, Rick. I never said I knew anything." She glanced up at Roman, her eyes wide and imploring. "Did anyone see you tonight? Anyone know you're back other than us?"

He shook his head. "Despite the small-town bit, I really don't think anyone noticed me." He'd kept to himself intentionally, though he didn't think Rick would appreciate him pointing that out.

"Rick, if I did know something, I wouldn't tell you unless you promised me two things. One is to never use the information I give you and the second is to never tell another soul Roman was back in town tonight."

His brother's face flushed a deep shade of red. "You can't mean to bribe a police officer."

She rolled her eyes. "In that case, I don't know anything. It's been nice seeing you, Rick. Good night."

Roman hadn't a clue what was going on, but he was putting an end to it now. "This is ridiculous. Charlotte, whatever you know, you have to talk. And Rick, you promise her anything she asks."

Rick burst out laughing. "Yeah, right."

"Samson's responsible for the panty thefts and if you repeat that, arrest him, question him, or so much as lift an eyebrow his way, I'll deny ever having said anything. I'll pay for his lawyer and we'll sue you for harassment. No hard feelings, by the way. I really do like you, Rick." She treated Roman's stunned brother to her sweetest smile.

That sugary grin would have Roman groveling at her feet. Unfortunately, Rick wasn't Roman, and his cop brother was livid. He turned even redder. "You knew this and withheld the information? For how long?"

"What good would it have done to tell? He's a harmless old man who was looking out for me. I'm nice to him, so he figured he'd drum up interest in my business. Roman being blamed was completely unplanned."

"But beneficial." Roman saw the humor in the situation even if Rick didn't. His high school prank benefited Samson's cause.

"What he did was illegal," Rick pointed out. "Or did you lose sight of that?"

She jerked her hand out of Roman's and placed her hands on her hips. "Tell me who got hurt. And then tell me who will benefit by hauling the poor man in for anything. It's over now. I promise. He won't do it again."

Roman leaned close and whispered in her ear. "You probably shouldn't make promises you can't keep, sweetheart. You have no control over the man." No more control than Roman had over his body now that he'd inhaled her delicious scent and those long strands of tousled hair had tickled his nose and cheek, arousing him.

It was time his brother made a quick exit, Roman thought. "She's right and you know it, Rick. You aren't doing anyone justice if you prosecute the guy."

"He won't do it again. Please?" Charlotte asked in a soft, pleading voice.

"Argh. Fine. Since I don't have a witness, I'll lay off Samson, but if this happens again—"

"It won't," Charlotte and Roman said at once. Roman assumed they'd be making a joint trip to visit the "duck man" and make sure he understood the break he'd been given.

"And since Samson went to the trouble of replacing the underwear in order to exonerate Roman during his absence, you never saw Roman in town tonight, right?" She said in a determined voice. "The first time you'll have seen him since he left over a week ago is—"

"Twenty-four hours from now, when I knock on your door," Roman decided. "Until then, *we're* incommunicado." He put his palm on Rick's back and shoved him toward the door. "If anyone asks, Charlotte's got the flu."

"I don't believe this," Rick muttered as he took a step into the outside hall.

"You're a good man, Rick Chandler," Charlotte called out to him.

Rick turned. "The things I do in the name of love," he said, and disappeared down the steps, muttering to himself the entire way.

The next twenty-four hours. The words reverberated in Charlotte's brain as she shut the door behind Rick and turned to face Roman. "Dare I ask where you plan on hiding out for the next day?"

Twenty-four hours, she thought once more. A long, long time for two people to remain incommunicado. Alone, together. Was that all the time they had left? Or did Roman have something different in mind?

"Your bed was pretty cozy. Of course, it would be more cozy if you were in there with me."

Once again her heart picked up a frantic rhythm. "Tell me about Washington."

He held out his hand, and next thing she knew, he led her back into the bedroom until they were comfortably settled on her frilly double bed. As comfortable as she could be with sexual awareness and anticipation humming between them and a soft mattress beckoning.

"Washington's hot and humid already. It's a great place to live. Fun, upbeat."

"Are you planning on switching your home base? Leaving New York City for Washington, D.C.?"

"The job offer was for an editorial position, but then I wouldn't have the freedom—"

"To travel?" she guessed, sensing by his tone he'd turned the well-known paper down.

"Yup. I want to be able to work from a laptop. Editorial is too much desk-sitting and I'd need to be available for the people working under me."

She gnawed on the inside of her cheek. "I can see where being stuck in D.C. wouldn't suit you. You being used to world travel and huge stories and all."

"I've gotten used to you." Taking her by surprise, he brushed one finger down her cheek. "I can't very well be stuck behind a desk in D.C. if you've got a business to run here."

She was confused and frustrated and hopeful at the same time. Most of all, she was sick of him talking in circles without making a point she could grab on to. In a move that shocked even her, she managed to take Roman down, pinning his shoulders onto the bed and straddling his waist. "Let's try this again, and try English this time. Did you or did you not take the job?"

He stared at her wide-eyed, obviously amused and, from the feel of his erection between her thighs, very aroused. "I didn't take the editorial job."

She picked up on his subtle nuance. "Which job did you take?"

"The one for op-ed columnist. They were very impressed with a recent piece of writing I'd done while home, a slice-of-life that showed them I can cover every angle. I resigned from the AP and I can now work primarily from home, while commuting on occasion to D.C. And taking vacations to exotic parts of the world when we feel like it."

"We." She would have swallowed, but her mouth had grown dry. She could barely speak, but she managed. Some things were too important. "Where's home, Roman?"

"Wherever you are, Charlotte." Those incredible blue eyes stared into hers.

She blinked, unable to believe this world traveler had given up imparting world news to settle in D.C. and Yorkshire Falls. With her. She shook her head. "You can't give up everything you love," she told him.

"I can't give up you. It was hell being a couple of hours away in D.C. I can't imagine anything more long distance. I'd die of loneliness." He grinned.

"Don't get carried away." She caressed his cheek and

held his face in her palm. "But I want you happy. I never want you to resent me or the choices you made."

"You said it, sweetheart. They're choices I made."

Before he'd even had Charlotte's okay, she realized. He'd taken concrete steps toward changing his life. He'd already quit his AP job, already taken another. All without a firm commitment from her about their future. He'd made choices he wanted to make, she realized now. And though he hadn't mentioned children or the coin toss, Charlotte knew Roman well enough to know he hadn't made this decision because of a bet or out of family obligation. Instead he'd followed his heart.

Just like she'd been ready to follow hers, she thought, taking in her open suitcase. The silly bet had become a moot issue for her before he'd ever returned.

"Washington's the best compromise I can come up with," he said. "You'll really like it during the time you're there and Beth can run Charlotte's Attic when you are. I found an apartment, but if you don't like it, we can pick something else there and buy or build a house here. And the best thing is that there's an easy flight into Albany that should work for us both. If you're willing."

"And if I'm not?" She had to ask. Had to know he'd be doing this anyway. Because if he planned to go back to his AP job if she turned him down, they didn't stand a chance. Charlotte held her breath and waited.

"We have many awkward run-ins for the rest of our lives. I've made my choices, Charlotte. I want them to include you, but they're final either—"

She cut him off with a sizzling kiss that had been too long in coming. His tongue met hers and he thrust deep inside her mouth, taking possession, letting her know she was his now and forever. She felt the words and the thoughts in every movement he made. And though she'd started as the aggressor, she soon found herself in the opposite position, flat on her back, clothes on the floor, and Roman devouring her with a wicked gleam in his eyes. "I realize we have details to work out."

"They can wait." Her breaths came in sudden pants.

He struggled to divest himself of his shirt while she unzipped his jeans and wrapped one hand around his thick, hard length.

"God." The word came out a sharp exhale. "Give me a second or I'm going to explode."

Charlotte laughed and let go, not wanting to ruin the fun before it began. Was this the lifetime she had to look forward to? she wondered as she watched the man she loved undress. Suddenly a commuter-type relationship didn't seem half bad. Not when it involved Roman.

Just as suddenly, she was able to understand her mother a bit more. Why she'd held on to the man she loved despite the distance and her own inability to move with him. Perhaps she and Annie weren't so different after all, and perhaps that wasn't such a bad thing, Charlotte thought.

Roman resettled himself on top of her, then reached for the bowl of ice cream. "Remember I said I was hungry?"

Charlotte tipped her head to one side, unrestrained desire in her green eyes. "I remember promising to feed you," she said, a sassy note in her voice.

He dribbled the melted ice cream down her skin. The cool liquid had her belly quivering and she felt the need pulse low and deep between her legs. "Ah, yes." She let out a low moan. "Rick was right, you know," she said to Roman.

"About what?"

She met his molten gaze. "I do love you."

"I love you too." And he proceeded to show her how much, starting with the ice cream that had pooled on her belly. He took a warm lap with his tongue. The heated contrast to the cold ice cream caused her stomach to ripple and her legs to quiver, as need built inside her.

And as he bent his head to take care of that need, Charlotte thought that she could indeed handle Roman's kind of life. For the rest of hers and beyond.

Epilogue

Charlotte lay naked on top of white sheets. Sunlight filtered through the sheer curtains, but privacy wasn't an issue. Their hotel room was on the fifteenth floor, with no other high buildings surrounding them. As Roman studied her, he was struck yet again by the beauty she possessed inside and out, as well as his complete and utter good fortune.

How had he almost tossed this gift aside, thinking he didn't want long-term? How had he ever thought he could be apart from her as a way of life?

He leaned over and dangled a cluster of grapes enticingly. She plucked one into her mouth with her teeth, then grinned. "You're spoiling me."

"That's the point."

"How can a girl argue with that? What's on today's agenda?" she asked.

They'd seen castles in Scotland and the home of the Loch Ness Monster. "I was thinking we could call the travel agent and add a quick trip to California on the way home next week." Roman held his breath for her answer because he'd already booked the trip. Wanting more time to gauge her reaction, he'd waited before springing it on her. He could always cancel and they'd fly straight home to Yorkshire Falls, check on her mother and his, as well as the shop, before starting their life in D.C. He hoped she'd want to see everything Hollywood had to offer, but he couldn't be sure whether the memories would still be upsetting despite the reconciliation with her father.

"I thought you'd be anxious to get home to Raina by now," Charlotte said.

"You know as well as I do, heartburn never killed anyone."

"Then I'd love to see Hollywood with you. Maybe Russell can give us a tour." Her green eyes glittered with pleasure.

That was the surprise plan, but Roman didn't reveal all now. "Maybe."

She fell back against the pillows and laughed. "I *still* can't believe the lengths your mother went to in order to get you boys married off." She was obviously thinking of Raina's antics again.

"Thank God I figured it out. All that tea and Maalox were the first clue she was dealing with indigestion more than a heart ailment; so were the over-the-counter acid-killing medications. But she also exhibited the classic symptoms of a bad liar." He shook his head, remembering, "She'd never look me in the eye when I questioned her about her health, and when she thought I wasn't around, she took the stairs like a sprint runner." He rolled his eyes at the memory.

"Not to mention the fact that she forgot to hide her exercise clothes?"

He chuckled. Before his trip to D.C., he'd tossed in a load of laundry and found his mother's damp sweats and T-shirt in the wash. No way he'd been looking at anything other than freshly worn exercise clothing. He'd wanted to strangle her when he put the facts together, but he'd needed his story confirmed first.

It had been easy to corner Dr. Leslie Gaines and pretend his mother had confided in him about her condition. He led the doctor to believe he knew his mother's health problems weren't serious, but was concerned that liquid antacid wasn't too healthy either. Dr. Gaines had agreed that gastric reflux wasn't as severe a problem as the heart attack they'd thought Raina had the night she was brought into the ER. The doctor assured him she was still monitoring Raina's heart anyway, and said she'd consider stronger prescription medication for her reflux.

"How could your mother not realize she was dealing with Chandler men with inherited reporters' instincts?" Charlotte asked.

"Because she was dealing with sons who put love and concern first and never once thought to look beyond." Hell, if Roman hadn't lived with her, he'd never have caught on.

"And you're sure you're doing the right thing not telling her you know?"

Roman grinned. "She thinks she's got the start of a winning track record. Why ruin her good mood? Besides, once I got over the shock and anger, I paid her back, didn't I?"

Charlotte stretched against the mattress, her lean body tempting him as much as the first time he'd laid eyes on her. "By telling her she wouldn't be getting grandchildren anytime soon because we want time alone together first, I know. And I still feel guilty lying to her."

"She deserves payback," he murmured. "And I don't know if I deserve you, but I'm going to enjoy you anyway." He dipped his head to trail lazy kisses around her breast, teasing her with quick darts of his tongue, but never latch-ing on to the nipple that begged for his touch, his tongue, his teeth.

Charlotte arched her back and moaned, a supplication and a plea for him to put her out of her misery and latch on to that distended tip. He'd come to know her body signals and signs well within the last few weeks and he'd never tire of learning more. "Not yet, sweetheart."

"We need—"

"I know exactly what we need," he said, his groin throbbing and ready to enter her slick body. He tormented her with his fingers first, gliding them between her legs and slipping one into her slick folds.

She squeezed her legs together tight, trapping his hand between her thighs and stilling any more movement. "We need to let Chase and Rick in on her condition."

Roman groaned. "*How* can you think about anything at this moment, including—or should I say especially—my brothers?"

"It's called prioritizing, and it isn't easy, believe me. Don't you think I'd rather be making love to you instead of rehashing this?"

They'd had this same argument before, Charlotte telling him it was unfair to keep Chase and Rick in the dark about Raina's decent health. "Honey, when we get home, we'll talk about telling Rick and Chase. In the meantime, the longer we keep them in the dark, the longer they'll be at Mom's mercy, and the better chance they have of finding the happiness we have together."

She sighed. "Maybe you're right."

"I know I am."

"Then why do I feel so guilty?"

He grinned. "Because you have too much time to think. Which means I ought to distract you completely."

Roman raised himself up and over her, settling himself on top of his wife. His *wife*. The word, which once would have sent him running abroad, now filled him with complete satisfaction. And all because of Charlotte.

She not only loved him, but she adored his family and looked out for them the same way she did for her own. This beautiful, caring woman was his, and would be forever. And he intended to enjoy every living, breathing moment of married life, while making all Charlotte's dreams and fantasies come true.

His groin pulsed against her soft feminine mound. "Open for me, Charlotte."

Her lips turned upward in a sexy smile at the same time her thighs parted wide. She was already wet and ready for him, and he thrust inside her easily and quickly, but there was nothing quick about how he intended to make love to her.

Her sigh of satisfaction was complemented by her body's reaction, as she clenched and closed herself around his hard erection. "Oh, yeah," he muttered, the slick heat filling him not just with hot need, but also with a deep emotional warmth. His bachelor days were long and happily behind him.

"I love you, Roman," her lips whispered against the skin on his neck.

"I love you too, Charlotte," he said. And then he proceeded to show her just how much.